MORE THAN JUST FRIENDS

ASTON FALLS BOOK 2

SARA JANE WOODLEY

Cover Design by
CANVAPRO

Ella & Austin art by
ARISTARH VIA DEPOSIT PHOTOS

ELEVENTH AVENUE
PUBLISHING

A THANK YOU TO MY READERS

In August 2020, I released my first book in the Legacy Inn series. I was passionate about this project, and I was hopeful that people would like my stories as much as I loved writing them. But, I never could have imagined that I would be blessed with the most amazing community of readers!

I can't begin to tell you how thankful I am for each and every one of you. I've loved every message, email, and review, and always appreciate hearing from you. Your support and kind words have been some of the *best* parts of this journey.

To my Advance Reader Team, thank you for your incredibly valuable and consistent feedback. It means so much to me to have such a wonderful group of dedicated readers.

If you'd like to connect further, drop by my Facebook Page, Instagram or Tik Tok! I like to engage with my readers and share my book inspo, new releases, and photos of my cat's antics.

Thank you again for everything you do.

Love always,

Sara Jane

1

ELLA

*W*hat's worse than being dumped? Going back to your tiny, gossipy hometown the next morning for your baby sister's wedding.

Great.

As I scrambled around my tiny bedroom, daylight barely shining through my window, I cursed myself yet again for not packing earlier. It wasn't like I hadn't made this journey before—I'd taken the 6am flight from La Guardia to Bozeman, and then the train to Aston Falls several times in the past couple of years.

Although, this trip was different. Because this time, I was going to be in Aston Falls for an entire month.

A very, very long month.

Maybe that was why I'd put off packing. Even before being dumped, the last thing I wanted was to go home. Zac, the guy I'd been seeing, had been my only shot at a saving grace. And I used the term "seeing" loosely as we'd been out on a grand total of one date and an accidental walk after a run-in at Central Park.

So, last night, when I'd panicked over the overcooked

mac-and-cheese I'd made, and asked Zac to meet me in Aston Falls next month for my sister's wedding, I shouldn't have been surprised when he hastily made an excuse to leave. As he flew out the door, he didn't bother pretending he was going to call me.

Not that I blamed him. I hadn't even kissed the man and I'd already asked him to meet my family. Crazy, much?

Zac was a sweet guy and it stung that we were over, but if I was being completely honest, what hurt the most was that it meant that I'd be attending my sister's wedding alone. I was already dreading my family's reactions to learning that the eternally single Ella was *still* single.

I dragged my suitcases off my bed and they landed on the floor with a *thud*. I winced, listening closely for any noise from the room next door. Janice, my roommate, despised being woken up by anything that wasn't bird sounds from her sunrise alarm clock.

I hoped that Janice's friend, Holly—the girl who was subletting my room for the month—was ready for recycled bird chirping followed by the incessant whir of the blender in the mornings.

Janice was a health freak. I was not.

My phone buzzed loudly on my nightstand and I almost face planted on the stained beige carpet as I dived for it. I checked the text and my stomach sank.

Hey Ella Bella, my mom wrote, *we can't wait to see you later today. And to meet the mysterious Zac!*

She ended the text with about 29 smiley faces and hearts. I rolled my eyes—I'd only told Mom about Zac a week ago, and she'd been the one to suggest I bring him home for Carly's wedding. In my brief moment of panic last night, I should've remembered where the idea had come from.

My family—Mom, especially—had become increasingly curious about my love life over recent years. My two older brothers were married, so the weight fell on my shoulders next.

I thought I could hold them off. I thought I had time. I thought I was able to keep searching for "The One."

But then, Carly—who was a whopping five years younger than me—had gotten engaged to the love of her life.

I was the last single Williams sibling. Which meant that my love life was Mom's only focus.

In the past, it was easy enough to get around her questions and nagging. I always had the same excuse: "I'm too busy with work, my career comes first." But, there was one problem—I'd been laid off from my journalist job recently due to budget cuts. My boss at the Brooklyn Chronicle insisted that he'd hire me back as soon as he could, and I tried to feel thankful for that.

It was perfect timing anyway, seeing as my sister was getting married. Carly had asked me to be in Aston Falls to help her before her wedding, so I was happy I could be there for her.

As quietly as possible, I placed my suitcases in the living room, then returned to my room and picked up my daily journal—my one true companion over the years. Obviously, it wasn't the same journal as when I'd first started journaling at 12, but this leather-bound one with parchment-style, deckle-edged pages had to be one of my favorites.

I clutched it to my chest as I took a final sweep around my bedroom. I'd left a box of chocolates for Holly to enjoy when she arrived. There was nothing like small-town hospitality, my mom used to say. And it was hard enough finding any hospitality in a city as big as New York.

As I turned to leave, I caught sight of one final item I could *not* leave behind—a gray hoodie, balled up on the floor next to my desk. I lunged for it and put it on, snuggling into the cozy fabric. The hoodie was far too big for me, the sleeves almost down to my knees, but was there anything better than a huge sweatshirt on a long flight? Especially seeing as the hoodie had once belonged to my childhood best friend... who happened to be 6'2" and very athletic.

I smiled as I wrapped my arms around myself. Being able to see my best friends—Grace and Austin Bell—was the one bright spot in the dark abyss that was my return home. The three of us had grown up together; we used to call ourselves the "Three Musketeers."

We didn't have any secrets from one another. Until Grace started dating Nicholas King, Austin's best friend last year.

As much as I wanted to tell Austin at the time, I couldn't. It wasn't my story to tell. And, in the end, when Austin found out, he couldn't have been happier. Grace and Nicholas got married this past spring in a gorgeous, intimate ceremony at the Aston Falls chapel. Soon after, they'd moved into a cute, modern bungalow that they were currently renovating together.

Which left Austin and I to bond over our shared single-dom. Though he did get a bit weird when I told him I'd joined a dating app around the time of Nicholas and Grace's engagement. Probably just upset at the thought of losing his single buddy.

Not that the app had done much for my dating life.

I shot a furtive glance around my empty bedroom before sniffing the arm of the hoodie. It still smelled vaguely like Austin—like soap and his mild woody cologne. It was the kind of smell that could soothe any post-breakup blues.

Not that I smelled it often or anything.

That would be weird.

I had about five minutes before I had to leave, so I tiptoed to the kitchen and opened the fridge. I'd made Janice a few jars of sugar-free strawberry jam—her favorite —for while I was gone. I leaned in to grab a jar for her, but I knocked over another jar in the process and it slammed to the floor.

"Nooo." I swore as I fell to the ground and collected the glass pieces.

My friends called me a klutz and, unfortunately, I lived up to that moniker more often than not. But, why did these things always have to happen when you were in a rush?

I cleaned the sticky pink mess, keeping a careful eye on my watch. With every tick of the minute hand, a little voice counted down within me.

In just a few short hours, I'd be back in Aston Falls.

2

AUSTIN

She's back.

I stood by the exam table in my office, listening to the voices at the front desk.

I recognized the high-pitched, feathery voice almost immediately and cool dread licked at my stomach. The reasonable tone of my receptionist, Becca, followed and I crossed my fingers that she would be able to handle this. I didn't have the mental space to deal with another appointment today.

Especially not with Sophie Moore.

I filed away Mr. Devi's chart—my last appointment for the day—and tucked my pen into my white coat. It had been a hectic week at the clinic, trudging through a couple of 14-hour shifts, and I was exhausted. Tomorrow was my day off, and I wanted nothing more than to go for a run by the river, take a hot shower, then collapse on my couch with a movie and popcorn.

But, the voices at the front desk continued to murmur. My head swam from exhaustion. Hopefully Dr. Rob was still here.

I approached the door and peered down the hall towards Dr. Rob's office. His door was closed—meaning he'd gone home while I was with Mr. Devi.

"Dr. Rob" was the name I'd lovingly given my coworker... even though Dr. Robert Lopez was old enough to be my dad and experienced enough to be Yoda.

Since opening the Aston Falls Medical Clinic a couple of years ago, patient intake had steadily grown. I hired Dr. Rob a few months ago, and he and his wife were happy to relocate to Aston Falls from California.

But, hiring one doctor wasn't enough. My practice had gained a lot of traction—not only within Aston Falls, but throughout Montana. We had patients come to see us from every corner of the state, and for this reason, I was expanding my practice to provide better medical care to more people.

I couldn't wait for my small hometown to have its own state-of-the-art medical center, and I was happy to help bring it to our community. After a scare with my dad last year, having better facilities in Aston Falls felt more urgent than ever.

It was a ton of work, though. As I was spearheading the project, I was in near-constant contact with the construction manager for the center, and I knew that I'd have to hire more staff. Dr. Rob was happy to assist me, but with an already massive patient load, this was going to be a busy year.

Yet, despite the dedication and care I had for my patients, I couldn't summon the energy to deal with another one of Sophie's "ailments."

As I stood by the door, praying for Sophie to turn on her stiletto heels and leave my practice, it occurred to me that I never thought I'd see the day when I wouldn't be interested in the advances of a beautiful woman.

Don't get me wrong, I'd enjoyed dating in the past. I'd done the whole single, bachelor thing. But, none of those dates ever led to anything long-term. And dating casually, making mundane conversation got old after awhile.

So much so that I stopped dating all together.

It was something Grace, my misguided but well-meaning twin sister, couldn't accept. Now that she was happily married to my best friend, she'd decided to make it her mission to find me someone to settle down with.

And where did she start? She spilled the beans to the town gossips that I was "single and looking." This was categorically untrue, and the last thing I wanted was to lead anyone on. Because, while Grace and Nicholas were cute as could be, I realized long ago that I would never have a love like that. I would never be a "forever" guy.

Unfortunately, the damage was done, and the town rumor mill started spinning. The flurry of women hunting me down became unrelenting. I was flattered by their attention, of course, but I had to tell them the truth—that, while I was single, I wasn't looking.

Despite numerous attempts to be honest with her, Sophie never got the message. She visited the clinic almost every day to flirt with me, making it abundantly clear that she was recently divorced and had received a healthy amount of money through the settlement.

If it was just harmless flirting, I would've dealt with it and moved on. The problem was that Sophie insisted on making appointments to discuss her varied "ailments"—which ranged from checking how toned her arms were, to examining her "slightly *too* silky" hair. The part that irked me was that she was taking my time away from patients who needed help.

The murmured voices at the front desk faded out and I leaned forward, listening closer.

The front desk was silent. Blissful, easy silence.

Becca must've dealt with Sophie after all.

A wave of relief washed through my body as I walked towards my bag, eyes barely open. I had to get into my running shorts, and fast. I blinked hard a couple of times in a feeble attempt to wake myself up.

Knock knock.

"Dr. Bell?" Becca said from the doorway. "Sophie Moore is here to see you."

A couple of four letter words danced through my head as I faced Becca. Miraculously, Sophie wasn't hovering behind her. "Can you tell her I'm wrapping up for the day? We're open again tomorrow morning, and Dr. Rob can help her then."

"But, *Doctor*," a voice whined from around the corner. Becca tumbled to the side as a very wide-eyed and pouty Sophie Moore stepped into view. "It's an emergency!"

My heart sank to my toes but I forced a smile. "Hi Sophie. What seems to be the problem?"

Sophie flung her long, pearly hair over her shoulder and fluttered her fake eyelashes at me. She was tall and slim, and her skin glowed the kind of nutty orange commonly seen after a session at the tanning salon. She was beautiful... if you liked the overly made-up look.

Sophie shot Becca a rude sneer, then marched into the room, heels clacking on the linoleum. Becca rolled her eyes behind Sophie's back, and I hid my smile as she walked away. Sophie hopped up on the exam table, her black skirt swishing around her legs.

"Right, Sophie," I grunted. "What can I help you with? Is it your blood pressure again?"

Sophie stared at me quizzically. "What?"

I was so tired my thoughts were moving like molasses. Wasn't that why Sophie came to see me last time? My memory was normally good.

"Sorry," I said as I searched through my files for her chart. "I thought that, when you came in yesterday, it was about your blood pressure. I must be mistaken."

"Oh." Sophie's mouth formed a perfect "o," brown eyes wide. "You're right. I *did* see you about my blood pressure. You were just so good at putting that blood pressure thingy around my arm."

She slow-blinked a couple of times and I stared at her, a familiar ache starting to build at my temples. Sophie's arrival was often accompanied by a pounding, incessant headache—especially when I was running on practically no sleep.

"Anyway," she continued, catching my "get on with it" expression. "I'm having some problems with my knee."

"What about it?"

"It clicks. Every time I move it," she simpered. Then, she lifted her leg. "See?"

I listened closely as she bent and straightened her leg. I didn't hear anything, but that didn't mean much. I was working on a grand total of 15 hours of sleep over the past five days. I bent closer to her leg, and turned my ear towards it.

Nothing.

Still, I opened the cupboard to grab the tool to check her reflexes. "I don't see or hear anything, but I'll do a quick exam."

Over the next several minutes, I took Sophie's vitals,

then examined her knee, turning her leg left and right to check for injuries. She chattered away but I was barely listening. My eyes were drooping and I thought I might pass out on the floor of my exam room.

Finally, I completed the exam. "Looks fine to me. But, maybe an x-ray would be helpful?"

Sophie giggled, her nose crinkled in a way that I can only assume was meant to be cute. Then, she flipped her hair over her shoulder. "You know what, silly me. I think it might actually be *this* knee that's bothering me."

She held her other leg towards me and it took everything I had not to pinch the bridge of my nose and leave the room. But, she was my patient and bedside manner was important. I smiled at her flimsily while I grabbed her other ankle.

Sophie giggled again. "Bad day to wear a skirt."

I ignored the flirtatious tone behind her words and examined her other knee, resolving to be as professional as possible... and not rip out my hair and send her packing.

Then, like an angel sent from heaven, my phone rang.

"Excuse me." I dived towards it. I didn't normally answer my phone while with patients, but things were different with Sophie.

"No problem," she said with her feather-light voice. "Is it hot in here, though? It feels warm."

I frowned. I kept the clinic at a nice and brisk 64F at all times—there was no way she found it hot. I'd checked her temperature earlier, but maybe she *was* feverish. I glanced at her and her eyes immediately locked on mine. She stared at me boldly, unblinking, as she undid the buttons of her pink sweater, revealing a white blouse underneath.

The blood rushed from my face as I hurriedly turned

away. I pressed the "answer" button without checking the caller ID.

"Austin speaking." I tripped over my words, my tired brain barely keeping up. I was hoping for Dad, Grace, or my best friend, Ella Williams.

"Is this Dr. Bell?" a man asked.

I stood ramrod straight and cleared my throat. "Yes, this is Dr. Bell."

"Fantastic." I could hear the man's smile through the phone. "I'm Dr. Mendoza, calling from the National Association of Family Physicians. Is now a good time to talk?"

Not really. But the sooner I got off the phone with Dr. Mendoza, the sooner I'd have to deal with Sophie. And I didn't particularly want to do that right now. So, I said, "yes."

"Myself and the NAFP Conference committee have been exceedingly impressed with your work," Dr. Mendoza said. "We've been following your career for..."

"Doctor!" a whispered voice spoke from behind me.

I half-turned and Sophie was waving at me. Her sweater was off and her white blouse billowed in the air conditioning. She must've been shivering.

"What do you think about getting dinner tonight?" Sophie whisper-shouted, and then batted her mile-long fake eyelashes.

I raised my eyebrows with alarm, pretending I didn't hear what she said. I gestured that I was on the phone and turned away. Meanwhile, I barely registered what Dr. Mendoza was saying. All I heard were the words "keynote", "conference", and "Seattle".

"Dr. Bell, what do you think?" Mendoza's words finally broke through. "Would you like to do it?"

Yeesh. I wasn't listening at all. Do what?

"I'm sorry?" I asked.

"Would you like to do it?"

I bit my lip, wishing I could ask him to repeat himself. But, I didn't want him to know I wasn't listening.

He was probably just asking if I wanted to come to the NAFP Conference in Seattle, happening around mid-August. I'd been waiting for an invite and, despite the situation with Sophie, I was pleased and flattered that he'd called to invite me personally.

"Sure," I said. "Absolutely. I'll do it."

"Amazing." Mendoza clapped his hands. "We'll announce that you'll be the NAFP Conference's keynote speaker. I can't tell you how excited the committee will be to hear that we have Dr. Austin Bell as our keynote. You've made a real name for yourself in recent years. I'll have my receptionist send you the information now. Ciao."

The line went dead, but I kept the phone pressed against my ear.

My body had gone very cold, my lips tingling. I was barely aware of Sophie as she got up from the exam table with a huff, sweater in hand.

Did Dr. Mendoza just say what I think he said? Would I, Austin Bell, be keynote speaker at a conference? Not just any conference, but the biggest medical association conference in the country?

My mouth went dry as cement on a sunny day. There weren't many things I was afraid of. There certainly weren't many things I shied away from.

Public speaking was my one exception. And I didn't do exceptions.

3

ELLA

I shoved another handful of popcorn into my mouth and chewed loudly. The sound cracked and echoed through the empty theater and I was, once again, grateful that I was the only one here.

A piece of popcorn dropped from my mouth and onto my—Austin's—gray hoodie, bounced over my lap, and rolled to a rest on my suitcase in the aisle. I unashamedly picked it up and popped it into my mouth. If no one was around to see you eat sketchy suitcase popcorn, did it really happen?

I turned back to the screen, half-watching the movie—some cheesy, overdramatic romcom about two friends agreeing to a fake relationship to appease the main actress's stuck-up family.

I sighed, thinking about my own family at home. Where I should be right now.

Instead, I was sitting in the one viewing room of the Aston Falls Cinema, a tiny, completely unique movie theater. The projection screen took up half the wall at the front of the room, and a small stage was set in front of an assortment of couches, armchairs, La-Z-Boys and bean bags. Those then gave way to regular theater seating, which I favored.

Picking popcorn out of couch cushions wasn't a fun way to end a trip to the movie theater.

I chomped on a kernel and grimaced. I felt like a coward. I'd gotten off the Aston Falls Express over an hour ago, and I was meant to go straight to my parents' house. But, I couldn't bring myself to do it. I knew what awaited me— Carly flapping through the house like a rabid goose, chattering about her wedding plans, Mom badgering me with questions while Dad sat with today's paper, staying out of it all.

And, if Marc and Phil—my brothers—were over, they would no doubt be giving each other a hard time. They'd drag me, unwilling, into their arguments. Sure, they were both dads now, but their own child-like behaviors always came out around the other.

So, I retreated to my favorite oasis in the entire world.

Despite my mood, I smiled as I gazed around the small, deserted theater. It was a wildly different experience going to the theaters in New York. The ones that were always cramped and overcrowded, no matter when you went. The ones that smelled vaguely like cigarettes and old milk. The ones that were never silent because, even during the loudest of movies, there was always a group or two chatting like they were in a bustling cafe instead of a movie theater.

I coughed, my throat coated with butter. I was thirstier than a desert gerbil on a hot day. I waited for a lull in the movie before making my way to the concession stand for a drink.

"Orange soda, please." I smiled kindly at the teenage cashier.

The boy eyed me suspiciously, pushed his glasses up his nose, then sighed. Like my request was a major inconvenience.

"Sorry," I muttered as he slammed the soda on the counter. I reached into the pocket of my hoodie for my wallet, then realized I didn't have it. I shrugged bashfully. "I forgot my wallet. Mind if I run into the theater and grab it?"

"Sure," the cashier sneered, more or less ripping the soda from my hands. "But, I'm about to go on my break so you'll have to come back in half an hour."

I frowned, irked. "Can't you wait for me to get back? It'll literally take two seconds."

The boy crossed his arms and stared down his nose at me. "This is already cutting into my break time. Sorry."

My mouth fell open. Was the kid serious? Talk about a power trip.

I scrambled to find something to say, some quick, witty comeback. Nothing came to mind. I was normally on my game when it came to snappy remarks. But, I was *not* good with confrontation, and I couldn't get mad at the kid. Maybe he'd had a bad day at school.

Pre-school.

Now I was the one being petty.

The cashier started to turn away with my refreshing orange soda when a large, warm hand landed on my shoulder.

I squeaked, almost jumping out of my skin.

"I got it," a familiar voice said.

The boy turned back, annoyed, then straightened as soon as he saw the owner of the voice—my best friend, Austin Bell.

I watched Austin as he reached into the back pocket of

his black slacks for his wallet. I watched the way the firm, taut muscles of his forearms shifted beneath the rolled-up sleeves of his dress shirt. The way his clear blue eyes glanced at his wallet as he took out a couple of dollar bills. The way his sandy hair, tousled from the wind, fell across his forehead.

"Keep the change," he said, eyeing the cashier as he plucked the orange soda from his hand.

He turned to me, ocean eyes dancing. He was clean shaven today, showing off the perfect right angles of his jawline, and his strong, grecian nose was freckled from the sun. He smirked at me, his trademark smirk, and it occurred to me that my stomach would flip at how hot he was if I was attracted to him.

Which I wasn't.

"You're lucky I came by, Els," Austin said smoothly. "Not every damsel in distress has a handsome hero to rescue her from the evil teenage soda guardian."

"Some hero." I laughed. "That's what I get for forgetting my wallet."

Austin's eyebrows rose. "You forgot it? Like, in New York?"

"No, weirdo." I rolled my eyes. "In the theater. In what universe would I—"

Austin's smirk grew and blood rushed to my cheeks.

"Fine," I acquiesced, unscrewing the top of my soda. "But, it only happened one time."

"You're lucky we were watching a movie together." Austin laughed. "If it wasn't for me, you would've been scrounging through the couch cushions for snacks."

"Well. Whatever snacks I came across would've undoubtedly been better than those bizarre seaweed thingies you basically forced me to eat."

"I don't remember forcing you to do anything," Austin said easily, his eyes glinting at me.

For some reason, my cheeks grew warmer than ever. I changed the subject. "What are you doing here anyway?"

"Watching a movie."

"Duh." I rolled my eyes again.

"You tell me and I'll tell you."

I took a long pull of my soda, relishing the way the cool drink soothed the dryness in my throat. "Avoiding my family," I muttered. "You?"

"Looking for you." Austin smiled as he slid his hands into his pockets, making his biceps pop. "I went by your house and you weren't there, so I knew you had to be here."

I smirked at my soda, picking at the label on the bottle.

Growing up, the Aston Falls Cinema became mine and Austin's "thing." Grace didn't particularly like coming to the movies—especially when Austin and I were going through our horror movie phase. This was something Austin and I would do together, just the two of us. We'd throw popcorn at each other across the empty theater, pile into the bean bags, make blanket forts... It was a highlight of my childhood.

"Mind if I join?" Austin asked now, running his fingers through his thick hair. A dark shadow crossed his features, then disappeared as quickly and unexpectedly as it had arrived. "Had a long day. A movie and popcorn sound good."

4

AUSTIN

I followed Ella into the theater, and my shoulders relaxed for the first time in what felt like weeks. I smiled at her back as she walked, noticing that she was wearing my gray hoodie from high school, the sleeves rolled to her wrists. Her dark leggings were definitely too warm for a summer evening, but I wasn't exactly complaining.

It was the sort of cute-casual look that used to drive me crazy in high school. Crazy like I wanted to jump on her and shower her with kisses and feed her popcorn until we were old and gray.

But, that was high school Austin. Adult Austin didn't think that way. About anybody.

Especially not his best friend.

When I walked into the theater lobby and saw the kid at the cash register giving Ella a hard time, it took some effort to walk over calmly. I'd always felt that way about her—I hated seeing her in trouble. My gut instinct was to protect her, keep her safe. The same way I'd do anything to keep Grace safe.

Ella looked so funny when I offered to pay for her drink,

her big brown eyes even larger than normal. Like she was an adorable owl. Her curly brown hair was wrapped into a messy bun on top of her head, and she was wearing her thick-framed black glasses. Her pink, bow-shaped lips stretched into a smirk as she snapped at me. The same smirk I'd seen my whole life. The one that always made me smile.

I heard somewhere that yawns are contagious. Ella's smile was even moreso.

"Where are you sitting?" I whispered as we entered the theater.

Ella threw a glance over her shoulder. "Take a guess."

I frowned, making a show of searching the theater. I even cupped my hands before my eyes in the form of a tele-scope. Finally, I squinted and pointed to the seat that was very clearly hers, just ahead of us. "Aye matey, I think I see it there."

Ella let out a little snort. "You're insane."

"You're only discovering that now?"

We approached her seat. The theater was dark—so dark I almost didn't see the large, dark blobs in the aisle.

Her suitcases.

Apparently, Ella had forgotten about her bags because, the next second, she yelped. She fell forward, head over heels. Luckily, I was ready. I grabbed her arm and righted her before she could hit the ground, or spill even a drop of her drink.

"I swear." I laughed under my breath. "How do you survive in the big city without me?"

Ella shot me a glare that could freeze the earth's core. "Just fine, thanks."

She then took a hilariously huge step over her bags and sat. Meanwhile, I walked into the row behind and hopped over, plopping down in the seat next to hers. I stuck my hand into the bag of popcorn on her lap, but this time, Ella was quick.

"Mine," she hissed, swatting my hand.

"You're like a seagull when it comes to food."

"You oughta know better," Ella shot back and shoved popcorn into her mouth. She missed a couple of pieces and they dribbled down her front. Not that she noticed.

I sat back in my seat, clutching my victorious handful. Spending time with my best friend was just what I needed after such a long week.

As soon as I managed to get rid of Sophie, I checked my phone and saw Ella's text—that she was boarding the Aston Falls Express. Suddenly wide awake, I decided to change my evening plans. After all, I couldn't think of anyone better to talk to about this disaster with the NAFP Conference.

And, in the end, look where we'd ended up—watching a movie with popcorn. Just like I wanted.

I glanced at Ella, thinking about having another go at her popcorn bag. But, the expression on her face made me pause.

The corners of her mouth pulled down slightly, and there was a small quirk in her eyebrow. I knew what that meant—something was bothering her. When it came to Ella, though, I couldn't just straight out ask or she'd brush it off.

I watched her face closely, hazarding a guess. "How's Zac?"

A weird, bitter taste filled my mouth as I spoke his name. I stole her soda and took a long swig.

Ella shrugged and the bag of popcorn bounced on her lap. "Don't know."

I frowned. "How can you not know?"

She shifted in her seat once, twice, and raised her fingers to her mouth to bite her nails. She dropped her hand when she realized she'd cut her nails too short.

"Spit it out, Els."

"He's..." Ella started. "We're... We broke up."

My eyebrows shot up in surprise. Then, my heart thumped and my fists clenched. "What did he do? Should I be tracking this guy down?"

"No, no. It was nothing like that." Ella shook her head. "It was for the best. We just weren't meant to be."

I bit my lip, processing her words. A hot flash of emotion rushed through my chest and I did my best to restrain it, to keep control.

I'd been trying to restrain a lot of emotions since I'd learned that Ella had joined a dating app last fall. She hadn't gotten serious with anyone and, as far as I knew, she'd only dated Zac for a week or two. I couldn't help but dislike the guy, though. With his rimless glasses, his job as a museum curator, the tiny, stupid mustache that I wanted to twist anytime Ella showed me a photo of him.

I was sure the guy was perfectly nice. It was just that I didn't want to lose my best friend. She'd moved to New York two years ago, and a part of me was—irrationally—dreading the day I'd lose her forever. That was what happened when your friends got married, right?

"You're not ready to tell your family," I guessed.

"I can't exactly go home and say 'surprise! I'm still single.'" She chuckled dryly. Her glasses reflected the bright movie screen so I couldn't see her eyes. "Besides, imagine how angry Carly would be to have the conversation venture away from her wedding."

"Angry." I nodded, and then shivered.

I mentioned that my biggest fear was public speaking? Dealing with a grumpy Carly Williams was a close second.

Ella shuffled in her seat so she could rest her head on my shoulder. The smell of her mango shampoo permeated the air around me, and my breath hitched.

"How do you do this whole eternally single thing, Aus?"

I focused on the screen, trying not to wonder whether her body lotion might smell like mangoes too. "It isn't always easy."

"Man, then what chance do I have?"

Her cheek was warm where it pressed into my shoulder. "What do you mean?"

"Isn't your tagline that you're a 'never forever' kinda guy?"

I smiled to myself, enjoying her turn of phrase. "Something like that."

She sighed and her breath brushed my neck, sending goosebumps across my skin. "Finding an endless line of people to date sounds easier than finding someone to spend your life with."

Her words gave me pause. I didn't dare shoot a glance her way. "You could also argue the other way."

"I guess," Ella whispered, then she exhaled in a raspberry. "Let's just watch the movie."

I nodded, the hint of a smile crossing my lips. I found myself fighting a crazy urge to pat her hair and kiss the top of her head.

The movie played out in front of us—some ridiculous comedy that didn't require a ton of concentration. But, all I could think about was spending endless days on a beach somewhere, the smell of mango wafting all around me.

5

ELLA

The credits rolled and I sighed as the theater lights brightened. Austin yawned and stretched before standing up.

"Great choice, Els. That was a masterpiece."

"Oscar-worthy?"

"Hands down."

I giggled as I took a step over my bags, narrowly avoiding wiping out again. I winced at the memory of tripping over them during the movie. Thank goodness Austin was there to catch me.

Not that I'd ever tell him that.

Austin snuck past me and slung the lighter of the two suitcases over his shoulder before lifting the heavier one. I raised my eyebrows, refusing to notice the way his biceps bulged and strained against the sleeves of his shirt.

"Alright, time to face the parents," I said, my mouth dry. "Might as well tell them I'm still on my streak of singledom."

"What about Zac?"

I swatted my hand. "A blip. Barely a second date. He just wasn't my type."

"Really?" Austin smirked. "And, what is your type?"

If only you knew.

I bit my tongue. "I don't know. Tall, smart, likes to read. Doesn't mind overcooked mac n' cheese for dinner."

"Have anyone in mind?"

I picked at my sweater, self-conscious. "Nope. I don't know anyone like that." I laughed it off. "It's stupid, anyway. Even if I met someone like that, I doubt they'd want to date a girl like me."

I expected Austin to laugh along with me. Instead, his face went strangely serious. He looked at me with such intensity that I almost took a step back. "Any guy would be lucky to date you, Els."

My heart skipped wildly as Austin's eyes bore into mine. A weighted silence fell between us and I found it hard to breathe. Like some warm, not unpleasant pressure was squeezing the air from my body.

Then, I remembered who I was speaking to—Austin. My best friend. He legally *had* to say that.

I forced my lungs to expand as I drew in a breath, then laughed shakily. "Yeah, right. You're hilarious, Austin. Ha. Ha."

An unreadable expression crossed Austin's face. But, a moment later, he laughed too. "We should probably get you home."

I sighed, the heavy moment dissipating into thin air. "You're right."

"Unless..."

I perked an ear and turned back towards him. "Unless?"

Austin chuckled. "You don't remember our tradition? Come on, Els. Movie then dessert. You're really going to leave me hanging?"

A warm glow bloomed in my chest and I smiled.

Though Austin and I had gone to a few movies at the Aston Falls theater over the years, we hadn't had a "movie and dessert night" since high school. I'd always assumed he'd forgotten.

"Can't let good traditions die out," I said gravely.

"That would be a shame."

Austin and I exited the theater and made our way across Center Street. We chatted easily, catching each other up on recent events. He told me about the progress on the medical center, and I told him about being "temporarily" laid off at the Brooklyn Chronicle. Though Austin and I spoke almost every day, it was much more enjoyable speaking to him in person.

Though it was later in the evening, Center Street was busy. As we walked, more than a few women literally stopped and stared at Austin. I was used to this—Austin had been popular with the ladies since his growth spurt in ninth grade. After all, he was an outrageously hot doctor who had a heart of gold, and the cutest smile to boot. It didn't hurt that he was also kind, and when he turned on that charm...

Well, let's just say it made sense that plenty of women were after him.

The funniest part was that Austin was completely oblivious to these attentions. And, though he dated a lot—and I mean, *a lot*—he never seemed eager to settle down.

It didn't take long for me to realize where Austin was leading us. I picked up speed, almost jogging up the steps of Morning Bell Cafe. I threw open the door—it was just about closing time, so I felt confident that no one but my friends would be around to witness my oddities.

"Honey, I'm home!" I shrieked as I slid into the cafe.

Unfortunately, Mrs. Applebaum was sitting at the counter, and she stared at me and my grand entrance incredulously. My face immediately turned the same shade of red as my suitcases.

"Sorry, Mrs. Applebaum. I—"

"ELS!"

Something hard hit me in the ribs, taking the wind out of me. When I finally managed to stand upright, two slender arms were wrapped around my body in a hug.

"You're back?" Grace squealed. "Finally!"

I laughed. "Just got here."

"Amazing." Grace's blonde hair was in a ponytail and her green eyes sparkled. She clapped her hands and turned towards the back of the cafe. "Nicholas, I'm taking my break. Look who's here!"

Her husband appeared from the back office. Nicholas King—ex star quarterback for Chicago—walked into the room wearing a blue t-shirt and a frilly "Morning Bell" apron. It said a lot that, even with frills, he looked just as strong and masculine as ever.

"Hey, Els." Nicholas smiled warmly as he wrapped an arm around Grace's waist.

By now, Austin had dropped my bags in our favorite booth by the window. Nicholas gave Austin a fist-bump and we all caught up for a few minutes. Then, Nicholas kissed Grace before going to the counter to ring up Mrs. Applebaum's meal.

Grace turned to Austin and me excitedly. "What can I get for you guys? Butter pecan ice cream?"

I stared at her, surprised. "You have that?"

"We always order a few containers from Sweets n' Sundaes for Austin. And now, for you."

Though butter pecan ice cream was one of my all-time favorite things, ever, I shook my head. I was in the mood for a change. "Actually, I think I might try the chocolate s'mores cheesecake."

Grace smiled. "Coming right up."

Austin looked at me. "Unlike you to try something different."

"Unlike you to eat something with sugar." I shrugged.

Austin laughed, a most gratifying sound, and I smirked back at him.

We sat in our booth and had a little sword-fight with our spoons (Austin won the first round, I won the second). Then, I sat back and looked around the cafe. Grace and Nicholas had given Morning Bell a facelift recently— working on their house together had apparently inspired them to paint and re-decorate the place. It looked amazing.

I caught sight of my suitcases on the floor and dropped my head in my hands. "I can't imagine living at home for an entire month. I don't even know if there'll be space for me with all of the wedding stuff crammed into my old room. Mom said we might have to move some of it to the garage. If my dad allows that in his little library man cave."

Austin grimaced. "Sounds... cozy."

"Yeah. Not to mention it'll be a full month of dealing with Mom's nagging and Carly's obsessive planning and my brothers fighting."

"Can't you leave the room when it gets bad?"

"I've tried, but Mom follows me. Even to the bathroom."

Austin laughed, then cut his laugh short when he noticed my serious expression.

I bit the inside of my cheek. "What am I going to do?"

"You could stay at Austin's." Grace spoke from behind my left shoulder before she placed my cheesecake on the table. She passed Austin his ice cream, then put a small basket of fries on the table for herself. She looked at her twin brother. "You still have that room to spare, right? Why can't Ella stay there?"

Austin and Grace shared a glance, looking almost the mirror image of each other.

"I'd ask you to stay with Nicholas and me," Grace continued, chewing on a fry thoughtfully. "But, the guest room is an absolute mess. Filled to the brim with paint cans and odds and ends from the work we've been doing around the house."

She glanced at her husband, and as if on cue, her diamond ring glinted in the light. I chewed my lower lip.

Grace stood from the table, fries in hand. "Think about it? I'm sure my stinky brother can make room."

As if Austin was stinky. He smelled like the woods after rain—earthy, fresh, masculine.

She mussed up Austin's hair before skipping towards Mrs. Applebaum's dirty dishes. Nicholas finished with the till and they chatted back and forth, settling up for the night. They moved so seamlessly, the two of them. They ran the cafe like some sort of intricate ballroom dance.

"You're more than welcome to stay, Els," Austin said, tearing me from my thoughts.

I dug into my cheesecake, bringing a larger-than-life bite to my mouth. I chewed thoughtfully and swallowed. "I wouldn't want to intrude."

"You wouldn't be. Besides, it's been awhile since I lived with someone. Probably good for me."

"I thought you didn't like having roommates."

"Correction. I didn't like living with 21-year-old guys who drank every weekend when I was in college. You are neither a big drinker, nor a 21-year-old guy."

"Nice of you to notice." I took another bite of the slightly-too-sweet cheesecake, wishing I'd gotten the ice cream instead. Served me right for trying something new. I shot Austin a glance. "Would it be weird, though? The two of us living together for a month?"

"You've stayed in the spare room before."

"Only for a night or two. This is a whole month."

Austin shook his head. "It isn't weird for me if it isn't weird for you."

I nibbled my fork and stared out the window towards Center Street. Austin was right—it would be fine. It would be better than fine. His penthouse apartment would be a welcome escape after spending too much time with my family. Before I could talk myself out of it, I nodded. "Alright. Let's do it."

Austin smirked. "There is one condition, though."

"What's that?"

"I've been looking for a jogging buddy. You up for it?"

I groaned. I wasn't into jogging. Or running. Or cardio of any kind. My jogging speed was closer to that of a leisurely walk. But, Austin was letting me stay at his place. I could probably join him for a "jog" or two over the next month. "Deal."

Austin's eyes danced and he looked so smug, he might as well have invented the sport. "Excellent news. Roomie."

I laughed and Austin chuckled. Though we were best friends, I never expected to have Austin Bell as my roommate.

But, as we finished our desserts, the question nagged at me—*would* it be weird to live with him? I'd never stayed at his place for longer than a week. Now, we'd be together for a whopping thirty days. That was a long time.

The more I thought about it, though, the more this arrangement made sense. Austin and I used to stay over at each others' places all the time when we were little. We even used to share beds. This was basically the same thing. Minus the whole bed-sharing aspect, of course.

Austin and I were friends. Platonic, casual, easygoing friends.

Even if his glance earlier tonight made my heart skip a teeny, tiny beat.

6

ELLA

*S*unlight shone directly on my face when I woke up the next morning, blinding me as soon as I opened my eyes. I rolled over in bed, groggy and disoriented, and took in the somewhat-familiar surroundings.

Where am I?

I gazed around the room, slightly panicked. This wasn't my room in New York. For one thing, there was ample space, and the desk in the corner wasn't piled high with books, headphones, and hand lotions. Then, I remembered.

Austin's. I was living in Austin's penthouse for a month.

I smiled wide as I stretched. My back ached from sleeping on the futon—the glories of approaching 30—and I gingerly sat up. I'd have to remind Austin to buy a proper bed for his spare room at some point.

I checked my watch and saw that I'd slept in much later than expected—the combination of the trip here, the "breakup," and the stress of seeing my family had been a particularly draining mix. I also had twelve messages on my phone, all from Carly and Mom. All reminders for Carly's bridal shower, starting in an hour.

I opened my suitcase and took out my daily journal, hiding it under the covers. Though I trusted Austin with my life, I didn't particularly want him happening upon my innermost thoughts. Then, I turned to my small selection of dresses and skirts. I couldn't help but grimace as I assessed them. I wasn't a dress person, but Carly definitely was, and she expected me to convert for her wedding.

In the end, I donned a pastel blue dress with a sweetheart neckline that cinched at the waist. I'd bought the dress last year for a work garden party, and hadn't worn it since.

I was frowning at a pair of dangling silver earrings when the doorbell rang.

My feet padded loudly on the wood floors as I walked through Austin's beautiful living room and down the steel staircase. Austin was meant to have the day off, but he'd texted me early this morning to say that he'd picked up a shift to help Dr. Rob.

I whipped open the front door and a rush of strawberry blonde hair launched itself onto me.

"ELLA!" the ball of hair screeched. "You're here!"

"Hey JJ." I hugged her back. "Got in last night."

JJ stepped back and smiled wide, her big, honey eyes dancing in the sunlight. JJ Sutton—or, if you wanted to live dangerously, "Jessica Jade"—was one of my best friends. In high school, she, Grace and I had formed our own little group. Like us, JJ was a bit of an oddity. She was loud and confident and constantly put her foot in her mouth. But, she was easily one of the nicest people I'd ever known. Not to mention her singing voice was literally sweet as apple pie.

"Am I glad to see you." JJ shook her head. "I thought I'd have to spend days hunting you down. Gracie told me this morning that you were staying at Austin's."

"I would've found you at Sweets n' Sundaes, don't you

worry." I giggled, and then gestured for her to come in. She was wearing a jean jacket over a brown sundress that kissed her curves. I'd always been jealous of JJ's curves. Don't get me wrong, I had curves... but they seemed to be in all the wrong places.

I linked my arm through hers as we climbed the stairs. "How are you doing, JJ? It's been awhile."

"Too long," she said gravely, then smiled. "But I'm good, I'm happy."

"And how's Ted?"

JJ hesitated and I could swear her smile faltered. But, the next moment, she was all sunshine again. "He's fine. Still looking for a job. Same as always." She gestured around the penthouse. "How is it living with Austin? You're here for a month?"

"Wow, word really does get around fast here."

JJ shrugged. "I work for the biggest gossip in town."

I chuckled, remembering seeing Mrs. Applebaum at Morning Bell last night. She and her husband owned Sweets n' Sundaes and were, effectively, JJ's bosses.

JJ turned her doe eyes on me and wiggled her eyebrows. "A month is a long time, Els. Won't Austin's myriad of dates bother you?"

She gazed at me keenly, her eyes intent. I knew what she was getting at and I scoffed. "Once again, JJ. There is *nothing* between Austin and me. We're just friends."

"So you've repeatedly said since we were kids. A little *too* adamantly, I might add."

I laughed as I went to the kitchen and took out a box of Austin's ridiculous antioxidant-fueled quinoa and raisin cereal. It definitely wasn't my favorite breakfast food, but it would have to do. I poured a bowl for myself and one for JJ as well.

JJ had been pestering me about Austin since high school. She and Ted, her fiancé, got together the first day of her freshman year, and she probably thought that everyone should marry their high school sweethearts. Or, in my case, my hilarious, smart, and completely out-of-my-league best friend.

"We'll agree to disagree," JJ said, putting the subject to rest. For now. "How're you feeling about Carly's bridal shower?"

My jaw tensed. "Dreading it, to be honest. Mom's going to be all over me. And don't get me started on my nosy aunts."

JJ grabbed spoons from the drawer and took a seat next to me at the counter. "Well, what time is the party? I have the day off. Want me to come with you?"

I took a bite of cereal, careful not to spill any on my dress. "I couldn't ask you to do that. My family is the mother of all handfuls."

"I'm well versed in matters of over-involved family members. I can help."

I stared at my friend as she slurped up her cereal. JJ had so much energy, and her enthusiasm was contagious. If she wanted to dress up and keep me company at my sister's bridal shower, I wasn't going to say no. Goodness knows I needed the support. And, maybe seeing me with a friend would appease my mother somewhat.

"If you're sure," I said. "I really would appreciate the company. But, you have to promise me one thing."

"What's that?"

"That you do not encourage my mother's behavior with any talk about Austin and me."

JJ thought for a moment, chewing loudly. Then, she extended her hand. "Deal."

Strips of tulle and lace adorned the exterior of my parents'
house, and flowers in all of Carly's favorite colors lined the
walkway to the backyard. The back patio was nearly unrec-
ognizable with all of the frilly white decorations and piles of
gifts. Proclamations of "Bride To Be" were posted on nearly
every surface that didn't already boast adorable, framed
photos of Carly and Ben.

Screeches echoed from the patio as Carly and her gaggle
of friends stumbled outside, giggling and cheering. Mom
and my three aunts followed close behind, holding flutes of
orange juice.

Carly caught sight of JJ and me, and her eyes went wide.
Her lovely face exploded into a smile and she dashed down
the porch steps, basically throwing herself on top of me.

"Ella Bella!" she shrieked.

I hugged her back, smiling at the scent of her floral
perfume. Though I'd only seen her a couple of months ago,
I couldn't believe how grown up my little sister seemed. Her
brown hair was cut to a neat bob and her face was perfectly
made up. She was no longer a girl, but a woman getting
married.

"Hey, Car." I laughed. "Great to see you."

Carly stepped back and held my hands in hers. Her
hazel eyes scanned my dress. "You look amazing, sis. That
dress is gorgeous on you."

JJ nodded vehemently, and I blushed and swatted a
hand.

"Look at you, Car!" I exclaimed, examining her outfit in
return. She was wearing a delicate, eyelet lace white dress
that billowed around her knees. "You're stunning."

"Thanks. I know, though." Carly winked. Then, her eyes

shone bright as she squeezed my hands. "Oh, Els. I'm just so happy. Like, so happy. Settling down with Ben is the best decision I could ever make."

"And marrying you is the best decision *I* could ever make." Ben appeared at Carly's side, planting a sweet kiss on her cheek. He looked at JJ and I with a kind, though apologetic, smile. "Mind if I steal the bride away for a moment? I have something to give her before I leave you to it."

JJ and I smiled as Ben took Carly away, sweeping her back into the house. Ben Lyons was about the same height as Carly and me, but his kindness was above and beyond anything I'd experienced. Plus, he basically worshipped the ground my sister walked on, and I knew that he'd be a caring, devoted husband.

A warm breeze blew through the backyard and the sounds of happy chatter and laughter were almost deafening. Mom and my aunts were standing at the other end of the yard, and Mom caught my eye and waved at me. I smiled feebly and waved back. I needed more food in my stomach before I broke the Zac news.

I leaned towards JJ and spoke out the side of my mouth. "You hungry?"

JJ rubbed her stomach. "Always."

Together, we proceeded up the porch stairs, where I added my gift to the pile for Carly. We entered the house and proceeded straight to the kitchen.

"Ella!" Dad was standing by the food table, a huge smile on his face. His brown eyes sparkled as I walked into his outstretched arms. His familiar smell of old books mixed with spicy cologne soothed me instantly. Dad's hugs were the best.

"How're you doing?" he asked when I pulled away. "Are you all settled into Austin's place?"

"I am." Then, my smile faltered. "Was Mom upset that I wasn't staying here?"

"Not at all. With all of the wedding excitement, she just wants you to feel comfortable. You *are* comfortable, aren't you?"

I smiled at the concern in his tone. "Definitely. I'm happy not to be living in the midst of the chaos, to be honest."

"A good decision on your part." Dad winked as he slipped into his jean jacket. "Ben and I are going to grab a bite to eat in town. Enjoy the bridal shower!"

With a final wave, Dad disappeared towards the front door. JJ and I grabbed plates and started stocking up. The food table was piled high with finger sandwiches, chocolate-covered strawberries, fruit salad, spring rolls, and charcuterie boards.

I was about to dive into a particularly tasty-looking turkey sandwich when, outside, Mom clapped her hands.

"Ladies. Ladies!" Her voice echoed around the house and backyard. "It's the moment we've all been waiting for... PRESENTS!"

All at once, there was a mini stampede onto the patio, and JJ and I followed the crowd outside. There, Carly was sitting, regal as ever, on a plushy armchair. She even wore a crown.

One by one, Mom brought Carly her gifts and, one by one, she tore off the wrapping paper and exclaimed in delight. I couldn't wait for her to open my gift—a stunning Le Creuset casserole set that she'd been fawning over for months. I'd saved up over a few paychecks, but I had a feeling that her reaction would make it all worth it.

"This is amazing," Carly said repeatedly as she opened her gifts. Small, shining drops appeared in her eyes and she dabbed at the corners. Carly was like that—the epitome of sweet and delicate... until you crossed her path. Then, those kind eyes turned to fire. "I can't wait to share all this with Ben."

"Ben?" Carly's college friend, Abby, laughed. "This day is for you, sweetie!"

"I know." Carly sighed. "But, I want to share it with him. That's what love is."

I was overjoyed for my sister. She deserved this day, she deserved all the happiness in the world. And yet, I felt something else in my heart, too. A pang, an uncomfortable tear.

As happy as I was for Carly, I couldn't help but consider how nice it must be to love someone that much. To have someone love *you* that much. I wasn't jealous—not at all— but as I watched her unwrap gifts for this next chapter of her life, my thoughts automatically drifted to the sad little dating app on my phone. The one that hadn't brought me anyone to feel excited or happy about.

All of a sudden, I felt too warm.

"I'm going to grab some water," I whispered to JJ. I didn't even wait for a reply before I darted inside the house.

I went to the kitchen and swallowed one, two glasses of water. Then, realizing that I'd somehow spilled mayo on my dress, I dabbed a cloth over the blue fabric. Eventually, I gave up, staring at the gift opening celebrations through the window. I felt very detached from it all.

"What a beautiful day! Perfect for a bridal shower, wouldn't you say, Ella Bella?"

I bit the inside of my cheek as Mom came to stand next to me, a huge bouquet of roses in her hand. Mom was what you'd call a firecracker. She was at least half a foot shorter than me, with wild, unruly black hair and huge eyes framed by long lashes. But, her loud and vivacious personality dominated any room.

People said that we looked alike, but I'd never seen it. Carly was the one who looked like Mom. Or, my brother Phil—a comment he'd never really appreciated.

I grabbed a vase and filled it with water for her. She stuck the roses inside and held a manicured hand to one of the flowers, inhaling deeply.

"A beautiful day," I echoed half-heartedly.

"I'm so happy that you brought JJ, honey. But, where is the mysterious Zac? Your aunts and I are all *dying* to meet him."

My stomach twisted into a knot. Here it was. The moment I'd been dreading ever since I left New York.

"We split up," I said quietly, my eyes riveted on the scene outside the window.

"Oh." In that single word, I heard the disappointment, the sadness, the pity. "Well, that's okay, Ella. There are plenty of single 28-year-olds in the world."

I winced at her dejected tone, then covered the reaction by rolling my eyes. "I know, Mom."

"Don't let it get you down, honey." Mom wrapped an arm around me and booped my nose. Then, she took a step back and examined my face more closely. "Speaking of being 28, it might be time for you to start using eye cream. You want to avoid those wrinkles best you can, keep that skin young. Especially if you're still in the dating game."

Great. Now my mom was lecturing me on skincare.

Just what I needed.

I forced a smile. "Thanks, I'll keep that in mind."

Mom tutted. "Anyway, when it comes to relationships, it's best to get back on the horse right away. And I know just where to start."

"Mom, please, no. I'm happy. I'm single—"

"And focusing on your career, I KNOW." Mom finished my sentence with a chuckle.

I rubbed the back of my neck. I hadn't told her I was temporarily laid off and, if I played my cards right, maybe I wouldn't need to. Maybe the Brooklyn Chronicle would hire me back sooner rather than later.

Before I could say or do anything, though, Mom whirled around and placed her hands around her mouth.

"Martha, Laura, Jos!" she bellowed. "Ella's single again. Let's find someone to set her up with!"

My body went cold and red alert signs flashed inside my head.

I didn't want to be set up. I didn't want to be forced on any dates. Not again. I just wanted to attend Carly's wedding in peace, and get back to New York as soon as possible. I thought bringing JJ might appease my family, but it seemed that wasn't enough.

The pounding of footsteps thundered down the hallway as my aunts approached.

I had to think of something. Fast.

7

AUSTIN

hat have I done?

I slumped into the chair in my exam room, pinching the bridge of my nose. I stared at my phone screen until it faded to black.

I'd just gotten off the phone with Dr. Mendoza and the NAFP Conference committee. I'd told them that I'd changed my mind and could no longer act as keynote speaker for the conference in August.

But, it was too late. The committee had made their announcement last night. They'd sent the brochures and marketing items to the printers, emailed their network of doctors, and alerted the news media covering the conference.

"We're very sorry, Dr. Bell," Mendoza had said, his deep voice grave and sincere. It occurred to me that he was probably pretty good at breaking bad news to patients. "But, there's simply nothing we can do. If you pull out now, it'll look horrendous for the conference's image."

I couldn't fight Mendoza on that. And, in truth, I knew that pulling out of the conference was no longer an option.

At this point—accidentally or not—I'd made a commitment. I couldn't let down the NAFP conference committee by reneging. It was an honor to even be considered as a keynote speaker and, when I thought about that one, isolated aspect, I felt incredibly proud.

Until I remembered that being keynote meant I'd be presenting to a crowded room full of doctors. All looking at me.

That's when the world went sideways.

I was a doctor; I was good with practicalities—assessing people and figuring out solutions for their problems. Speech writing was simply not an effective or efficient use of my time. When I told Ella that last night while we were having dessert at Morning Bell, she laughed in my face. She waxed on about the joys of writing, but it was all so easy for her to say. Her job was to write; mine was to speak with patients. One on one.

Yet, in a month and a half, I'd be giving a 45 to 60 minute keynote speech to hundreds of people.

Amazing.

Ring!!

My phone screen lit up and I jerked in surprise. I saw the name on the display and answered with a smile.

"Hey, man. How's it going? How's the big city treating you?"

The gruff chuckle of my friend, Christian West, echoed down the line. "Same old. You know LA."

"Never a dull moment."

"I could go for some dull moments," he said ruefully in his trademark gravelly, melodic voice.

Christian was known for that voice. For the words and poetry he expressed with that voice.

Christian West was a country star. Like, a huge country

star. I'd met him on shift one evening at the hospital, when he brought in a woman after a small accident he'd witnessed. He and I got to talking, and it turned out that the country star was hilarious and sharp as a tack. We'd kept in touch over the years, even while his star rose.

"You planning on visiting soon or what?" Christian asked now.

"Nah, I won't be back in LA for a while."

"Understandable. I mean, after what happened, how could you not?"

I froze, mouth half-open. Then, I realized the game Christian was playing and I exhaled in a laugh. "You almost got me."

"You'll have to tell me what happened sometime." Christian chuckled. "I'm still dying to know why you left."

I ran my fingers through my hair, tugging at the ends. I'd never told a single person the real reason I left LA. I had no plans to change that now.

Living in LA was a wonderful experience. I learned a lot over the years I was there for med school and part of my residency. I loved the city—the excitement, the opportunities, the fast-paced lifestyle. I missed it sometimes.

After finishing at the top of my class, I had the option to move anywhere I wanted—Brazil, Australia, Switzerland. Instead, I returned home to Aston Falls and opened my medical practice here. At the time, it seemed like the right thing to do.

Though things turned out differently than I'd hoped, never once did I regret my decision to come back. And now, I was taking the secret behind my return to the grave.

There was a light knock on the door and Becca popped her head into the room. She smacked her gum, eyes thoroughly disinterested. "Dr. Bell, Dylan Murphy is here to see you."

I checked the time. I wasn't supposed to meet with the construction manager of the medical center for another ten minutes, but I appreciated his punctuality. "Thanks. Let him know that I'll be two minutes."

"No probs." She turned on her heel and disappeared out the door, but the scent of bubblegum lingered.

"I can't talk for long, I'm supposed to get an update on the building permits for the center," I said. "How's touring been?"

Christian sighed heavily. "Just got back from Europe and I'm exhausted. These huge concerts in massive auditoriums with all the lights and fanfare... it's awesome, don't get me wrong. But, it makes me miss the simplicity of small performances. Just me and my guitar."

"No wonder you're exhausted." I bit down on the lid of my pen and scribbled a couple of questions I had for Dylan Murphy. "You were gone for, what, ten months?"

"Something like that. I've been thinking of taking a break, but now Josh is insisting we film the music video for my next single first."

Josh was Christian's manager and, while they'd been working together for years, the money and fame had really gone to Josh's head. The guy was almost unbearable. Christian, meanwhile, cared mostly for the art, for connecting with people. He was a hard worker, focused and dedicated to his music. He put everything he had into it.

"Why don't you lay low for a while? Take it easy?"

He chuckled dryly. "If only I could. Things have been nonstop for years, and I've been fine with it. But now, it's starting to feel a little much."

His words triggered something within me. I thought of

my crazy patient load, the medical center, the freaking keynote speech. "I know what you mean. Well, if you ever want to take it easy, you're welcome to come back to Aston Falls. It's the exact opposite of overwhelming."

"I liked it a lot when I visited last year," Christian mused. "Seems like a great place. Aside from that one bossy chick."

I laughed. Christian had gone on and on about this mystery girl over the past few months. They met when he was walking by the river one evening, and I often wondered who she was. Probably visiting from out of town.

"I have the spare room if you want to stay with—" I cut myself off. "Never mind, the spare room is occupied for the month. Ella's in town."

"Ella?" I could hear Christian's smirk. "Like, your beautiful best friend, Ella?"

I shifted in my seat and cleared my throat. I suddenly felt very put on the spot. "Yes, she's my best friend. Yes, I suppose she's beautiful. What does that have to do with anything?"

Christian laughed. "Come on, dude. You *know* she's beautiful, you've said so yourself after a beer or two. You couldn't be more oblivious if you tried."

"I don't know what you're talking about." I frowned. "Anyway, I've got to meet the construction manager so I should go. Later, man."

I put away my phone and hastily got ready for my next appointment. Yet, I found my mind drifting back to Ella. Christian was right—from an objective, completely impartial perspective, Ella was beautiful. With those big, brown eyes, her perfect lips, her slim body with curves in all the right places.

But, what made Ella even more beautiful was her personality. She was sweet and kind, and she had a heart of gold. I might've been the doctor, but Ella had been there for me every single time I needed her.

I chuckled as I remembered having dessert last night at Morning Bell. She dropped a bite of her cheesecake thing on herself and tried to clean it up before Grace, Nicholas or I could notice.

I noticed, though. I couldn't help but notice Ella.

8

ELLA

*I*t'd been a few days since the bridal shower, but bits of tulle and lace remained strung around my parents' house. As I stood on the front steps, I self-consciously fiddled with my coral-colored halter dress. It was a warm July evening and my skin was sticky from the heat. My legs still felt like jelly from the jog Austin and I had gone on earlier.

Well, "jog" was a generous term—I'd lagged minutes behind, sweating buckets, while Austin literally ran circles around me. It was the opposite of my idea of a good time, and yet, I knew that what awaited me on the other side of this door would be worse. I couldn't bring myself to knock—no matter how much I was dying to be in an air-conditioned room.

Mom had called earlier to say that the photographer was coming by to take photos in preparation for the wedding. She asked—insisted—that I dress nicely and join them.

I didn't particularly want to get into another dress; I was the kind of gal who sported jean shorts and faded t-shirts in the summertime. Wearing two fancy dresses within the span of a week was a definite step outside of my comfort zone. And being photographed wearing said fancy dress? An even bigger step.

I didn't like being dressed up, I didn't like being the center of attention. I preferred to stand on the sidelines, observing from a comfortable distance. After all, my job required me to remain detached and impartial.

But, I would do anything for my little sister, and I had an obligation to be where she wanted, when she wanted. Today, I would stand in front of a camera and attempt to smile, look normal, and behave normally. Even if the thought stressed me out.

What if I sneezed when the camera flashed? Or, if the photographer's wind machine was too strong and every photo of me featured a sort of "squinty eye" situation? Or, if I tripped on the photography equipment and it broke?

Not that those exact situations had happened to me before. Of course not...

I checked the time on the pink plastic watch that Austin had given me when we were kids—the only watch I hadn't broken. I'd been standing outside for ten minutes.

It was time.

I took a deep breath and knocked. My knuckles had only rapped the door once when it swung open.

"Ella!" Mom exclaimed, smiling wide. She skimmed my outfit carefully, head to toe, and her eyes widened. "That dress is just stunning on you. You look amazing."

"Thanks, Mom." I pursed my lips as I noticed that she wore dark jeans, a floral blouse, and slip-on sandals. Her hair wasn't done and she was only wearing lipstick. "You look... casual?"

Mom grabbed my arm and dragged me into the living room. Carly was nowhere to be seen, but my aunts were all gathered by the kitchen. When I looked at them, they exploded into giggles.

The hairs on the back of my neck stood and my stomach churned. Something wasn't right.

"Mom," I said, my voice low. "What's going—"

"Ella, meet Steve." Mom cut me off as she pushed me in front of our sofa, where a man was sitting. A man without any photography equipment.

He stood and his eyes scanned my body in a way that made me want to skitter into the kitchen and hide. Steve was just a couple of inches taller than me, but he exuded over-confidence. He was also extremely buff—like, he hit the gym three times a day. He wore a maroon V-neck shirt that was a touch too much V, and his jeans were rolled up at the ankles. His hair was gelled and stiff, and I could smell the over-whelming scent of his Axe body spray from four feet away.

"It's Stevo. And you're Ella, huh?" he said, so poetically, as his eyes returned to my face. "Your mom did not do you justice. You are smokin'."

I held back a grimace as Steve—Stevo—took my hand and pressed his strangely moist lips onto my skin. I reminded myself not to judge the guy so quickly. Despite his air of arrogance, it seemed like he was trying to be nice.

"So, you're the photographer?" I squeaked hopefully. Desperately.

Stevo's thin brows furrowed. "What?"

Mom burst into laughter. High-pitched laughter that hinted at embarrassed guilt and secrets exposed. "No, no. Steve is the son of a friend of Ms. Rodriguez's dog walker."

I faced Mom, eyes narrowed to slits.

"Anyway," Mom continued as she took careful back-wards steps away from us and towards my aunts. Still giggling in the corner. "Steve is single too, and we thought you two might hit it off."

The hopeful look in her eye softened my aggravation a touch. I knew she was trying to help, trying to make me happy. But, as I'd told her on numerous occasions, she had to stop forcing me on surprise blind dates with any random single man she could find.

I glanced at Stevo, who was unashamedly leering at me while he thought I wasn't looking. So much for him being "nice."

He affected a power stance, arms crossed so his biceps bulged. He looked down his nose at me, which wasn't easy given that he wasn't much taller than me. "Your mom tells me you're a bookworm. I like reading but, like, only my Facebook newsfeed. Reading books is kinda boring. But hey, I've never gone out with a hot nerd before, so what the heck?"

My eyebrows nearly shot off my head and my jaw dropped. Did Mom even have a proper conversation with this guy before she tried to set us up? Or, was she so desperate to find me a man that she thought this apparent book-hater would do?

Fire exploded in my veins and my blood boiled.

This had to stop. Once and for all.

For some inexplicable reason, the romcom Austin and I saw the other night popped into my head. Before I could consider what I was doing, words were tumbling from my mouth.

"I'm not single anymore, Mom. I have a boyfriend," I blurted.

Mom's hand flew to her chest and a shocked silence fell across the room, our house, the town. The entire world went quiet in the face of my big, fat lie. Even my aunts were stunned.

"Who?" Mom asked.

I scrambled, mind racing. "It's a surprise."

She frowned, head tilted as she stared at me. She crossed her arms. "Why didn't you tell us? This is awfully embarrassing for Steve."

"It all happened so fast," I said, breathless. I hated lying.

Mom stared at me skeptically for a few more moments. I kept my eyes wide and innocent.

Then, she clapped her hands. "Fantastic! Ella, this is great news. When will we get to meet this surprise boyfriend of yours?"

Dang it. Didn't consider that.

"Soon," I squeaked.

Mom rushed over and wrapped me in a hug, squeezing me tight to her body. She patted my cheek once before darting towards my aunts. They all burst into quiet, excited conversation.

Meanwhile, my stomach was in a terrible knot and I rubbed a hand over my face. What did I do? Did I really just lie to my mom and aunts? Not to mention Stevo?

I still had weeks left in Aston Falls. My lie would be found out sooner rather than later, especially seeing as I'd now promised my mom that she'd be meeting my supposed boyfriend "soon." What a mess.

I needed to find a boyfriend, and fast. But, what were the chances I'd stumble across one of those?

9

AUSTIN

I shuffled the papers into the right order before filing them away. Then, I checked the time on my Fitbit—9pm—and stretched. The sky was a dark shade of blue as the last of the daylight faded into night.

I was alone in the clinic, catching up on days' worth of paperwork. Dr. Rob and Becca had gone home hours ago, and I was grateful for the quiet.

If I was being honest, I was stalling. The paperwork was urgent, but it wasn't nearly as urgent as my speech for the NAFP Conference. There wasn't a single part of me that was looking forward to getting back to that.

In short, it hadn't been going well.

A bitter taste filled my mouth at the prospect of working on it now. Maybe I'd go for a run instead, get the juices flowing. Or, maybe Ella was home and we could make dinner together.

The thought made me smile. Since Ella's arrival in Aston Falls five days ago, we'd barely spent any time together. Between my insane work schedule and meetings with the medical center's construction manager, along with Ella's various errands for the wedding, it really was starting to feel like we were roommates instead of friends.

I packed up my things, removed my doctor's coat, and turned off the lights. I unbuttoned the top button of my dress shirt. I couldn't wait to get into more comfortable clothes.

I was locking the door of the clinic when I heard a car door shut behind me.

"Woohoo, Doctor!"

My muscles tensed in response to the familiar, feathery voice. I squeezed my eyes shut, wishing the ground would swallow me whole.

It didn't. So, I turned around slowly.

"Hey, Sophie," I said, my voice detached yet professional. "Funny seeing you here at this hour."

"I was just out for a drive." Sophie swatted her hand casually. She was wearing a tight, black leather skirt, red heels, and a light blouse. Not exactly your typical outfit for driving. "Are you done for the day?"

I smiled wanly and a dull ache started pounding in my temples. Right on time. "I am. I'm just about to start dinner."

Sophie pouted her ruby lips and flicked her hair over her shoulder. "I haven't had dinner yet either."

"Too bad." I waited a beat. "Anyway, I should get going. I have a pile of work to do."

"I have an idea," Sophie said brightly, disregarding my statement. She beamed like she'd just discovered fire. "What if we get dinner together? My treat."

The ache in my temples grew more pronounced and I suddenly felt very, very tired. My entire body sagged. "Sophie. As I've said before, I'm not really dating right now."

She waved a perfectly manicured hand, approaching me

slowly. "Don't be silly, everyone's dating. You haven't given me a single good reason why we shouldn't."

My jaw clenched as I held up a hand and counted down the reasons I'd given her in the past. "Because you're my patient and I'm your doctor. Because you just got out of a marriage and it's a bad idea. And, mostly, because I don't think we're a good match. I'm sorry."

"Good match?" Sophie smirked. "What does that even mean? I—"

"Aus!" a voice shouted from around the corner. "Is that you? You'd better have my dinner ready, you—"

Ella stopped dead on the sidewalk. Her gaze ping-ponged between me and Sophie's back. Her cheeks turned pink as she assessed Sophie's short skirt and heels.

"Oh, gosh. Sorry," Ella stammered. "I didn't realize you were speaking to someone."

She backed into the light of a street lamp and my breath caught. She was wearing a pink dress that I'd never seen before. And trust me, I would've remembered.

The soft fabric skated over her curves, caressing each one perfectly and showing off her delicate shoulders. The pink color played off her naturally tan skin, and her silver heels made her legs look a mile long. Her hair was whipped into a gorgeous updo that framed her face and showed off her swan-like neck.

My pulse quickened as I gazed at her.

There was no denying it. Ella was beautiful. Truly, unbelievably beautiful.

She took my breath away.

"Ella?" Sophie's screech pierced the air and I was wrenched back to the present moment. "I thought I recognized your voice."

Immediately, Ella's face went from pink to ghostly white. "Sophie. Hi."

Sophie and Ella didn't have the best track record. Namely, Sophie used to terrorize Ella in middle school. She'd make fun of Ella's curly hair, or the fact that Ella used to bring comic books to class. She was a bully, and it wasn't until high school that she laid off. Mainly because, at that point, Ella was hanging out with two guys on the football team—Nicholas and myself.

Sophie being Ella's bully was another reason I never would've dated her.

"Well, don't you clean up nice." Sophie was saying now, her voice sugary sweet as she prowled towards Ella. In response, Ella shrunk back and crossed her arms. "I never would've guessed you could tame your hair like that. You certainly didn't look like this in high school. I seem to remember—"

"Let it go, Sophie." My voice was a crack of thunder.

Sophie wheeled around, teetering on her heels. Her blue eyes were wide and her mouth popped open. "What?"

"Leave her alone," I said, not unkindly.

Sophie's face went slack as she looked between Ella and me. Then, her shocked expression cracked and she laughed. "What? Is she your girlfriend or something?"

I gazed at Ella for a moment, noticing how stunning she looked, but how dejected she seemed facing Sophie. I had a sudden burst of inspiration and I flew forward, sidestepping around Sophie and rushing to Ella's side. I placed my arm over Ella's shoulders, pulling her close.

Ella looked up at me, bewildered, her brown eyes huge as they gazed into mine. Her shoulders felt so soft, so small under my arm and it took everything I had not to wrap both arms around her. The smell of her mango shampoo was comfortingly familiar, and I shot her a quick smile, hoping she'd trust me.

I looked at Sophie and smiled my biggest, brightest smile. "That's right. Ella is my girlfriend."

10

ELLA

I'm his WHAT?

I twisted my neck to look between Austin and Sophie. My best friend and my school nemesis. It was weird enough that they were talking to each other. But then, for him to make such an announcement...

Was Austin aware of what he'd just said?

"She's my girlfriend," Austin repeated, squeezing me closer to his firm upper body.

Guess he was aware.

But, why on earth would he say that? And, why was Sophie here?

My thoughts were a chaotic, confused mess. But, the worst part was that I wasn't even fully focused on this bizarre situation. Instead, I was thinking about Austin's strong grip around my shoulders, his big hand heating the surface of my skin. Jolts of electricity seemed to tangle and travel through my body. I noticed how the side of his body fit perfectly with mine.

Plus, the mild, masculine scent of his cologne was making me light-headed.

"I can't believe this," Sophie scoffed. "You two? People used to joke around in high school, but I never really thought..."

Sophie trailed off, her eyes riveted on where Austin's arm lay across my shoulders.

Then, her jaw set and she turned to Austin. "When this thing ends, you know where to find me."

She gave me a final cool once-over, and then pushed past us to return to her car. The engine roared and she peeled away from the curb, disappearing into the night.

Feeling mildly breathless and more than a little warm, I peeled Austin's arm off my shoulder. "Want to tell me what *that* was all about?"

Austin chuckled as he stared at Sophie's retreating tail lights, hands in his pockets. "Just the resolution of a particularly nagging problem. Thanks, Els."

He turned on his heel and walked towards the front door of his penthouse, and a rush of confused frustration spread through my body. Frustration because Austin and Sophie were speaking quietly in the intimate darkness before I arrived, which bothered me for some reason. Frustration because Austin had lied and said that I was his girlfriend when I evidently was not. Frustration because my body felt weirdly cold and lonely without his arm wrapped around me.

"Hello!" I burst out, agitated, as I followed him into the spacious vestibule of his penthouse. "You're not going to tell me?"

"Maybe." Austin smirked that annoyingly confident little smirk of his. The smirk that drove women wild.

I kicked off my shoes, my entire body pounding with some red hot emotion. Anger?

He began to walk up the stairs and I followed him. "Honestly, Aus. What's the deal? I need to kn—OH!"

My toe caught the edge of a stair and, suddenly, I was falling. Going down, headfirst, onto the steel stairs.

I braced myself for impact, hands out and eyes squeezed shut.

This was going to hurt.

But then, a pair of strong, warm arms wrapped themselves around my body, and I stopped falling. I was safe.

I opened an eye and found myself staring into Austin's gorgeous blue ones. And, all of a sudden, that red hot emotion seeped out of my body. Everything was good. I was back in Austin's arms.

Even if it was only because he'd saved me from some horrible staircase-related injury.

Austin held me close, then he lifted me in his arms and walked the rest of the way up the stairs. Like I was weightless as a sheet of paper. He placed me on my feet and it took a minute to get my legs back under me. My mouth was dry as the desert and my heart raced. From fear, of course.

"Look, Els." Austin chuckled easily, like he hadn't just carried me up a flight of stairs. "I haven't had dinner yet. So, what do you say we get changed, meet in the kitchen, and I'll tell you while we're making food?"

I nodded dumbly, feeling completely out of sorts. "Okay."

My voice cracked embarrassingly but I turned and ran to the guest bedroom before Austin could say anything. I was feeling slightly feverish and I hoped I wasn't coming down with something.

I slammed the door shut and took in a few deep gulps of air. Being away from Austin, away from what happened on the staircase, I was starting to feel better.

I took off my dress and briefly thought of Mom saying I looked stunning tonight. Not to mention the positive reactions from Stevo, and even Sophie. Austin didn't seem to notice at all.

Not that I was surprised. Not that I wanted Austin to notice, anyway.

I forced the thoughts from my mind and focused on finding my pajama shorts and a hoodie. Austin's story had better be good.

Minutes later, I was sitting at the kitchen counter while Austin took out the makings for a salad and a cauliflower crust pizza. Only healthy food, of course. The guy was going to kill me with this health business before I could make it back to New York.

I was telling him about my unfortunate surprise date with Stevo, and Austin was in stitches, holding his sides because he was laughing so hard. He was wearing gray sweatpants and a crisp white V neck t-shirt. Even at his most casual, he looked amazing.

"Really, Els? He thinks that reading books is boring?"

"Unless it's his newsfeed, apparently. In all honesty, I'd be surprised if the guy even knows how to read."

Austin laughed harder. "Clearly, he's doing something wrong. There's nothing like sitting on the couch with a good book and getting lost in a story."

I smiled in total agreement. Then, I crunched down on a kale chip. I hated to admit that it wasn't the *worst* thing I'd ever eaten. "So. Are you gonna tell me the story with Sophie?"

Austin chuckled as he moved about the kitchen. "Long

story. But, essentially, Sophie has been visiting my practice daily for months just to flirt with me. She's asked me out several times, and no matter how many times I say no, she refuses to get the message. I'd almost admire her persistence if she wasn't such a pain."

I shifted in my seat as a strange burning sensation flitted through my chest. I didn't like the idea of Sophie hitting on Austin. She'd been an absolute terror in school. Not only to me, but to everyone. A person like that didn't deserve Austin, even in her wildest dreams.

"I was nice to her at first," Austin continued, washing lettuce for the salad. "I let her down easy. But, over time, I had to become more firm with her. And I honestly think she liked that."

"What do you mean?"

"I think she thought it was a game. Like, she had to keep playing to get a date with me. Not realizing that I don't play games when I'm dating someone. When I'm with someone, I'm all in. Hook, line and sinker."

I rolled my eyes. "This coming from the 'never forever' guy."

"You're right." Austin smiled. "I guess that's just how I'd want to be if I ever *am* in a long-term relationship. I want to treat her right, make her happy, be completely committed. There's no sense in playing games when you're happy with someone."

"Ooh, tell me about this lucky lady you envision," I said, against my better judgment. I didn't really need to know who Austin pictured as his future forever person. But, my curiosity was nagging me forward.

He took out some carrots and started slicing them. He glanced at me, and then back at the cutting board. "Let's see. I'd want to be with someone who's about 5'4", doesn't care what people think about her, wears shorts all the time. Maybe she likes to read—that'd be cool, too. And, she has to love at least some of the same foods I do."

My mouth went dry. Those qualities sounded familiar... Like, very familiar.

Austin put down the knife and placed his hands on the counter. His eyes gave nothing away. "If she can make jam, that's a bonus."

That's when I knew he was joking.

I punched him in the arm, laughing it off. "Hilarious, Aus."

Austin looked down to wipe his hands, then laughed along with me. When we calmed down, he shook his head. "Anyway, when Sophie asked if you were my girlfriend, it all just came together. Not even Sophie would go after someone who was already taken." He shot me a look under his lashes. "Sorry for using you like that, Els. I hope you don't mind."

I chuckled, but the sound was a bit shrill. I didn't mind that Austin used me to get rid of Sophie, but the weirdest part in all of this was that I'd told the same sort of lie to my mom earlier tonight—I told her I had a boyfriend when I absolutely did not.

Austin often joked that he had a twinny sixth sense with Gracie. But, I'll admit that there were times when I wondered if he might have it with me too.

I shook off the thought. "Can you imagine if we actually committed and went on fake dates and stuff?"

Austin laughed. "I'd ask you out for dinner and a movie."

"Dinner and a movie?" I asked, mock-shocked. "Definitely not. If you're taking me out, we're doing something wild. Like, dancing barefoot in a barn under twinkling lights."

"And I'd buy you flowers and wear a fancy suit."

"And the town gossips would have a frenzy because we're living together before marriage."

"We'd have to get fake married!"

By now, we were both doubled over, laughing our butts off. The mere thought of Austin and I dressing up for a date, like two people in a play, was just too much to bear.

Yet, as our laughter died down and I wiped the tears from my eyes, something occurred to me. Something crazy.

But, who better to share your craziest ideas with than your best friend?

"Okay," I said slowly. "I might be clinically insane, but what if we actually did it?"

Austin's smile quickly flipped to a frown of confusion. "Did what? Get married?"

"No. Fake date."

His jaw dropped. "What?"

"Hear me out." I stared hard at the granite countertop, tracing my finger along its cool surface. "I made a similar announcement tonight as you did. To my family."

Austin's eyes narrowed. "Els, what did you do?"

"I kind of maybe... told them I had a boyfriend."

Austin's eyebrows almost disappeared into his hairline. "And do you?"

"No," I said hurriedly. "Of course not. Which is why I was wondering if you... I mean, if we..."

"Spit it out, Els."

"If *you* could be my boyfriend."

Austin froze, dropping the carrots into the sink. Two spots of pink appeared on his cheeks and he blinked slowly. "I'm sorry?"

"It would be fake, of course. Just for the month. Until Carly's wedding." The words tumbled out, one on top of the other, and I suddenly wondered whether this was a terrible idea. Maybe there were some things you just couldn't ask your best friend. "My family is being unbearable, they keep setting me up with random strangers, and guys named Stevo, and I'm sick of it."

"Your mom has set you up with some stinkers." Austin pressed his lips together. "Remember the fireman?"

I grimaced. "Oh, he definitely didn't look anything like his photo."

"And that guy who spent the whole evening talking about his pet ferret."

"Smelled like his pet ferret, too."

"You've dated some real winners, Els."

I sat back, surprised. "And, apparently, you remember them all."

Austin tapped his ear. "I do this thing called listening."

I rolled my eyes. "Anyway, you get the point. If you act like my boyfriend for the month, my family might finally leave me alone. Then, after the wedding, we can 'break up' and everything will go back to how it was."

Austin frowned and the light, humorous vibe from moments ago was replaced by a serious one. He ran his fingers through his hair and leaned against the counter, legs crossed at the ankle. "Won't your parents be suspicious that you and I are dating out of the blue? Plus, I have a lot on my plate right now."

"Like?"

"Like... Like this keynote speaker thing. It's a big deal, and I don't know what to do about it. The presentation is in a little over a month now."

I raised my hand like a kid in class. "I can help. I'll help you write it."

"I have to present, too," he muttered.

"Ohhh." A smile snuck onto my lips and I snorted involuntarily. "Well, sorry friend, but a month isn't enough time to perfect your presentation skills."

"Thanks, Els."

"I don't think I'll ever forget the time you got up to present Shakespeare's Sonnet 18 in class. Remember? 'Shall I compare thee to a summer's day?' You shifted back and forth so much, the teacher thought you had to pee."

Austin winced and turned away to peel the carrots. "I remember."

Sensing I'd touched a nerve, I clamped my lips together. "Sorry, Aus. But, I swear I can help you. If you can just help me with this one teeny, tiny thing."

"I wouldn't call it 'teeny, tiny.'"

"Alright, it's big and huge-y. But, I would so appreciate your help and I would owe you forever. Please?"

Austin was silent, his back to me. I frowned, weirdly desperate for Austin to get on board with my plan. He was the closest thing I could find to a fake boyfriend at this point. And, though I would've helped him with his speech anyway, a trade felt more fun.

I watched Austin's back as he peeled carrots, then I slowly rose from my stool and grabbed a couple of carrot peelings that had escaped onto the floor. I tied them into a makeshift flower and got down on one knee behind Austin.

"Pretty please?" I begged, proffering my carrot flower. "With a cherry on top?"

Austin glanced back, saw my ridiculous offering and immediately burst into laughter. He rolled his eyes. "Alright, fine. I'll be your fake boyfriend. Now, can you please get off the floor and help me with dinner?"

11

ELLA

*S*weets n' Sundaes was uncharacteristically quiet for a Friday afternoon. The old-school ice cream parlor was a real throwback to the 1950's, complete with the traditional pink, white and turquoise color palette, and normally, the booths were full. Groups of teenagers, older couples, and hyperactive children would mill around, trying the dozens of flavors of ice cream and sorbet.

But, today, it was only Grace and me. And JJ working the counter.

"Got any butter pecan ice cream?" I asked JJ as I sat in a booth opposite Grace.

"Coming right up." JJ twirled away.

"Like you had to ask." Grace laughed. "You and Austin are so consistent with your ice cream choices. No surprises with you guys."

Not quite true, my friend.

I smiled at Grace feebly and played with my napkin. I hadn't told anyone that Austin and I were doing this fake relationship thing, and I still wasn't sure myself whether we were doing the right thing. I was beyond nervous to tell my friends; I had no idea how Grace and JJ were going to take the news.

"About that, Gracie." I took a deep breath. "I have something to tell you—"

"Hello, ladies!" Mayor Davis's cheery voice interrupted me as he appeared next to our table. "Beautiful day, isn't it?"

"It is," I agreed, peeking at Grace. If I didn't get this out now, I wasn't sure I would. "I was just telling—"

"Aston Falls is the best place to be in the summertime. And winter, too," Mayor Davis added with a chuckle. "But, summer is such a popular season for tourists."

"Sure is. But—"

"On that, mind if I ask you both a couple of very quick questions? I'm taking a poll to see how many of our towns-people would be interested in building a paved road to Aston Falls. I'm *finally* making progress with the county commissioner—thanks to a few rounds of golf." He nudged my shoulder and winked. "But, I want numbers to back it up. Have you got a minute?"

Grace and I looked at each other, and I exhaled. Mayor Davis was relentless when it came to this roadway issue. We weren't getting out of this anytime soon.

So, we grinned and bore it as we answered the mayor's rather tedious questions. By the time he left Sweets n' Sundaes to continue his poll, our ice creams were more or less melted. JJ joined us as soon as the mayor left. Smart girl.

"Man." Grace shook her head. "The mayor's been working on that since before Nicholas and I got together."

"That long?" I asked with a wink.

"Oh, ha ha." Grace rolled her eyes and took a bite of Rocky Road slush. "We haven't been together nearly as long as JJ and Ted."

"Woah, throw me under the bus." JJ laughed, hands up.

I smiled. "She's right, though. You guys have been together since high school, and engaged for, what, four years now?"

JJ shrugged, her gaze intent on a cookie. "We've just been too busy to get married. Ted's still looking for a job so he can move out of his parents' place and help pay for the wedding. We have the apartment together, but technically, my name is on the lease. Didn't stop him from moving his stuff in, though."

She wiped her hands on her pink and white apron. I could swear there was a note of bitterness in her voice, but it was probably nothing. When you were together as long as Ted and JJ had been, there were bound to be moments of frustration.

"Married life seems to be treating you well though, Gracie," she added.

Grace giggled, pink rising to her cheeks. "Things have been great. Nicholas's football camps are blowing up this summer and he's spending most of his days coaching the kids. Now that we have more staff at the cafe, I get to go with him sometimes. It's a lot of fun." She sighed, the picture of happiness. "I love watching him with the kids. He'll be the best dad someday."

I took another bite of ice cream, enjoying the smooth, buttery taste. Butter pecan ice cream was one of the few healthy-ish food items that Austin had sold me on—pecans were healthy, right? "Best dad? You guys talking about having kids?"

"Absolutely, we'd love to have a couple of little kiddos running around. Do you and Ted want kids, JJ?"

At this, JJ nearly choked on her cookie. She patted her chest and smiled.

"Not sure yet." Her voice was clipped and she hastily turned to me. "But, enough about us and our boring love lives. How's work, Els?"

I reflexively checked my phone. "Funny you should ask. I got a voicemail from the Brooklyn Chronicle's HR department this morning asking for me to call them."

"Do you think they're giving you your job back?" Grace asked.

"Yeah, maybe."

"Isn't that good news?" JJ frowned. "Because your face is saying the opposite."

I sighed and sat back in my seat. "It is good news. Really good news. But, in all honesty, the job is not what I expected. I thought that I'd be telling stories and writing something meaningful. But, my boss only seems interested in having my articles be as short and snappy as possible. It just doesn't sit right."

Grace bit her lip. "That sucks, Els."

I grimaced. "And, on top of that, my mom and aunts are still committed to setting me up with any single man they can find."

JJ rolled her eyes. "Who is it this time?"

"Have you heard of Stevo?"

Grace and JJ both shook their heads.

"Consider yourselves lucky. But, I do have a potential solution to that particular problem." I paused, my stomach filled with nerves. *Here goes nothing.* "Austin and I are going to fake being in a relationship. For my family."

I held my breath as a heavy silence dropped over our little group.

"A fake relationship," Grace repeated quietly.

"With Austin?" JJ burst into laughter. "Never saw that coming."

I shifted in my seat and hazarded a glance at Grace. Austin was her brother, after all. If anyone was going to have anything negative to say about this, it would be her. To my dismay, her brow was furrowed and she was glaring at her Rocky Road slush like it had personally insulted her.

"You okay, Gracie?" I asked gently, placing a hand on hers. "What're you thinking?"

Grace's lips pressed into a thin line as she met my eyes. "Are you sure this is a good idea?"

"Not at all," I attempted to joke. It didn't quite land. "I know—*I know*—it's not a good idea to lie to your family. But, I can't deal with any more of these blind dates. I can't deal with any more Stevos." I shuddered. "If my family thinks I have a boyfriend, maybe they'll leave me alone. And Austin and I will 'break up' right after the wedding anyway. No harm, no foul."

Grace continued glaring at her cup in silence, stirring the chocolate goop. It seemed like she wanted to say something but couldn't get the words out. I watched her closely, waiting.

"Alright, Gracie. Get on with it," JJ butted in, rolling her eyes.

Grace faced me again. This time, her eyes were clear, but concerned. "It's just that... Austin is a casual dater. Sure, I'd love for him to settle down and commit to someone, but I'm not sure when—or if—that'll happen."

I bit my lip as I patted Grace's hand.

"Not that my brother could ever deserve you," she continued quietly. "But I just want to make extra sure that, if this is fake and just for show, you're keeping your heart out of it."

Out of all the concerns Grace might have, I did not expect this one. I couldn't help but laugh as I leaned in and hugged my friend. "Oh Gracie, of course I'm not putting my heart into it. Austin and I are friends. That will never, ever change. Austin is helping me with this, and in exchange, I'm helping him with his keynote speech. It's a gentleman's agreement—a trade among friends. You don't have to worry about me."

I squeezed Grace extra tight and another pair of arms circled around us.

"Group hug!" JJ bellowed.

When we pulled away, Grace nodded and tucked a strand of hair behind her ear, appeased.

JJ, meanwhile, darted across the room to the radio. "This is my JAM!"

She cranked up the volume, and I immediately recognized the gravelly voice and the heartfelt strums of the guitar. The song was by Christian West, a country star from LA and a friend of Austin's. Christian West must've been doing pretty well to get his song on a radio in small-town Montana.

JJ burst into song, following the beats and harmony effortlessly. Her voice was silky smooth as it matched Christian's on every word. If I closed my eyes, I could almost believe the two were performing together.

Goosebumps rose over my skin, as they often did when I heard JJ sing. The girl could've easily taken her talents to New York or LA. Sometimes, I wondered whether she regretted not taking a chance and leaving Aston Falls. Any time I asked, though, she insisted that she could never leave Ted.

"Has Austin ever introduced you to Christian, Gracie?" I asked.

"Never. It's like he's ashamed of me or something." Grace

laughed. "Like I'm going to take a billion photos of him and sell them on the internet. Nicholas will always be the most handsome man I've ever seen, but Christian is a close second."

I smiled. "I haven't met him either, but his photos didn't look anything like I expected."

"I would never want to meet him, or see a photo, or anything." JJ pressed her fingers to her temples and closed her eyes theatrically. "I have a perfect idea of what he looks like in my head and I don't want to ruin it."

As the song picked up again, the three of us sang and ate ice cream and laughed. Man, I'd forgotten how much I needed time with my girlfriends. As much as I loved my friends in New York, there was nothing like childhood best friends.

Like Austin.

I thought about Grace's sweet, but unrealistic, concern that I might fall for Austin during our fake relationship. But, I'd told her the truth—Austin and I would always just be friends.

And yet, I couldn't help but think about the way he'd slung his arm around me the other night when we were speaking with Sophie. Even though she was in the middle of our conversation, at that moment, the air between us felt tense and electric. Like we were the only ones there. I remembered the way he spoke to me, the way he defended me... No one had ever done that for me before. No one except Austin.

I closed my eyes against the memory of him carrying me up the stairs after I fell. The way my skin sparked and tingled at his touch. The way he made me laugh when we cooked dinner in the kitchen.

If Austin ever *did* decide to settle down, he would make a great boyfriend to some lucky girl. A girl who had her life together, and was organized. A girl who had a job and an exciting, successful future.

A girl who wasn't me.

12

AUSTIN

y muscles burned as I sprinted forward, my eyes on the football as it arced across the sky. The world stopped and time slowed as I threw my body into the air, arms outstretched.

My hands made contact with the ball.

I held it close and landed in a roll.

"Touchdown!" I cheered, holding my hands in the air in victory.

Across the Aston River Park, Nicholas whooped as he jogged towards me. He gave me a fist bump and we walked towards the river, where we'd stashed our gym bags. It was another warm day, but a welcome breeze rolled off the river. The smell of pine trees and sunshine was in the air.

We collapsed in the shade, and I used the bottom of my red jersey to dab the sweat on my face.

"You've still got it, 13." I chuckled, slightly out of breath. Playing football with Nicholas was about as effective a workout as spending hours in the gym.

"Helps when you've got a good teammate." Nicholas's black hair stood on end and a light sheen of sweat shone on his forehead, but his gray eyes were clear and happy. He took a swig of Gatorade. "What's Ella up to today?"

"She's sticking around the house. She got some bad news on the job front last night." I shook my head, remembering coming home to find Ella bundled onto the sofa dressed in sweats and holding a bucket of figs. The tip of her nose was red and her eyes were teary. "Apparently, the Brooklyn Chronicle let her go. Permanently."

Nicholas rubbed the back of his neck. "That's rough."

"Yeah. I guess she was laid off and was expecting to be hired back. She didn't love working there, but she's pretty upset anyway."

I understood why. Even if Ella didn't like the Brooklyn Chronicle, it was always hard to lose a job. I knew it was especially hard on her given the job turnover she'd been through over the years. So, last night, I gave her a hug, and we sat on the couch together watching silly movies. Between her sniffles, Ella told me all about the phone call from HR. She also made it clear that figs did *not* qualify as comfort food.

"We're meeting up later for a jog," I continued. "I told her the endorphins would cheer her up. She seems skeptical, but I'm optimistic."

"As always. You enjoying having her as a roommate?"

"She's got her moments." I smiled. "She's surprisingly neat and tidy for someone who constantly drops food and is hands-down one of the clumsiest people I've ever known."

Nicholas snorted. "I seem to remember you loving those particular qualities back in high school."

"I don't know what you're talking about."

I took a long swig of water. Nicholas wasn't wrong—I always did like Ella's klutzy side. It was one of her most endearing and disarming qualities. She had a way of making things feel easy, comfortable. She didn't put on a show, didn't try to appear a certain way. She just was who she was, and it allowed me to be who I was, too.

After Mom passed away when Grace and I were in high school, I relied on Ella and her friendship more than she knew. She was my rock, the person who kept me tethered in place when it felt like the world might crumble.

Ella truly was a great roommate, though. I loved cooking meals with her, and watching TV on the rare evenings that we were both around. She'd also started a game where she re-arranged the books on my shelves, just a little bit. Just enough that I knew something was out of place. I enjoyed finding the wayward book and putting it back.

"Why are you smiling?"

Nicholas's voice brought me back to the moment and I cleared my throat. I wiped my face with my jersey again and tried to recover my normal, neutral expression. "No reason."

His eyes were playful but intent. "I recognize that face. Is something going on with Ella that you're not telling me?"

"No, dude. We're just friends. Always will be..." I trailed off, then bit the inside of my cheek, realizing this was technically a lie. "Except for the next few weeks."

Nicholas's eyebrows shot up. "What do you mean?"

"Ella and I have made an agreement, of sorts."

"What kind of agreement?"

I ran my fingers through my hair. "Ella's been having a hard time with her family—her mom and aunts are bent on setting her up with any single man they can find. She's basically asked me to be her blocker. She wants me to act as her fake boyfriend at family events until Carly's wedding. And, in exchange, she'll help me write the keynote speech for my conference."

Nicholas's brow furrowed and he took another long swig of Gatorade. "Aren't you worried?"

"Worried about what?"

"Worried that faking your relationship—faking your feelings—might make those feelings come rushing back?"

"Rushing back from where?" I laughed, rolling my eyes. "I never had feelings to begin with."

Nicholas's eyes sparkled mischievously. "Just checking."

For years, Nicholas had been trying to get me to admit that I had a crush on Ella when we were in high school. I always carefully avoided the subject with him, never quite giving him the answer he was looking for.

Because Nicholas couldn't know that I had a crush on her back then. At the time, her friendship was like oxygen to me. Especially after Mom died.

He also couldn't know that that crush had lingered past high school and all the way to the day I returned home to Aston Falls after LA. The day I discovered that Ella moved to New York.

I would never tell Nicholas any of that, though. There was no way he could keep a secret from Grace, and I couldn't risk this information getting back to Ella. I valued our friendship far too much, and she'd made it abundantly clear over the years that she wasn't interested in anything more.

Besides, she *just* ended things with Zac. Even though she insisted that they'd barely dated, I needed to respect that. Respect her.

But, when she appeared on the sidewalk the other night wearing that pink dress that hugged her body just right... Well, the image stuck with me. As was the feeling of her body in my arms as I carried her up the stairs, her hands clasped behind my neck.

When she'd asked me to be her boyfriend that night, it felt like the world tilted on its axis. A spark lit within me, a fire that raged through my limbs and down to my toes.

Then, she'd backtracked. Added the words "fake" and "temporary."

And, even though her ask was a bit unconventional, I never could've said no. I would've done anything for her, and I folded immediately when she countered my one attempt at resistance.

The truth was that Ella and I were never going to work. She was my oldest friend, and risking our friendship was simply not an option. Plus, she was Grace's best friend too. And Grace would be *furious* if I ever made a move.

"Earth to Austin." Nicholas waved a hand in front of my eyes.

"Sorry, man." I cleared my throat. "Went off in my own world."

"Sure did. I asked if you have plans for your day off tomorrow."

I leaned back on my hands and let the sun warm my face. "I'd love to go to the Aston Falls rodeo, if I can talk Ella into it. You sure you and Gracie can't come?"

"We can't. Working." Then, he lightly punched me in the arm. "Maybe you and Ella can use the rodeo as practice for your fake relationship."

I chuckled. "Maybe. It's not like it's a big deal, though. We'll just be going to a few family events together, and then we'll break up. Easy."

"If you say so." Nicholas smiled cryptically. "But, look at Ace and me. Things change, just keep that in mind."

13

ELLA

I twirled in front of the mirror, checking out my newest pair of light jean shorts. I paired them with a frilly, white button-down blouse, and I imagined the cowboy boots that would complete my outfit. But, something didn't feel right.

With a sigh, I returned to my bed, where I'd laid out a pile of clothes—all of the denim, blue and white variety. Once again, I picked through the items.

Why was this so hard? I never cared about how I looked. But today, I was struggling.

Maybe it was because summer was well underway, or because today was the rodeo. Or maybe, it had to do with the fact that I was now involuntarily unemployed.

I still couldn't believe that I'd lost my job at the Brooklyn Chronicle. I was so sure that HR had called to say that I could return to work after being laid off. Instead, they informed me in clipped tones that they were letting me go. Permanently. Budget cuts and all that...

I tried to see this as a good thing, as an opportunity. After all, I wasn't crazy about my job at the Brooklyn Chronicle to begin with. But, all I could feel was a distinct lack of motivation at getting on the job hunting train. Again.

I grimaced at my outfit in the mirror, deciding it wasn't what I wanted.

I rifled through my closet, and came across an item of clothing I'd forgotten—a dark wash button-down denim skirt.

I changed into the skirt and, when I saw myself in the mirror, I smiled. I tucked a strand of curly hair behind my ear. Even the pink watch looked okay with this ensemble.

As I gathered my things, I reminded myself that there really was no reason for me to look good today, no reason to feel embarrassed or self-conscious if I didn't. After all, it would only be Austin and me at the Aston Falls rodeo today. I shouldn't care at all about my outfit, or my makeup being done right, or anything.

And yet, I changed about fourteen times this morning.

"Rodeo time," Austin said when I walked into the living room. He stood from the sofa and passed me a to-go mug.

I frowned as I took it. "What's this?"

"I know how you get in the morning without caffeine."

I stuck my tongue out at him before we made our way downstairs. I tried not to notice the way his blue jeans fit him just right, the way his green checkered shirt had the top button undone to reveal a tanned triangle of his muscular chest. His sandy hair was lighter than usual from the hours he'd been spending in the sun.

He looked pretty great as a cowboy.

We donned our boots and left his penthouse, strolling towards the river where the rodeo was being held. As we walked, I noticed that Austin was checking his phone a little *too* often. I wondered whether there was a woman he was texting. Someone special?

"What's going on, Aus?" I asked, trying to sound casual. "Your eyes have been glued to your phone since we left the house."

"Sorry." He ran his fingers through his hair and I had a sudden, indescribable urge to do the same. "I'm waiting on a call."

"From who?"

"Maybury's Furniture Store." He shot me a smile, his blue eyes dancing. "Your bed's getting delivered today."

I stopped on the sidewalk, mouth open. "You're buying me a *bed*?"

"Well, not you." Austin rolled his eyes. "It's a bed for the guestroom. You were right, the futon won't cut it. Especially for my geriatric friends."

He elbowed me playfully and I almost toppled over. I'd only mentioned the back aches I'd had on the futon once. I'd actually started getting used to the thing. I couldn't believe that Austin went out of his way to make me feel more comfortable in his home.

"I can help pay for it," I stuttered. "Given that you're letting me stay for free."

"No need. Just write something nice about me in your daily journal."

"That I can do." I smiled. My insides felt warm and gooey. Probably just from the hot drink.

Austin had been pestering me for years about my daily journaling obsession. He, JJ and Grace sometimes joked that it was my only addiction, but it seemed like a pretty healthy addiction to me. There was something comforting about journaling at the end of the day, and it had become almost a religious practice.

What I liked was that it helped me establish some sense of control over my life. Which was necessary when everything—my career, my love life, my future in New York—felt like they were teetering on a precipice.

"I'm very curious to know what you've written about me over the years," Austin said.

I feigned a doe-eyed look. "Who says I've ever even mentioned you?"

"Oof." Austin winced, then smirked. "Touché."

I winked at him and took another sip of coffee. He didn't need the ego boost of knowing just how often I wrote about him. How much I thought about him when we were apart.

We chatted easily as we walked down Center Street in the direction of the park. The shops and restaurants were open and streams of people flowed from one store to another. We passed by Sweets n' Sundaes and Morning Bell, and both had line-ups out the door. The excited energy in the air was contagious, and I was vibrating as we approached the rodeo.

Austin, Grace and I used to go to the rodeo every summer when we were kids and, in high school, Nicholas and JJ joined us. It was a tradition of sorts. But, today, everyone else in our group was working.

Today, it was just Austin and me. Me and Austin. Going to the rodeo.

As friends.

We were almost on the grounds when Austin stopped walking and gently grabbed my arm. He twirled me to face him and we stepped out of the crowd, his expression serious.

"Els, I have something to confess," he said.

I was suddenly intensely aware of just how close we were standing. Close enough to feel the heat coming off his body. "What's that?"

Austin's ocean eyes met mine. "I had an ulterior motive in asking you to come with me today."

"Yeah?"

He nodded, brow furrowed. Then, he looked around the crowd with a half-smile. "I was hoping to lay to rest all of the rumors that I'm 'single and looking.' I know we agreed to do this fake dating thing in front of your family, but would you mind if we pretended to be together today too?"

My mouth was dry and I swallowed with some difficulty. "You want us to act like, well, a couple?"

"Yeah, the whole town's here. If people see us together, it might get around that I'm not available. Plus, it'll be good practice for us."

"I see."

"So, with that in mind..." Austin smirked and, to my utter embarrassment, he took my hand and very obviously kissed it in front of the crowd. "Ella Williams, would you be my fake girlfriend for the day?"

A blush rose to my cheeks as the imprint of his kiss burned deliciously on my skin. In my peripheral vision, I saw a few heads turn to look at us. To look at the gorgeous, model-worthy man kiss the hand of a woman who wasn't nearly beautiful enough for him.

I pulled my hand away, cheeks flaming, and cleared my throat. "Uh... sure?"

"Great." Austin smiled wide, but he didn't drop my hand. Instead, he tenderly cupped his palm against mine, interlacing our fingers. Our hands locked together easily.

Together, we entered the Aston Falls rodeo.

14

AUSTIN

*E*lla's hand was soft and warm in mine as we walked around the rodeo grounds. The sun was hot, and a fresh breeze blew among the booths selling homemade jewelry, clothing, and cowboy paraphernalia. We passed a lemonade stand and I bought us both a drink. The tangy, sour taste was wonderfully refreshing on this cloudless day.

As we walked together, hand in hand, I was doing my very best not to sneak glances at Ella. She looked incredible in her jean skirt and white blouse. She'd taken off her jacket and I was holding it for her, unable to ignore the way her dark hair fell across her shoulders.

We took a detour to the food trucks on the way to the rodeo tent. The smell of churros and french fries made my mouth water, and we stopped by a truck that sold donuts. Ella bought a cookies n' cream flavored one, while I got an apple fritter.

"You sure you want to ingest all those calories?" Ella teased, eyes innocent.

I took a huge bite of my fritter. "It's worth it."

"You're too healthy for your own good, Aus."

"I'm a doctor." I laughed. "That is literally my job."

"Whatever." Ella shrugged, a smile playing on her lips. "You've always been so set on being a doctor. Remember when we were kids and you would run around with your toy stethoscope?"

"I loved that thing," I murmured, recalling fond memories of using the stethoscope to listen for heartbeats on every tree trunk, fire hydrant and river rock. Mom was all too happy to humor me, listening with me.

"It's the star of most of your home videos, I bet." Ella chuckled.

"Hey, don't knock the home videos."

"I'm not knocking them. I actually think it's really impressive that you and Gracie have collected so many great memories over the years."

"They're memories of you, too," I said, knocking my hip against hers. "You were basically family when we were growing up. Still are."

Ella smiled, her expression dreamy as she got lost in the past. My eyes locked on her and I couldn't help but smile, too. I wondered what she was thinking, what memory she was conjuring up.

Before I could stop myself, before I could even think about what I was doing, I reached out and lightly wrapped my arm around her small shoulders. A fire burned where my skin met hers and I noticed how perfectly she fit there, in the crook of my arm.

But, Ella snapped out of her trance and, when she looked at me, her face was all business. "So. I have some thoughts on this fake relationship thing."

I dropped my arm, pretending that I was checking my phone. But, there wasn't much to see aside from a message from Maybury's to say that the delivery had been made. "Oh yeah?"

"There are a few events that I'll need you to come to, including my sister's bachelorette party next week, the rehearsal dinner, and the wedding. Then, we can break up."

I took another bite of my fritter. If she was going all business, so was I. "And what, exactly, will be expected of me as your fake boyfriend?"

"What do you mean?"

"Like, what do I have to do to fulfill my duties?"

Ella pursed her lips. "How about you do what you do with every girl you date."

I raised an eyebrow and smirked. "So, take you somewhere nice and kiss you at the end of the night?"

I watched Ella's face for a reaction. To my gratification, a bright shade of pink rose to her cheeks and her nostrils flared. "Hand holding is fine. Kissing is not."

"We're meant to be in a relationship. How are we going to prove we're together if we don't kiss?"

She shrugged.

"So, really, no kissing?" I said, my voice low and my eyes intent on hers. "At all?"

Ella's cheeks turned an even brighter shade of pink. "Well. No kissing on the lips. Obviously."

I bit my lip to hold back a smile. I loved getting a rise out of Ella, loved seeing her flustered and unsure. It occurred to me that, to an outside observer, it might've looked like we were flirting. But I knew the truth—Ella and I didn't flirt. We just teased each other, joked around.

No matter the fact that there were times in the past when I did wish I was flirting with Ella.

"The wedding's in early August anyway," Ella said

quickly, finishing her donut. "So, we don't have to keep up this charade for too long."

I frowned. "When in August again?"

"The 2nd. Why?"

"The NAFP conference is mid-August." I exhaled. "Do you think you can help with my speech before that?"

Ella smiled the kind of smile that could light any room. "Absolutely. I got you, Aus."

I smirked, happy to hear that we had time. "I probably just need a few writing tips for the speech. Then, it would be helpful if I can present it to you and get your feedback. Nothing major."

Ella smiled and punched me in the arm. "Anything for my best friend."

I winced. Ella sure did pack a good punch.

15

ELLA

*B*y the time the main rodeo event was over, my throat ached from cheering and screaming. I'd jumped up and down so many times, my blisters would be singing to me by the time we got home. For now, I barely noticed—Austin and I always got invested in the rodeo.

Though, I wasn't so invested that I missed the flirtatious looks women were sending Austin from across the crowd. I saw the way their eyes scoured his body, perusing every inch of his hot, cowboy self. Bless him, he didn't seem to notice.

As we followed the crowd out of the rodeo tent and back onto the grounds, Austin slid his hand into mine again. I almost jumped at his touch. In the past few hours, it had occurred to me several times that Austin didn't need *me* to be his fake girlfriend. He had so many more realistic options. He must've asked me purely out of convenience.

"How're you feeling about the job thing, Els?" he asked and his velvet voice brought me back to the present. "Have you started looking for a new one?"

I tucked a strand of hair behind my ear. "In all honesty, I

haven't tried very hard. There's just not a lot of good journalist jobs out there. Every time I apply, it's like starting from the beginning. Plus, there's thousands of applicants for every position—so my resume is a needle in a haystack."

"You could go back to freelancing."

"I loved freelancing when I was younger, but I'm looking to do something more long-term—find a magazine or newspaper to grow my career with. And breaking into that section of the industry feels impossible."

I loved New York, loved the city. But, the thought of going back and struggling to find yet another job that I'd likely eventually lose? Well, let's just say that I wasn't excited by the prospect.

Besides, there were much more fulfilling things to do— like reading on Austin's couch, or getting lost in a YouTube hole about how to perfect salad dressing.

"Have you told your parents yet?" Austin asked.

I laughed, too long and too hard. "Absolutely not. Can you imagine what my mom would say to hear that I'm single *and* unemployed?"

"Well, not single anymore." Austin smirked. "As far as they know."

"You make a good point."

All of a sudden, Austin froze, stopping dead in the middle of the crowd. A couple and their children shot us dirty looks as they sidestepped around us. I tried to drag Austin forward, but he was harder to move than a marble statue. When I faced him, his mouth was pressed into a line.

"Aus, what's wrong?"

"Sophie," he whispered. "Coming right at us. Don't look now."

I wasn't known for my subtlety, however, so I whipped

right around. And Austin was right—Sophie's pearly hair was breaking through the crowd, beelining straight for us. Her blue eyes locked on mine and a shiver of fear ran down my spine.

I turned back to Austin. "What are we going to—"

"Trust me."

Austin placed his hands on my hips and dragged me towards a wooden wall away from the crowd. His grip was firm and my stomach jumped as his hand pressed against a sliver of bare skin on my back.

Before I could think or speak, Austin unceremoniously shoved me against the wall and his body covered mine. He lowered his lips towards my neck, tantalizingly close.

I couldn't breathe, couldn't move even if I tried. My heart skipped and my legs felt numb. All I was aware of was Austin—the smell of his woodsy cologne, his strong body so close to mine, the tickle of his breath on my neck. My head spun and I closed my eyes to soak in this unexpected moment.

"Is she gone?" Austin whispered, his breath washing over my skin.

Somewhat reluctantly, I pried my eyes open and peeked over his shoulder. Through the people milling around, I caught sight of Sophie's retreating back. She cast an angry glance over her shoulder before disappearing.

"She's gone," I confirmed, my voice more breathy than I would've liked.

Austin immediately pulled away and I stumbled forward, lightheaded.

"Well." Austin smiled, holding out a hand to steady me. "I kept my promise."

"What promise was that?"

"I didn't kiss you."

He chuckled and I wanted to laugh along. Truly, I did. Instead, I emitted what sounded like a dry cough.

I'd never felt anything—ANYTHING—like that before.

16

ELLA

"*A*ustin, let's go!" I hollered for what felt like the thirtieth time in as many minutes.

I opened a cupboard and grimaced at the healthy food inside. Every once in a while, I'd find a small bag of chips hidden in the back, but today was not my lucky day. Instead, I took out a box of homemade seaweed crisps, sniffed the offending substance, then changed my mind and put the box back.

When a girl was craving salt and vinegar chips, seaweed just didn't cut it.

"Austin?" I bellowed again.

From his bedroom, I heard a muffled, "Coming!"

I rolled my eyes and collapsed on the couch with my book.

Since losing my job last week, I'd managed to get through some of my "to be read" pile. I was grateful for the time off, for the opportunity to rest, relax, and read. I hadn't done much reading in New York, there was too much going on. In the city, it felt like I was always a step behind, constantly scrambling to keep up.

But, if New York was a race for hares, Aston Falls favored the turtle. And I enjoyed the slower, more leisurely pace. The days felt longer here, the hours more pleasant. I didn't even want to think about going back.

I sighed and readjusted the straps of the little black dress JJ had let me borrow. Tonight was Carly and Ben's joint, semi-formal bachelor/bachelorette party. That's right, they were so in love that they didn't even want to spend a night apart celebrating their last few days of singledom. They'd invited all of their friends to join them on a massive Carly-and-Ben-themed scavenger hunt around Aston Falls, starting at the Aston Falls Express train station.

As eager as I was to get going—and indulge in the catered food—the anticipation of attending the party gave me heart palpitations.

Why? Because, tonight, I would introduce Austin as my boyfriend to my entire family. It was our debut. Sure, my parents knew Austin as my best friend, childhood buddy, and the town doctor. But tonight, he would arrive as my "surprise boyfriend."

The thought made my stomach roll. One, because I hated lying and didn't do it often. And two, because, as a result of point one, I was a very bad liar.

I hoped Austin was a better actor than I was. Judging from his little performance at the rodeo last week, he certainly could hold his own.

I shifted on the couch as I remembered the moment he'd pushed me against the wooden wall. The memory was seared into my mind like sweet fire, and it filled me with enticing but unwelcome jitters. The feeling of his fingertips resting on my bare back. His breath tickling the sensitive skin on my neck below my ear. The warmth of his body pressed so close to mine.

The more I thought about it, though, the more clear it became that my reaction was just a fluke.

Before Zac, it had been a long while since I'd dated someone. And even longer since I'd dated someone I actually *liked*. My racing heart, the lightheadedness, feeling breathless... Those were nothing, just a series of strange coincidences.

Maybe an allergic reaction. To his cologne.

Yeah.

Austin was my best friend; the only thing I felt towards him was a friendly regard. And a touch of annoyance when he got on my nerves.

Or made me late for my sister's bachelor/bachelorette party.

In all honesty, I had no reason to feel frustrated with him this evening. Austin had gone out of his way to wrap up his workday early so he could join me. He even put off a few appointments until tomorrow, ensuring that he'd be working late tomorrow night. He'd come straight home, run into the shower, and gotten ready as quickly as he could.

And yet, I felt bristly and uneasy around him. I might as well have been pacing around like an animal in a cage.

I wondered briefly whether my annoyance was an overcorrection for some other feelings I was having. But, I shoved that thought to the back of my mind. I simply didn't want to be late, that was all.

Plus, Mom needed to be in the best mood possible when I dropped yet another bombshell on her. Because, not only was I going to announce this evening that Austin were together, but I was also planning on telling her that I'd lost my job and didn't have a new one lined up. I was totally and completely unemployed.

I was going to rip the bandaid off, feel the immediate sting, followed by the slow, dull ache. But at least, at the party, I might be able to snag some chips from the caterers to ease the pain.

"Almost ready?" I yelled over my shoulder. "This isn't *your* bachelor party, you know!"

"I know." Austin's voice was much closer than expected and I leapt from the couch. He was standing just behind me, and he smirked, his blue eyes lazy. "Tonight's a big night for us, though. I want your parents to be happy to have me as their daughter's fake boyfriend."

I wanted to laugh, to chuckle along with him, but the moment I laid eyes on him, my mouth dried. Austin's hair was still damp from the shower, and his skin looked dewy and warm. He'd trimmed his scruff so it accentuated his chiseled jawline, and his eyes looked bluer than ever as he slid into his dark gray suit jacket. The fabric strained around his strong shoulders as he buttoned his cuffs.

He looked good in a suit. Like, really good.

With extra cherries on top.

"Els?" His voice broke through the sound of the singing angels in my ears. He stared at me, his brow wrinkled. "You look a bit flushed. You good?"

I picked my jaw up off the floor, finally aware that my face was burning.

Sure, I'd seen Austin in a suit countless times over the years. But, this was different. This time, I noticed just how insanely handsome my best friend had become.

"I good," I responded eloquently.

Austin rolled his eyes. "I know that look. It's time for food. We should get going."

No, let me stare at you just a little while longer.

"Yeah," I said instead.

Austin walked to the top of the steel stairs, giving me a

fabulous view of the back of his suit, and held out an arm. I was still staring at him, dumbfounded. He raised an eyebrow and nodded towards his extended arm, and I took his cue. I rushed forward, almost tripping over my own feet, and linked my arm through his.

"Making us late again, *babe*." Austin shook his head teasingly. "I'm always waiting on you. What am I going to do with you?"

I took a breath, trying to calm my fluttering heart. "Beats me."

By the time Austin and I reached the Aston Falls Express train station, the nervous butterflies in my stomach had relaxed. Now, there was just the occasional butterfly. Though calling them "butterflies" was generous.

They were more like giant moths.

As we walked, I carefully avoided looking at Austin head-on. Despite being one of the best-looking people I'd ever laid eyes on, talking to him felt wonderfully normal. Easy. He was just Austin Bell, the boy I used to push into the mud. As long as I didn't look at him directly, I was safe. I would apply the same rules to him as I applied to looking at the sun.

Had to protect my eyes—and my heart—after all.

We came to a stop in front of the train station and Austin squeezed my hand where it rested on his arm.

"You ready, fake girlfriend?" he asked.

I bit my pinky nail as the nervous moths were reborn in my stomach. I couldn't remember the last time I'd felt so apprehensive. How would my parents react to the news I had to share tonight? What would everyone say to seeing me on the arm of Austin Bell?

I forced a smile. "Ready as I'll ever be."

I hazarded a peek at Austin and immediately regretted doing so. I was, once again, taken aback by his brilliance. He towered over me, his athletic frame seeming at once safe and dangerous. I had the urge to run my finger along his profile, capture his strong nose and angular cheekbones.

But, like magic, when he looked at me, my nerves dissipated. Our eyes met and he smiled, and the chaos in my head calmed. The confidence in his gaze made me feel confident, too. I straightened my shoulders and nodded once.

We stepped into the lobby of the train station, arms linked and heads held high.

Bustling, noisy chatter awaited us on the other side of the door. Austin and I strode through the crowd and I tried not to notice how conversations died around us. How women literally swiveled around to look at us, look at Austin. Many of them didn't bother hiding the fact that they were pretty much drooling in his wake.

I patted my dress as I shrunk back, self-conscious. I'd seen the women Austin had dated in the past—all of them beautiful, athletic, and intelligent. Was it realistic to think that a guy like Austin could date a woman like me? Would anyone believe we were together?

Right before I could call it quits and abort the entire plan, a hand landed on my shoulder and twirled me around.

"Ella Bella, so happy to see you! And, I see you brought another friend?" Mom nodded at Austin with a wide smile. "Nice to see you, Austin."

"Hi, Mrs. Williams." Austin wrapped Mom in a hug. He

glanced at me. "Actually, tonight, I'm here as something else entirely."

He trailed off and he looked at me again. Heat rose to my cheeks and I found it hard to swallow. It was now or never.

"He's here as my..." I paused. Cleared my throat. "Boyfriend."

Mom's eyebrows rocketed skyward. She leaned forward, cupping a hand around her ear. "Sorry? I don't think I heard that right."

I opened my mouth to repeat myself, but my voice was gone.

What was I doing? This was clearly a mistake. My stomach lurched like I was in freefall and I reflexively looked around for the exits, hastily planning my escape.

"I'm here as her boyfriend." Austin's voice broke through my panic as he wrapped an arm around my waist, effectively grounding me. My mouth slammed closed and my mind shut up, too busy focusing on the feeling of his firm body against mine.

Meanwhile, Mom's eyes bulged as she looked between Austin and me, uncomprehending. Then, she lunged towards us, wrapping us in a hug.

"Austin Bell is your surprise boyfriend?!" she shrieked into my ear. "That's the best news I've heard all year!"

Somewhere, in the far distance, I could almost hear Carly's offended, "Hey!"

"I always knew you two would get together. I bet this has been going on for months," Mom gushed, squeezing us even tighter. For being such a small person, Mom's hugs were a force to be reckoned with. She stepped back and looked at me. "Does this mean you'll be moving back to Aston Falls? Leaving your job and New York?"

I bit the inside of my cheek and tucked my hair behind

my ear. Here was bombshell number two, the chance to rip off the bandaid.

Austin squeezed my waist and I felt better knowing he was with me.

"About that, Mom," I started, shifting from foot to foot. "I was actually... I was let go."

I waited for Mom's reaction with bated breath.

But, instead of seeming sad or pitying, Mom looked confused. "What's the problem with that? Now you have nothing holding you back when you move here."

"No, Mom." I frowned. "I'm going back to New York. I want to find another job."

Her gaze clouded over and she turned to Austin. "You're okay with this? With Ella living in New York?"

"All I want is for Ella to be happy." Austin said this so genuinely, without a beat of hesitation, that even I believed for a minute that he was my caring, selfless boyfriend.

Mom grimaced, then she pulled me aside and dropped her voice so Austin couldn't hear. "Ella, does the job even matter? You're dating a *doctor*. What more could you want?"

Her words irked me and I leaned away from her coldly. "I want a career, Mom."

She just shook her head and continued to stare at me like I was the eighth wonder of the world. But, the truth was that I wanted a career. Especially seeing as this little charade with Austin was just that—a charade. I didn't have a doctor boyfriend, or any boyfriend at all. All I had was work.

"I couldn't help but overhear."

Austin's deep voice startled us apart.

"Mrs. Williams, with all due respect, Ella is an extremely talented writer. Her articles are brilliant. The one she wrote on fast fashion was eye opening, and I changed some of my spending habits after reading it. If Ella quits working as a journalist, it would be a massive loss for our society." Then, seeing our perplexed faces, Austin quickly added, "but that's just my opinion."

I stared at him, dazed and lost for words. No one had ever complimented my work like that before.

"Well." Mom cleared her throat. She looked at me, an apologetic smile on her lips. She placed a hand on my wrist and squeezed. "Sounds like I've got some reading to do. I'm sorry, Ella Bella."

All I could do was shrug. My brain was no longer functioning. In all the ways I thought this conversation might go, this was the absolute *last* thing I could've expected. "Apology accepted?"

Mom squeezed my wrist again and winked. "You've got a good one here, sweetie. Austin really believes in you."

I pressed my lips together, but I couldn't hide my smile. I glanced up at Austin and he nodded at me. His smirk sent shivers of warmth down to my toes.

Mom turned to leave, and then paused. She twirled back towards Austin and me, frowning. "Wait a minute. You two are dating, but aren't you still living at Austin's?"

We exchanged a glance. I nodded sheepishly.

Mom tutted, shaking her head. "It isn't proper for the two of you to be living together before marriage."

Austin was about to say something, but I cut him off. "You're right, Mom. Completely right."

"You're welcome to move into the house, if you'd like," Mom offered. Then, her smile faltered. "Of course, your old room is packed full of boxes of wedding things and furniture. Carly and Ben have started collecting items for their house, whenever they find one. But, I'm sure we can make room somewhere, maybe move the boxes into the living room or kitchen or something—"

"Don't worry about it." I chuckled. "I can find somewhere else."

With a final, slightly relieved nod, Mom disappeared into the crowd and it was just Austin and me again. His words still burned bright in my mind and I bit my lip. "Massive loss to society, huh?"

"I stand by that."

I bit my lip shyly. "Did you really read my articles?"

"Every one. What are friends for?"

I didn't think that friends would read *any* of my articles, but it meant the world to me that Austin had read them. And, apparently, enjoyed them.

"You have to believe in yourself, Els," Austin said seriously. "You have so much to offer the world, so much talent and intelligence. You've always been so quick to doubt yourself."

A small smile touched my lips. "But you haven't. Doubted me, I mean."

Austin shook his head. "I never have."

My eyes met Austin's and, for the first time, I noticed the flecks of gray in his otherwise blue irises. The world seemed to melt away and I was hyper aware of the way we were standing—my chest mere inches from his. My insides felt warm, and happiness radiated from my core out through my limbs.

Sometimes I really did wonder how Austin knew exactly what I needed to hear. Maybe he did have that weird sixth sense thing with me. It felt like he knew everything about me.

I don't know how long we stood there, staring at each other. But, I eventually forced myself to look away. I couldn't get carried away. A man like Austin was so far out of my league, we weren't even playing the same game. I couldn't ever forget that.

Austin ran his fingers through his hair. "Want a drink?"

"Sure." I nodded, careful to avoid eye contact.

As we made our way towards the bar, Austin placed a hand on the small of my back. It was a small, insignificant gesture. I was sure it meant nothing, just a reflex of his. And yet, the protective, possessive undertone made my heart race.

Try as I might to remember that he was just my friend, electricity tingled on my skin where his hand lay. And, as women turned to stare at the two of us, pride rose in my chest.

For a brief moment, I could almost pretend that none of this was fake.

17

AUSTIN

The day after the joint bachelor/bachelorette party proved to be a very, very long one. I treated three children for strep throat, helped an older gentleman with his rehab exercises after an accident, and—the cherry on top—called an air ambulance for a woman who had gone into premature labor with signs of complications. The woman had been taken to the Bozeman Health hospital, and last I'd heard, mom and baby were doing just fine.

I suppressed a yawn and rubbed my eyes. As exhausted as I was, I would've done it all over again. It was worth it for Ella's smile.

I knew that Ella was nervous for the bachelor/bachelorette party. She was practically exuding fear and foreboding as we walked to the Aston Falls Express train station last night. I did my best to act as her anchor, to help keep her calm.

After telling her mom the "truth" about us—and about Ella's job in New York—the entire evening turned around. Ella and I had a great time. We did the scavenger hunt together and came in second after the bride and groom.

Then, everyone rallied to a restaurant in town where I ordered a beer and Ella had white wine. We spent the evening joking around and chatting.

I couldn't remember the last time I'd smiled so much. Speaking on the phone and on video calls was fun, but there was nothing like spending time with Ella in person.

Plus, she looked stunning in her black satin dress. She told me that she'd borrowed it from JJ, but the dress was clearly made for her. From the thin spaghetti straps that grasped her tanned shoulders, down to the hem that brushed her knees, the soft fabric danced over every curve and swell of her body. And whenever she twirled, the dress twirled with her.

I noticed a few of Ben's groomsmen and friends checking her out. Their eyes slowly skated down her body, but I doubted they saw the sweet little birthmark on her shoulder, the scar on her ankle from when she'd fallen off her bike when we were eight.

Ella was more than hot, she was beautiful. And I'll admit a little green monster clawed at my insides to see other guys flirt with her.

At one point, after going to get us some water, I returned to find that a particularly buff guy had taken the seat next to Ella. She was cringing away from him, sitting on the edge of her chair. I bristled and, without thinking, strode forward and sat on her other side. I handed her a glass, slung my arm around her shoulder and smiled at the guy lazily.

"Hey, thanks for keeping my girlfriend company. What are you two chatting about?" I asked.

"This is Stevo," Ella said, gesturing to the man. He looked even more greasy close up. "He's been telling me about the secret perks of protein powder."

"Nice to meet you, man." Stevo looked me up and down,

then straightened and flexed his pecs. He still didn't come close to my eye level. "You're the town doctor, aren't you? Makes sense that a hot nerd would try for a doctor. Setting her sights high, am I right?"

He laughed, looking at me as though he expected me to laugh too. Instead, my nostrils flared as Ella blushed and looked away.

"You don't know what you're talking about," I said coolly. "And I think it's time you apologize."

Stevo snorted. "What?"

"Apologize."

Ella glanced at me quickly, but I just stared Stevo down, calm as ever.

The guy's beady eyes narrowed, but eventually, he exhaled a frustrated sigh. "Sorry, Ella."

"Louder."

"Sorry, Ella," he said at full volume.

"Good." I let my arm fall to Ella's waist. "And, by the way, I'm the one who set my sights high with Ella."

Stevo pressed his lips together, and stalked off. I felt a little bad for my behavior, but not bad enough to apologize when Ella stared at me questioningly. I knew guys like Stevo —guys who hit the gym and counted calories more than they cared to keep up with world events and debate political issues. There was no way he was good enough for a woman like Ella.

And even after a good night's sleep, I still didn't regret my decision to scare off Stevo. My relationship with Ella might've been fake, but I had resolved to do one thing—I was going to play a mighty fine boyfriend. Which meant protecting her from people who didn't have her best interests at heart.

And, it was fun to act as Ella's boyfriend for the night.

More fun than I expected. Sure, I'd never been in a serious, long-term relationship—Hannah McAdams, a fellow med school student in LA, was my longest one and it had lasted three months. Even in high school, the girls I'd dated hadn't lasted long.

Back then, though, the problem was simple—none of them were Ella.

Lots had changed since then, including the fact that I was now a "never forever" kind of guy... right? I mean, I barely ever made it to the second date with the women I went out with.

Yet, I couldn't help but consider that, if last night was my first "date" with Ella, we were pretty much guaranteed a second date. And then, probably, a third and fourth. How many of these family wedding events would we attend together as a couple?

I shook myself off and blew out a loud exhale. I clearly needed sleep—these "dates" weren't real. They didn't count. Ella and I were friends. Dressing up and going out together amounted to nothing more than fulfilling my side of an agreement.

I had to be careful not to slip up and delude myself into thinking any of this was real.

By the time I locked up my office for the night, it was pitch-black outside. I wondered what Ella got up to today. I couldn't wait to get home so we could catch each other up.

I unlocked the door to the penthouse and walked into the vestibule.

"Honey, I'm home! I—" My voice died and I frowned. "What's going on?"

At the top of the stairs sat two cherry red suitcases. Ella popped her head over the railing and smiled down at me. She wore a blue hoodie with the hood up, her glasses, and not a brush of makeup. She was still one of the most beautiful people I'd ever seen.

"I'm moving out," she said, somewhat apologetically.

I jogged up the stairs three at a time and faced her. "You what?"

"I'm moving out." Ella shrugged. "My mom was right. If my family is going to believe that we're a couple, we certainly can't be living together. I have to move out, for the sake of the lie."

I furrowed my brow. "I guess that makes sense. But, where are you going to go?"

"Well, I can't go home for obvious reasons, Grace and Nicholas's place is still a construction zone, and JJ doesn't have space either. So, I called Ms. Rodriguez and she has a room at the Aston Glow Inn that I can stay at for cheap." She pursed her lips. "Now that I lost my job, I might as well stay in town a little while longer, anyway. Holly was more than happy to extend her stay in New York, so my rent is covered."

"I see," I said, and my shoulders drooped. "Ms. R did always have a soft spot for you."

Ella laughed and we fell into a slightly tense silence.

"So. This is all your stuff?" I gestured lamely towards her bags. "I won't lie, I'm sad to see you go."

"Don't be sad, Aus. It's not like the Inn is far away. Plus, I'm not moving out until tomorrow morning, which means that we have one more night to make dinner, watch mindless TV, and work on your speech." She rolled her eyes. "And go for a jog if you really, really want to."

I laughed. "Later. I'd love some food first."

Ella skipped towards the kitchen, yammering about the NAFP Conference and my presentation. I gazed at her bags one last time, then pasted on a bright smile.

I was going to miss having Ella as a roommate. We'd fallen into a comfortable routine the past couple of weeks—whenever I got home, we'd cook dinner together, clean up, then go for a jog, play board games, or read and watch TV. Ella had made me her classic overcooked mac n' cheese a few times, and, I had to admit, it was better than I would've expected.

We spent hours laughing and chatting; I made fun of her whenever she dropped her food, and she made fun of my healthy food choices. Though, I had started leaving little bags of salt and vinegar chips in the cupboard for her. Like she was a little house mouse.

I changed into a blue t-shirt and black sweats, then joined Ella in the kitchen. Together, we made pizza pops (Ella's choice), a fresh green salad (my choice), and lasagna (a shared love of ours). While we cooked, we talked about my speech—about what I wanted to say and how I would deliver it. The thought of public speaking still made my stomach turn, so I decided to focus on the speech itself. I'd cross the "presentation" bridge whenever I came to it.

As I gave Ella the rundown of what I'd be covering—opening a modern medical facility in a rural community—she gave me pointers on how to organize my thoughts. Soon, I'd more or less abandoned her with the cooking so I could take detailed notes of her advice.

"The best thing you can do is tell a story around the facts you're presenting," Ella said as she cut the pizza pops into little squares. "People don't just want to hear cold, raw data and statistics. They want to know the consequences of that data, how it affects them."

I frowned. "Let me get this straight. You want me to stand in front of a group of doctors and tell a story?"

"Basically."

I rubbed my forehead as I stared at my notes. "I doubt medical experts are going to care about the story around the data, Els. Facts are all that matter."

Ella checked the lasagna in the oven, and then faced me, smirking. "That's where you're wrong, Aus. You need to loosen up. People are sucked in by stories, they want to *feel* something."

I pursed my lips, eyes narrowed.

Ella noticed my skepticism and she sighed. "Okay, I'll show you an example. Give me a fact, any fact."

I paused, and then decided to use data from my keynote speech on the benefits of bringing cutting-edge medical care to smaller towns and cities. Ella recited the information back to me, adding some additional context that really did tie everything together.

I sat in silence for a moment, mulling it over.

"So?" she asked, one eyebrow raised.

"You're right," I admitted, rather grudgingly. "Maybe there is something to this."

Ella smiled and leaned against the counter. "It's okay, you can call me a genius. I don't mind."

I rolled my eyes and scribbled a few more notes. "Is this always how it is when you're writing?"

At this, Ella hesitated, just for a moment. "Sometimes. Not so much when I was at the Brooklyn Chronicle. My boss didn't seem to care what we wrote, so long as we hit the key points and got our articles done well before the deadline. I think he cared more about looking good to corporate than actually producing quality work."

"And you didn't like that."

"No. I care about the writing, about the power behind words. There's so much we can communicate through writing, it's such a wonderful tool."

I shook my head. "You can do a lot better than the Brooklyn Chronicle, Els."

Ella scoffed and tucked her hair behind her ears. "I'm not sure."

"Of course you can. You should work somewhere that values how you write."

"Maybe," Ella said noncommittally. Then, she smiled and opened the oven door to check the lasagna.

I sifted through my notes—I'd taken pages and pages of her advice, and I felt better about my speech. Part of me was actually excited to start writing it. I never, ever thought I'd see the day.

But, that was what made Ella so special. That was why she was my best friend and one of the people I trusted most. She was brilliant, and her out-of-the-box thinking was exactly what I needed sometimes. Ella could've been anything she wanted to be, and as a journalist, I had no doubt that she had a bright future. I meant everything I'd said to her mom—Ella was talented.

Beep! Beep!

The oven went off and I scrambled to a stand. I pressed the "OFF" button, and then reached behind Ella to grab the oven mitts. She was cutting carrots, her back to me, and I instinctively placed a hand on her hip as I leaned across her.

When I stood straight, my hand lingered on her hip just a moment too long. I felt a sudden, inexplicable pull between us, an urge to kiss the side of her neck.

But, the next moment, I snapped out of it. I put on the mitts and opened the oven door.

18

ELLA

"Well, this is cozy." JJ lounged across the wood-frame double bed in my room at the Aston Glow Inn. She gazed out the window and sighed as she looked at the mountains. "Nice view. Ms. Rodriguez must love you."

"I wasn't expecting this." I chuckled. "Especially with the discount. I thought she'd give me a small, dark basement room. But, this must be one of the Inn's nicest ones."

"Gotta love small town hospitality."

I bit my lip as I looked around. The walls of my hotel room were made of brown wood, and met with a high, vaulted ceiling. Shag carpets graced the floor next to the bed and by the balcony doors. A red plaid comforter covered the plushy bed—it was almost as comfortable as the bed Austin had bought for his guest room. The one that had replaced the dreaded futon.

"Are you missing living with Austin?" JJ asked as she casually reached for my daily journal on the nightstand.

I swatted her hand, laughing. "I only moved out, like, four days ago. It hasn't been that long."

"And yet." JJ gestured around the room. "Looks like you've settled in."

Her sarcasm was not lost on me. The desk in the corner was piled high with my computer, books and toiletry items, my suitcases were overflowing with clothes, and a lone towel hung over the bed frame. It looked like someone had come in, started unpacking, and then abandoned the room completely.

"It does look pretty bad, doesn't it?"

"It doesn't look good, that's all I'll say."

Spurred on by JJ, I started to pick up my clothes and place them into the wardrobe. I did consider myself to be a pretty neat person—most of the time—but, after checking into the Inn I'd struggled. Part of me didn't want to unpack, didn't want to admit that I'd left Austin's place for good.

But, I couldn't continue living out of my bags. Austin and I were no longer roommates. Now, he was just my fake boyfriend. It was time I moved on.

JJ rolled onto her back. "Top floor rooms are the best. Look at the height of these ceilings!"

"They've got pretty good acoustics," I said. "You could sing in here, if you wanted to."

"I sing enough at the apartment. I'm surprised I haven't received any noise complaints."

"Anyone who issues a noise complaint against your singing doesn't have functioning ears."

JJ laughed, then her mouth puckered downwards. "Well, that won't be a risk for much longer anyway."

"What do you mean?"

"I'll probably stop singing when Ted moves into the apartment after we're married. He always asks me to keep it down. My singing often distracts him. And, I get it, he makes a good point."

JJ's voice was level and unaffected, but her words bothered me. JJ loved to sing, and she had the voice of a literal angel. How on earth could Ted have an issue with that?

She sat up on the bed. "You still looking for jobs in the city?"

Her firm gaze made it clear that she wanted to change the subject. As much as I wanted to discuss the whole "Ted doesn't want her to sing" issue, I knew better than to push JJ when she wasn't ready.

I nodded towards my computer. "I am. Though the search is going about the same as it was when I was in New York—nowhere."

"You know why it's going nowhere?"

I frowned. "Because I don't have the qualifications?"

"Because you're meant to move back here!"

I chuckled, rolling my eyes.

"Come on, Els, why not? Your family's here, your close friends are here... I have no doubt you could find an amazing job here, too." Then, she smiled teasingly. "Plus, Austin's here."

I froze for a moment, my coral dress bundled in my hands, before grabbing a hanger. When I spoke, my voice was calm and even. "What does he have to do with anything?"

"Nothing. Just thought it was worth mentioning." JJ blinked innocently. "He is your fake boyfriend, after all."

"That's right," I murmured, lost in a memory. "Fake."

JJ peered at me, her honey eyes scanning my face. "Ella, what's going on? Your whole face just turned a new, blooming shade of bright pink."

I turned away from her. "I don't know what you're talking about."

"I've known you since you were 14, Els. This act ain't going to work on me."

"It's not an act," I said stubbornly. "I just have nothing to say."

JJ was silent for a moment. Too long a moment.

I squeezed my eyes shut and tried to think of anything that wasn't Austin. I pictured shoes. Socks. Running around. Running in the grass. Running and laughing. Austin laughing. Austin holding my hand.

Nope, this wasn't working.

I sighed and faced JJ, and she raised her eyebrows at me. We stared each other down—two people stuck in a to-the-death staring contest. I couldn't lose.

But, as my eyes burned and my lids twitched, I quickly lost confidence.

In the end, JJ proved to be victorious.

I blinked my sore eyes, deflated. "Fine. But you can't tell Gracie any of this."

JJ crossed her heart. "I swear."

So, I told JJ about the small—probably insignificant—things that had happened between Austin and I lately. Him defending me to Sophie and to my mom. How he'd stood so close to me, his lips hovering above my neck, when we were at the rodeo. The bachelor/bachelorette party, when we'd spent the night laughing and chatting, and it felt more like a date than any other *real* date I'd been on in my life.

"The weirdest thing is," I finished. "I can't explain my reactions. My heart gets all fluttery around him, and I'm annoyed at him all the time for the stupidest reasons. It's funny, I feel like I should see a doctor, but he's probably the only doctor I *would* see. I don't know what's going on."

JJ crossed her arms and cocked an eyebrow. "Sure you do."

I shook my head.

"Duh!" She exploded, throwing her arms out wide. "You like him!"

My mouth dropped open and I blinked. Then, I snorted. Which quickly turned into giggles. Which then turned into full belly laughter. I keeled over, hands on my knees.

"Are you crazy?" I managed, collapsing on my desk chair. "I can't like Austin!"

"Yes, you can." JJ's calm, rational, reasonable tone was really killing my buzz.

"JJ, even if I *did*, by some crazy twist of fate, like Austin Bell, there's no way we would ever work. He's miles out of my league, and any thought that he might like me back is a joke!" I gulped in air, wiping tears from my cheeks. It had been a while since I'd laughed so hard. So hysterically. "Besides, we're best friends, I would never jeopardize that. And, could you imagine how angry Gracie would be if we tried to date and then broke up?"

I mimed my throat being slashed and JJ rolled her eyes.

"You're so dramatic, Els," she said, standing from the bed. She walked behind me, took my hair in her hands, and started french braiding it. Like she used to do in high school. "Face it. You and Austin are endgame. I've been saying it since we were kids."

"You've been delusional since we were kids."

JJ made a face in the mirror and we both giggled. But, as she slowly braided my hair—an intensely calming sensation —my mind strayed back over her words. She really was insane. Sure, there were times that I was attracted to Austin. Like at the rodeo, and at the bachelor/bachelorette party, and even when he was sitting on the couch wearing his sweats and no socks.

And yes, in the past, there were fleeting moments when I

might've considered that, maybe, I had a small crush on him. But, those feelings were about as consequential as our fake relationship. What I felt for Austin didn't matter—we would never be together.

Then, my mind paused on a particular moment just a few days ago, when Austin and I were making dinner and talking about his speech. He smiled. It was just a regular, everyday smile. More of a smirk, really. But, I could recollect each and every detail of his face at that moment. The sparkle in his eyes, the way his full lips curved upwards, the five o'clock shadow gracing his chin.

I'd remember that smile forever.

When I peeked in the mirror, my cheeks were flushed pink.

19

ELLA

*B*eads of sweat gathered at my temples and dripped down my back as I jogged along Center Street. It was way too hot to be running on this late July day —there wasn't even the slightest breeze, and the dark pavement just radiated the heat. Even the chirping of the birds and bugs had ceased.

In retrospect, I was grateful for the jogs Austin and I had done together. I was at least slightly faster than a snail's pace now.

Several people stared at me as I ran by, and I couldn't blame them. Not only was I exerting myself in weather that made any fitness almost impossible, but my get-up was definitely unusual. I was wearing jean shorts, a faded band t-shirt, old white sneakers... with my face perfectly made up, and my hair done in a classy updo.

I tried to ignore the bewildered looks as I took a corner fast and stopped in front of Aston Falls' one and only bridal boutique—Frills & Lace. I swiped a hand across my forehead and prayed that my mascara wasn't running down my cheeks.

I was late. Like, really late.

Mom and Carly had texted me about a half hour ago, wondering where I was. Unfortunately, with all of the job and moving drama, I'd completely forgotten about my final styling appointment for my bridesmaid's dress. They told me to come as I was, assuming I'd already done my hair and makeup.

I hadn't, of course. So, I'd scrambled around for a solid twenty minutes getting ready. All while my phone almost vibrated itself to death with Mom's texts asking where I was, how long I'd be, and if I thought I gained weight since my last fitting.

I felt terrible for forgetting the appointment, and I wanted to make it up to my sister any way that I could. Carly might've been annoying at times, but she was my sister and I loved her. I would've done anything to be sure that her wedding went as smoothly as possible.

I fanned myself and took a deep, calming breath. With a final, self-conscious hair pat, I opened the door to the bridal boutique.

Inside was mayhem.

Carly's entire bridal party, along with a dozen of her closest female friends, were crammed into the small, chic boutique. Laughter, conversations and cheers echoed across the store and the crisp smells of chiffon and lace were nothing compared to the overwhelming scent of perfume.

I squeezed through the store, smiling at Carly's girl-friends. I passed by Ana, Phil's wife, and waved, but the crowd pushed me onwards.

Finally, I reached Mom and Aunt Laura.

"There she is!" Aunt Laura said, grasping my shoulders. She looked me up and down, and kissed me lightly on both cheeks. She'd picked up this habit while vacationing in Italy last year. It had quickly grown old. "Late again, Ella?"

"My fault," I mumbled, then leaned in to hug Mom. "Where can I find my dress?"

"Ah, another bridesmaid's dress," Aunt Laura said fondly. "Your closet will be full of them! I remember when you were the bridesmaid at Phil and Ana's wedding, and at Marc and Diane's. And now, you're Carly's bridesmaid too. I'd almost say there's a pattern." She elbowed me playfully. "Though, I saw the way you and that gorgeous doctor were cuddling up the other night. Maybe the whole 'always the bridesmaid' thing doesn't stand up, after all."

She winked at me and I smiled feebly back. If only she knew the truth.

"Ella and Austin are adorable," Mom agreed and I was grateful for her interruption. She turned to me and clapped her hands. "Now. Speaking of Austin, where is he?"

"Austin?" My brow furrowed. "Why would Austin be here... at a dress styling appointment?"

"Didn't Carly tell you? He's going to be an usher for the wedding alongside your brothers. We need to get his suit fitted today at the very latest. It's vitally important that the ushers match."

I shook my head slowly. "I haven't heard anything about this. Why would he be an usher?"

"He's basically family now, Ella Bella," Mom said gravely, like she couldn't believe I'd asked such a senseless question. "It's only right that he joins your brothers."

"That's not necessary, Mom. Really. Austin's very busy, he's got his practice to run, and the medical center to coordinate, and all that—"

"Nonsense." Mom waved her left hand and reached for

her phone with her right. "I'll call him now. I'm sure he can pop by for a couple of minutes on his lunch break."

Mom tapped at the numbers on her screen, and a rush of adrenaline burst through my veins. I couldn't let her talk to him, couldn't let her convince him to come. I knew he'd do it, he'd drop everything for my family in a heartbeat. But, if he was busy, I couldn't let this derail his day.

"Let me call him," I said hurriedly. "I've been wanting to talk to my, uh... *honeypie* all morning."

Mom's face exploded into a beaming smile. "You kids. Alright, I'll leave you to it."

With that, she stashed her phone in her back pocket, grabbed Laura's arm, and charged through the crowd towards Carly. I exhaled a sigh of relief and clutched my head. My hair was already falling out of the updo, and tendrils hung along the side of my face. I had no doubt that I looked a mess, and part of me hoped Austin wouldn't have to see me in this condition.

But, I took out my phone anyway and dialed his office number, crossing my fingers that he wouldn't pick up.

"Dr. Bell speaking." His warm, smooth voice flowed down the line like melted chocolate.

Say more things.

Then, I realized that it was technically my turn to speak. "Oh! Hi, Aus, it's Ella."

"What's up, weirdo?"

"Please don't hate me, but I might need your help... only if you're not too busy."

He chuckled. "I'm always busy, but what's on your mind?"

I paused, the phone pressed against my ear as I debated my next move. Could I ask Austin to leave his practice in the middle of the day for this random errand? Could I take him away from patients who needed him?

No, I decided. This wasn't right.

I was about to insist that he ignore me and hang up the phone when his melted-chocolate voice spoke again. "Els, talk to me. What's up?"

I took a deep breath and squeezed my eyes shut. "It's stupid, but I'm at Frills & Lace with Mom and Carly, and apparently, they want you to be an usher. They'd like you to come in for a suit fitting. Now that we're 'dating,' you've been promoted."

"Mhmm," Austin murmured. "When?"

I bit my nail. "Soon. Today."

The phone line was silent for a long moment and I wondered whether Austin had hung up on me. Truthfully, I might've hung up on me, too.

"I'll be there in fifteen," he said. "Just need to transfer my next patient to Dr. Rob, and get changed."

"Are you sure?" I asked. "You really, really don't have to. I know you're busy, so if that's the case, we'll figure something else out. I'm sure I can get you out of being an usher, too."

"Don't be ridiculous, Els." I could hear his smile. "Don't you know after all these years that I would do anything for you?"

A series of strange, fluttering sensations started in my stomach and radiated out through my body. I found I was smiling the biggest, stupidest smile. I had no idea what to say to that.

"Is fifteen minutes okay, Els?" Austin asked after a few seconds of silence.

I snapped out of it, clearing my throat. "Yeah, of course, dude. Whatever works."

"Good." I heard his smile again.

I was about to hang up when I remembered one more crucial detail. "Oh, and Aus? I might be calling you 'honeypie' when you arrive."

"Sounds good, snugglekins," he answered smoothly. "I'll be right there."

Austin wasn't lying.

Exactly fifteen minutes later, he strode through the front door of the bridal boutique. A hush fell over the store as twenty pairs of eager eyes swiveled towards him. He stood by the entrance, confident as ever, and his gaze slid over the crowd. He was spellbinding, like a lion at the front of the pack. I couldn't tear my eyes away from him, and apparently, neither could anyone else.

To be fair, he did look handsome as ever in a pair of blue jeans and a gray t-shirt.

His eyes met mine and it was like the world faded away. He made his way through the crowd, never dropping my gaze, and I could swear that time slowed for him. My head spun and I didn't even realize I wasn't breathing until he was standing right next to me.

"Sorry, I'm late," he said with that same chocolatey voice. He leaned down and kissed my cheek. "I had a couple things to wrap up."

"No worries." I managed a shaky smile.

What was wrong with me today? It wasn't like Austin and I didn't see each other all the time, didn't text almost constantly. But, for some reason, I felt hyper aware of him, hyper aware of myself.

How do I normally behave around Austin Bell?

"Austin!" Mom shrieked as she broke through the crowd. "You're here. Fantastic."

"Wouldn't miss it for the world, Mrs. Williams." He slung an arm over my shoulder and I was hit by his masculine, woodsy cologne. "Can't let down my babycakes."

I held back a gag as he beamed down at me. I forced a smile back, signaling with my eyes to cool it.

Mom giggled like a schoolgirl. "We're so glad that you'll be an usher at the wedding." Then, she leaned in and wiggled her eyebrows. "Could be good practice for *another* wedding, hm?"

Horrified, I stepped out from under Austin's arm and propelled him towards the fitting rooms. "Sounds good, Mom. I'm going to try on my dress and get Austin help with his suit. Bye!"

Before Mom could say anything else, I'd pushed Austin far, far away. I had to be careful, I couldn't let her get *too* attached to the idea of Austin and me. After the wedding, we'd be "breaking up," and I certainly didn't want her heart breaking in the process.

"Alright, sugarpants. I think we're a safe distance from your relatives." Austin held up his hands and faced me, stopping so fast that I almost plowed headfirst into his muscular chest.

I wondered briefly what that chest might feel like under my fingers, and then immediately squashed the thought.

"Sugarpants? Babycakes? Really?" I asked, hands on my hips.

He smirked. "Just playing along, Boobear."

I almost vomited. "Oh, this is too much."

He laughed, the sound deep and melodic. How had I never noticed how nice Austin's laugh was?

"Hello there," a sing-song voice interrupted us. We both

whirled around to face a petite lady with voluminous blonde hair. Her blue eyes barely glanced at me before resting on Austin. "How can I help you today?"

I bristled at her flirty tone, and then remembered that Austin wasn't really my boyfriend and he could flirt with anyone he wanted. Even if the thought made my stomach turn a little.

But, to my intense gratification, Austin took my hand and brushed his thumb along the top of it. Shivers traveled up my arm, which I quickly attributed to the shop's air conditioning. The lady's face dropped just a touch before she recovered her beaming smile.

"My *girlfriend* here wants to try on her bridesmaid's dress, and I'm here for a suit. Any chance you can give us a hand?"

Man, he was good.

The lady's head swiveled between the two of us, and finally, her gaze rested on me. "You're with the Williams party? Your dress is in that fitting room there." She gestured to the room nearest to us. Then, she turned to Austin. "And, for your suit, I'll send over a salesperson who can help."

The lady wandered back towards the cash register, leaving Austin and I alone. He dropped my hand and nodded towards the fitting room. "You should try on your dress, Els."

"I'll wait until you have a suit."

Austin gazed towards the bustling center of the shop. He shrugged. "Could be a while. You might as well get the dress over with."

I sighed dramatically. "Never thought I'd see the day when you—Austin Bell, my *best friend ever*—would force me into a frilly ball gown."

Austin smiled, and it was positively devilish. "There's a first time for everything."

His words sent delicious chills down my spine and my cheeks grew warm. I scurried into the fitting room before he could notice my blush.

I closed the curtain securely, and then changed into the bridesmaid's dress. It was a long, purple thing with thick straps and an overabundance of frills. I couldn't help but grimace at my reflection in the mirror.

Whoever designed this dress didn't consider that putting this many frills would make the wearer look like a floating, purple orb.

I hoped that, by doing up the back, the "orbness" of the dress might decrease. I pulled the zipper up over my waist and midway up my back, but then, it caught. The zipper was stuck in the fabric.

I grunted a couple of times, dancing around the fitting room as I tried to pry the zipper free. But, it wouldn't budge and my arms were beginning to cramp. I felt very, very hot, and it occurred to me that I might never get out of this. I was trapped in the orb.

"Uh, you okay in there?"

Austin's voice shocked me and I froze mid-hop.

"I'm fine." My strangled voice wasn't convincing. I sighed. "The zipper's stuck."

"Let me help you." Austin's voice was closer now and I shot away from the curtain like it might burn me.

I dared look at myself in the mirror. I was a red, sweaty tomato with wild hair wearing a purple pompom. There was no way I was letting anyone see me like this, much less Austin. It didn't matter that he was my best friend and had seen me at my very worst—nine years old, hair in a bowl cut, covered in mud and grass stains after a particularly unruly day by the river.

"Els, seriously," he insisted, his voice right outside. "I can help."

I took three deep breaths, steeled myself, and then opened the curtain. Austin's blue eyes scoured my body and he pressed his lips together to conceal a smile.

"You look great." The sincerity in his tone was marred by his subsequent snort. "That looks like—"

"My prom dress, I know," I said impatiently, swishing around him and feigning an amount of confidence I absolutely did not have. "And, you can just keep your mouth shut before you try and make fun of me."

He saluted me, his cheeks puffed as he tried to restrain his laughter. "Sir, yes sir!"

Despite my burst of false confidence, I refused to look at myself in the big, flashy mirrors outside the fitting room. Instead, I looked at my feet, one hand hovering over my chest self-consciously.

"Honestly," Austin said after he'd calmed down. "The dress is cute."

I rolled my eyes and then glanced at him. It was a mistake. He looked perfect, as usual. "Are you seeing what I'm seeing?"

Austin shook his head, his gaze genuine. "You have nothing to be embarrassed about, Els. You just... you look like a giant loofah."

I snorted. "Thanks."

"No, seriously. You look like a loofah and you might as well own it. Be proud of the cute, giant, purple puffball that you are."

I giggled despite myself. He called me "cute."

I hazarded a glance in the big mirror. I really did look remarkably like a huge shower loofah.

Austin's brow wrinkled. "You said the zipper's stuck?"

I stared at the ground again. "Just the top of it. I can't tell if it's stuck in the fabric or if the dress is too small."

"I can try zipping it, if you'd like?"

I couldn't muster any words even if I tried. Slowly, I turned and thanked my lucky stars that I'd managed to get the zipper most of the way up.

He came to stand behind me and I could swear I felt the heat radiating off his body. His soft breath tickled the top of my hair, sending chills over my skin. An irrational part of me wanted to step back and lean against his firm torso. Just a little bit.

He placed his fingers on my shoulder blades and warmth extended from his fingertips through my limbs and down to my toes. He grasped the zipper and carefully maneuvered it through the fabric and up to the top of the dress.

He kept his fingers on my back for a moment, his skin electrifying my skin. I wasn't breathing, didn't want to disturb this intensely charged moment. But, charged with what, I wasn't sure.

Part of me wanted to turn around and... put my arms around him? Push him away? Something. But, before I could do any of it, there was a commotion at the front of the shop.

"Noooooo!"

The guttural shriek tore through the air and Austin and I jumped apart like we'd been caught doing something bad. We ran towards the entrance to find Carly in a pile on the floor.

"No, no, no," she was muttering, over and over, her head in her hands.

I dropped to the floor next to her, grateful I had the frills to land on, and held her close. "Carly, what's wrong? What's going on?"

Carly sobbed onto my shoulder. "It's the ba-and! They've dropped out. They can't p-play!"

"The wedding is in a week," Mom whispered, her face white. "We can't lose the band. This is the worst thing that could possibly happen."

I shot Mom a look. "Not helping."

Carly continued to cry, hiccuping and muttering. "No m-music. No music at m-my wedding. What kind of a wedding d-d-doesn't have music? What is Ben going to s-say?"

My mind raced as I tried to come up with a solution. Surely, there was another band in town who could play at Carly's wedding. There had to be someone else we could ask. And, if worse came to worst, I could probably learn guitar in a week. Right?

Then, to the surprise of pretty much everyone in the shop, Austin stepped forward. "I think I might have an idea."

20

AUSTIN

*M*y phone rang through my headphones and I jerked in surprise, my feet falling out of step. I'd been lost in thought about the goings-on at the bridal shop yesterday, and the high-pitched ring was a harsh return to reality. I took another couple of steps, pushing my body forward and getting my rhythm back, then I checked to see who was calling.

I smiled at the name on the screen and answered. "Hey, man, thanks for calling me back."

On the other end of the line, Christian chuckled. "Am I catching you at a bad time?"

"Not at all. Why?"

"Because it sounds like you've got a yeti hot on your tail."

I laughed, and had to slow to catch my breath. "I'm out for a run."

"Of course you are." Christian's deep voice was colored with sarcasm. "So, what's up?"

I rounded a corner to take me back to the park and slowed to a walk. I'd been out running for over an hour now, and it was about time I headed back anyway. "You're going to love this, but I have a huge favor to ask you."

"A favor?" There was a shuffling noise as Christian shifted his phone to his other ear. "What kind of favor?"

I crossed my fingers. "The kind that might interfere with your recording schedule."

Over the next couple of minutes, I gave Christian the rundown on the drama with Carly's band for the wedding. Unfortunately, it looked like Carly and Ben were hooped. Ella and her entire family had spent all night scrambling to find another act, even calling bands in Bozeman. But, with the wedding happening in less than a week, everyone was booked.

Now, Ella was insisting that she learn to play guitar, which, judging by her experience with high school flute, was not going to go well. As talented as Ella was with writing, she did not have an ear for music.

I figured I might as well try another avenue.

"Okay," Christian said after I'd finished the saga. "And, what does that have to do with me?"

"Well, seeing as you're sick of concerts and want a break, I was thinking that you could come to Aston Falls and play the wedding? It'd be a super low-key gig, just you and your guitar. Nothing crazy."

"Ha." Christian chuckled dryly. "Josh would have a fit. He's been an absolute pain lately trying to scout out locations for music videos. I can't exactly drop everything and leave."

"Of course you can," I said smoothly. I was prepared for this answer, I just had to execute my part perfectly. "You're not doing any of this for the money, you've said so yourself. You're doing it because your jackwad of a manager told you to. If you come here, you can play a small, simple gig, which

I know you love. None of the usual touring stuff. None of the high pressure."

Silence on the other end of the line. I was a tightrope walker approaching the dangerous middle.

After a short pause, I continued on. "But, if you can't do it, I totally understand. I know you're busy and have lots going on. Don't worry about it, I'll find someone else—"

"I'll do it," Christian cut me off. "I'm up for a challenge, and trust me, convincing Josh to let me go will definitely be a challenge. I'll count it as a work trip, say I'm helping him scout out video locations or something. Besides, the last time I was in Aston Falls, I wrote a ton of new stuff. He can't say no to that."

I smiled, internally rejoicing. Christian West was nothing if not ambitious.

"Awesome. Ella will be so happy."

"Ella?" Christian asked, a note of confusion in his voice

I squeezed my eyes shut and backtracked quickly. "Sorry, I meant Carly. Carly will be so happy."

"No, you didn't." I could hear Christian's smirk. "You meant Ella. You're doing this for her, aren't you?"

"No way. This is for Carly's wedding. I'm not even planning on telling Ella about it."

"So, what you're saying is... You're planning a secret concert to surprise Ella."

I rolled my eyes. "You're twisting my words."

"You're not denying it."

I forced a chuckle and picked up my pace again, breaking into a jog as a surge of adrenaline flooded my system.

Though I'd never admit it aloud, there *was* an element of truth to what Christian was saying. Due to sheer proximity to Ella, I'd come to see Carly as a sister over the years. I wanted the best for her, wanted her wedding to be a blast.

But, I'd be lying if I said that a part of me wasn't thinking about Ella, too. Almost constantly, these days. It was one of the reasons I'd gone for a run. I'd hoped to work through the strange swirl of energy that radiated from my chest any time I thought about the bridal shop.

Memories of yesterday overwhelmed my senses once again—Ella in her hilarious purple dress, hair billowing around her face. She smiled, shy and sweet, and I couldn't tear my eyes away from her. It broke me to see the way she refused to look at herself in the mirror.

And then, I thought about helping her do up her zipper. When my fingers made contact with her back as I pulled the fabric free. Her skin was silky smooth, but I noticed the trail of goosebumps left in the wake of my fingers. A fire lit within me as I slowly, so slowly, slid that zipper up the back of her dress...

I grabbed the bottom of my jersey and shook out the billowing fabric, trying to cool down.

"Aus," Christian said with a tinge of annoyance. "You still there?"

"Yeah," I croaked. Cleared my throat. "Still here."

"Where'd you go?"

"I..."

Was thinking about being in a bridal shop yesterday? Was remembering when I touched my best friend's bare back? Was wishing I had another moment with Ella, right here, right now?

"Well," I stammered.

Christian sighed. "Are you ever going to tell that girl how crazy you are about her?"

I froze, like literally stopped in the middle of the sidewalk. Usually, I was quick to retort, quick with an answer, a rejection. But, for the first time in my life, I was speechless. My throat was closing up.

It was like my body wouldn't allow me to deny it.

"You know me, I'm not that kind of guy," I finally managed.

"You *haven't* been that kind of guy," Christian corrected me smoothly. "But, man, you should listen to yourself. Every time we talk, it's 'Ella this' and 'Ella that' and 'did you hear about this hilarious thing Ella did the other day?'"

I bit my lip. Had I been talking about Ella that much?

"I haven't had much luck in my own love life," Christian continued. "But even I can see you're nuts about her."

"Funny, seeing as your love songs always make the Top 10," I joked, attempting to divert the conversation.

"My *breakup* songs make the Top 10."

I chuckled, shaking my head.

"Come on, man, be straight with me. Something's going on between you and Ella Williams."

I stayed silent and my face drew into a frown. Because Christian was right—there *was* something going on: our fake relationship. But, what he didn't know was that the fake relationship was starting to feel a little too real at times.

I'll admit that I was a pretty sappy fake boyfriend. I usually wasn't into PDA, I preferred to keep things neat and tidy. But, with Ella? It was hard not to want to be around her. I found myself using any excuse to touch her, be close to her.

The craziest part? Sometimes, it seemed like she wanted the same thing. The chemistry between us was undeniable, and I was sure she felt it, too. But, feeling something and crossing the line were two entirely different things.

And, technically, our fake relationship would end in a

few days anyway. The wedding was less than a week away, so Ella and I would soon "break up."

"It's not that easy," I said on an exhale. "Things are... complicated."

"Complicated, how? She's your best friend, dude. You can talk to her about anything."

"Not this. Never this." I raked my fingers through my hair.

"Have you at least kissed her, yet?"

I laughed, a little too loudly, as I remembered the almost irresistible urge to kiss her neck while we were cooking together last week. "You're out of line."

"I'm not," Christian said seriously.

"Listen, Ella's a great person, she's my best friend. She's sweet and brilliant and hilarious. Anyone would be lucky to date her. But, not me. Ella deserves better than me. Besides, I'd be breaking, like, thirty personal rules of mine."

"So? Some rules are worth breaking. Make an exception."

"I don't do exceptions," I said automatically.

Chrstian sighed. "Here we go again."

Luckily, Christian seemed happy to drop the topic, and he segued into questions about the wedding and what he'd need to bring to Aston Falls. I followed the conversation as best I could, but his words nagged at me long after we'd hung up.

That was the thing with Christian. He was too intuitive for his own good. Must be the artist in him.

Because all I could think about these days was when I'd next hold Ella's hand, or drape my arm over her shoulders. When I could nuzzle my nose into her hair, or shamelessly watch her laugh from across the room.

But, Ella needed a friend, and the last thing I wanted to do was risk jeopardizing that.

For so long, I'd successfully compartmentalized my life —placing my medical career in one box, my personal life in another, and so on. And, locked in the very depths of my heart were a couple of boxes I simply did not touch. Not anymore.

Everything had its place, my life was neatly organized. But lately, the lines were beginning to blur. And I began to wonder what it would be like to make an exception, just once.

21

AUSTIN

"What do you think they're talking about?" Ella's sweet whisper brushed against my cheek.

We were sitting on a white loveseat at one end of the quaint, old barn where Carly and Ben's rehearsal dinner—and tomorrow's wedding—were taking place. All afternoon, we'd stood outside rehearsing the ceremony—from greeting guests, to Carly's entrance, to cueing everyone so they knew when to sit and stand.

Ella's mom had gone all out for the dinner—even ordering a catered four-course meal. The venue, which would host the reception tomorrow evening, was already half-decorated and looked stunning with the chandeliers and twinkling lights surrounding the dance floor.

I felt a bit out of place in my casual black slacks and polo shirt. But, everyone was dressed casually for the setting.

Even Ella wore a plain t-shirt and her favorite jeans shorts. Her hair was up in a messy bun, and she wore only a brush of mascara. She looked cute, comfortable, and just like herself. And yet, I had to fight the urge to look at her, to memorize every detail of her face.

I shifted on the seat, and my thigh brushed against Ella's bare one. She didn't seem to notice, but I did.

We were sitting close enough to look like we were a couple, but there was a part of me, a surprisingly insistent part, that felt we weren't close enough. I could say that it was because I wanted to put on a show—really play up that I was her doting and caring boyfriend—but if I was being completely honest, I was finding it very hard to stay away.

I thought about my conversation with Christian the other day, and all I could wonder was when this happened, when things had changed.

Somewhere along the line, our fake relationship had stopped feeling so fake to me. The fake attraction, fake feelings... they'd become a little too real. And I'd realized one thing—I was powerless when it came to her. Powerless to stop the magnetism that seemed to draw us together. Powerless to fight the undeniable attraction I felt to her.

When she leaned over to whisper in my ear, it was all I could do not to wrap my arms around her and pull her into my lap. But, maybe that was a bit much for her sister's rehearsal dinner. Even if she *was* my fake girlfriend.

"Aus? What do you think?"

I forced myself to focus and I stared at the couple she was referring to—an older married couple at the other end of the room. They were speaking to each other in hushed voices, but the man kept glancing around, clearly bored.

I squinted at them, and, instead of answering Ella's question directly, I waited for the man's turn to speak. Then, I spoke as though for him, affecting the Mid-Atlantic drawl from old movies. "Golly gee, Martha, if I want another slice of cake, I'll have another slice of cake!"

Ella caught my drift immediately. "I'm not going to tell you again, Earl. Six and a quarter pieces is too much."

"But that was a mighty fine quarter."

As if on cue, the woman sighed, gazing dreamily off into space. Ella sighed with her. "You know who loves cake? Barkley. He would love this place."

I tried, and failed, to hold back a laugh. "Barkley wouldn't be allowed at a wedding."

"He's just a teeny tiny Great Dane. Besides, he looks flashy in a suit."

At this point, Ella and I were both cracking up laughing, and her body pressed against mine. Reflexively, I wrapped my arm around her shoulder. She didn't pull away. Instead, she leaned in and settled perfectly into the crook of my arm. I rested my chin lightly on the top of her head.

Just playing my part. Being a good fake boyfriend.

"This dinner wasn't nearly as bad as I expected," Ella murmured.

"You're welcome," I quipped with a smirk. She was right, though, her family had more or less left us alone—probably wanted to observe our couple-ness from afar. "Is tonight worthy of your daily journal, then?"

Ella faced me before rolling her eyes teasingly. "Wouldn't you like to know."

I really would, though.

"Aren't you two just precious?" a voice cooed behind Ella and me.

We sprung apart and whipped around to face Mrs. Williams. She was wearing billowing white pants and a matching top, and her arms were full of flowers and unlit candles.

"Thanks, Mom," Ella mumbled.

"I never thought I'd see you looking so happy and blissful, Ella Bella." Then, her eyes lit up. "And, just think! If you get married, you'll officially be 'Ella Bell'! Isn't that just the best—"

"Mom!" Ella said sharply, her mouth in a grimace.

"All right, all right." Mrs. Williams tutted. "I'm just so pleased to see you both so happy. And after all these years. Did you two ever think you might end up together?"

I stiffened and I noticed Ella shoot a glance my way.

Before either of us could answer, Mrs. Williams continued on. "Of course you did. I told Jos and Laura—"

"Mom." Ella interrupted, standing abruptly. "Can I give you a hand carrying those flowers?"

Mrs. Williams blinked. "Oh, don't you fret, honey. I'm just stocking up for the wedding tomorrow." She glanced between Ella and me, and I mustered an enthusiastic smile for her. "Anyway, I'd best be off. Come and find me later!"

With that, Mrs. Williams bustled off. I chuckled and Ella rolled her eyes as she collapsed back onto the chair.

"It wouldn't be a Williams family gathering without one awkward encounter," Ella grumbled.

"Ah, it wasn't so bad."

"Were you not just listening to my mom basically force us into marriage?"

I looked after Mrs. Williams as she approached the bar. The lilacs she was holding hit her in the face, and she did a remarkably good impression of someone putting out a fire as she blew the petals away. "Your family isn't so bad. They're endearing. Sweet."

Ella rolled her eyes again and laughed. But, I couldn't help but think about Mrs. Williams's words. In high school, I was crazy about Ella. I wondered whether we would end up together. It was funny the way life worked—that we'd wind up faking a relationship instead of being in a real one.

Suddenly, the barn lights dimmed and the music switched from an upbeat tune to an intimate ballad. The DJ —yep, the Williams had hired a DJ for the rehearsal— announced that the song was a request from the bride and groom to be. Something about practicing their first dance.

Carly waggled her fingers and made a face at the crowd as she and Ben swept onto the dance floor. I tried not to laugh at the way her flip-flops clacked and how Ben's overly casual khaki shorts didn't quite match the tempo of the song. But, as soon as they fell into step, my smile faded.

A hush fell around the room as all eyes turned to the couple. Carly and Ben moved seamlessly around the dance floor. Their gazes were locked on one another, and they were clearly lost in their own world. The love between Carly and Ben was so obvious, so genuine. I wondered, not for the first time, what it would be like to have a love like that.

"They're really happy together, aren't they?" I murmured, turning to face Ella.

She, too, was staring at Carly and Ben, a small smile on her lips. Her hand pressed against her chest, right above her heart, and her eyes glowed. Though everyone was looking at the couple dancing, I couldn't take my eyes away from her.

As soon as the song wrapped up, the dance floor became populated again, and Ella snapped out of her trance. I blinked as she turned away and rifled in her bag, pulling out a pile of papers.

"While we're here, we might as well read over your speech," Ella said, a thickness remaining in her voice.

"You brought my speech?"

"Of course. These wedding things always have plenty of down time, and I figured we should make use of it. If I've learned anything from living in New York, it's that you've got to make use of the time you have. And, we still need to work on your presentation skills."

I grimaced as a bitter taste filled my mouth. Ella and I had finished writing the speech a few days ago, and a part of me was hoping that she might've forgotten to help me with the actual presentation part. I was living in a happy state of denial—now that the speech was written, I could blissfully pretend that it was done. That the presentation would be perfect.

But, further reflection quickly quashed that idea. Public speaking still made me uneasy, and the thought of presenting to a group of doctors made my stomach turn right over. The conference was only a couple of weeks away now.

"Why don't you practice presenting it here?" Ella suggested.

I shifted, looking around. "Now? To all these people? Els, they came for a rehearsal dinner, not to hear me drone on about the medical center."

"No, weirdo." Ella laughed. "Present it to me."

I stared at my best friend skeptically, but she wasn't kidding.

And, I wasn't about to say no to her challenge. I sat up straight, cleared my throat, made a big show of getting ready, and then started to read. I'd only gone through a couple of sentences when Ella put her hand up to stop me.

"You trying to kill me, Aus?" she asked seriously.

I tilted my head, pretending to think hard. "Hmm, didn't have that planned for today."

"This is dry as a desert creek bed. Why are your eyes glued to the paper when you have the speech pretty much memorized?"

"I don't want to miss anything. Besides, it's more comfortable this way."

"Screw being comfortable," Ella burst out passionately, eyes flashing. "To be comfortable is to be boring. You gotta step outside the lines sometimes."

I smiled ruefully. If only she knew.

"Try looking at your audience," Ella said.

I raised an eyebrow. "The audience being these poor, unsuspecting dinner attendees?"

"Sure."

I pressed my lips together, but I decided to try it her way. What did I have to lose?

I felt ridiculous, but I sat on the edge of the loveseat and tried again. My voice was quiet, quiet enough that no one could overhear. Though I imagined that Martha and Earl might have something to crack up about if they saw me presenting to a whole lot of no one.

I steeled myself and visualized speaking to a room full of doctors. Apparently, my imagination was *too* good because I clammed up, the blood draining from my face.

"It's useless, Els." I shook my head. "I can't do this."

"Yes you can." Ella shamelessly grabbed my chin and wrenched my face to look at her. "Try it once more. But this time, look at me."

I rolled my eyes but did as she said. I glanced at the paper, my mind already twenty steps ahead and making contingency plans for when I tanked my speech and had to return to Aston Falls in shame. With a final sigh, I looked into Ella's eyes and spoke.

And, it was like magic. Some weird voodoo stuff.

Because, with my eyes firmly locked on Ella's, I managed to run through my entire keynote speech. The prospect of a judgmental audience faded to the back of my mind, and the words tumbled out of my mouth. Ella smiled and nodded encouragingly, and I found I didn't even need to glance at the paper. I even felt somewhat... comfortable.

By the time I finished speaking, Ella was chuckling.

"How'd I do?" I asked, nervous for her answer.

"Amazing." She smiled and the world might as well have faded away. Then, she winked. "You're welcome."

22

ELLA

*A*ustin took a sip of his beer as he gazed over the room, and I tried not to notice the way his Adam's apple bobbed up and down. The way he bit his bottom lip after the sip. I'd never, ever been attracted to the way someone swallowed their drink before, but here we were.

It didn't help that Austin had, once again, brought his A-game to this rehearsal dinner. Though he wore casual slacks and a navy polo shirt, whenever his biceps flexed, I nearly swooned. Next to him, I felt like a slouchy, messy muppet. A muppet that was currently the envy of every woman here.

I had to keep reminding myself that this wouldn't last forever. In fact, it would only last until tomorrow—Carly's wedding.

What was my plan after that? It was a great question. I could hardly believe that a month had passed, it felt like I'd just arrived in Aston Falls. Time always went way too quickly when I was surrounded by the people I loved. When I spent time with Austin.

The prospect of my grand return had been like a hazy

cloud in the far distance. I knew I'd have to worry about it eventually, but not now. Never now.

And yet, the angry cloud was upon me.

To my surprise, no one had asked me about my plans to return to the city. My parents were usually all over me about it, but they hadn't said a word. Even Grace and JJ had kept their mouths shut. And Austin... he surprised me most of all. He was the most obsessive planner I knew. If he suspected that I didn't have my flight booked, he would undoubtedly be freaking out.

But, as I'd discovered numerous times since being home, the guy was full of surprises. Despite being my best friend— and the person I talked to almost every day—there was something different about this visit.

Austin folded up his speech and tucked the papers in his back pocket. A wave of gratitude flowed through me as I looked at him. He'd been so amazing this month—truly the perfect boyfriend. We had my family convinced, and it was probably the longest my mom and aunts ever gone without trying to set me up.

I didn't deserve him... a friend like him. I wanted to do more to help him in return. Sure, we'd written the speech, but I knew that the presentation was the part Austin was most nervous about. There had to be something I could do.

All at once, an idea began to form. It might've been the rush of the wedding, or the joy in the air, or the feeling of possibility whenever I was with Austin, but I knew what to do. A guaranteed way to get him out of his comfort zone and trying something different.

Before I could talk myself out of it, I turned to him. "Do you trust me?"

Austin cocked an eyebrow. "Mostly?"

"I have an idea to practice your presentation skills."

He narrowed his eyes, perhaps rightfully so. "And that is?"

I smiled at him, slightly manically, and shot to a stand. I plucked an empty wine glass from a table near us and clinked the glass. The room fell silent and the DJ turned down the music. Everyone looked at me, forty pairs of eyes, and I wondered whether I was making a big mistake. But, it was too late now.

"Good evening, everyone," I announced, sounding more confident than I felt. "I just want to say that I am very thankful for everyone who came tonight. Carly and Ben, your love is truly inspiring, and I, for one, cannot wait until tomorrow."

I cleared my throat and glanced at Austin. He was staring at me quizzically, his expression demanding to know what I was up to.

I looked back at the crowd. "I was just speaking to my bes—*boyfriend*, here, and he said the most beautiful thing. Austin? Care to take it away?"

I felt Austin's reaction before I saw it. His body stiffened, and I noticed his fists clench just a touch. When I looked at him, his face had gone white and he was staring at me, his eyes flaming. He looked... mad.

Of all the things you could've done, Ella.

My eyes went wide as I realized just how colossally stupid this idea was. I should never have put him on the spot like this.

With an embarrassed grin, I faced the crowd again. Time for damage control.

I scrambled to find something to say, something sweet. Just a single sentence.

But, my mouth was bone dry. As much as Austin hated public speaking, I couldn't say I loved it either. I broke out in

a full-body flush as I looked upon the smiling faces. I floun-
dered, racking my brain for an endearing childhood story
about Carly and me, but I was drawing a blank. A complete
blank.

You'd think I didn't know the girl.

And, just when the crowd was losing interest and my
never-ending mortification was about to swallow me whole,
a tall presence appeared next to me.

Shocked, I looked up to see that Austin was standing
with me, his trademark smirk on his face.

"Thanks for the lovely introduction, *honeypie*," he
said to me and I blushed an even deeper red as
laughter rippled across the room. He ventured a gaze
towards the crowd and his jaw clenched. He looked like
he might lose his train of thought, so I touched my
hand to his.

Austin glanced at me and I nodded encouragingly. He
could do this, I knew he could.

When he spoke, his eyes didn't leave mine. "I used to
think that love is untouchable, unattainable. But, I've come
to realize that love is in the little things. Like the way she
laughs, or the way you fight over the remote, or..." Austin
paused and a whisper of a smile crossed his lips. "Or, when
you cook together and make a huge mess, but you clean it
up together."

Another laugh echoed around the room. Austin faced
the crowd, but intertwined his pinky with mine. Then, he
smiled his biggest, brightest, most confident smile.

"I have Carly and Ben to thank for showing me that.
Showing me that a simple dance, a simple kiss can be the
most loving thing you ever do. As my ever-so-wise girlfriend
pointed out, your love *is* inspiring and I wish you both the
best."

Austin raised his drink and the crowd broke into applause and cheers.

But, I was frozen. Captivated. I couldn't say anything even if I tried. Austin's words, his bravery, his entire presence hypnotized me. Shivers crawled up and down my spine yet my body felt blissfully warm.

As soon as the attention turned away from us, Austin dropped my hand.

"How's that for being good under pressure?" he joked.

I unfroze long enough to say, "Uuung."

"Poetic." He smirked, then ran his fingers through his hair. "I can't believe you did that to me."

I found my bearings and flaming hot regret washed through me. "Oh, gosh. I'm so sorry, Aus. I thought it was a good idea, but then I stood up and saw your face and I knew I did the wrong thing. I hope you can forgive me, I—"

"No, no." Austin held up his hands. "That was brilliant, Els. Sometimes I need to be thrown into the deep end like that. You definitely put me out of my comfort zone." He winked. "And I'm actually grateful."

"Really?"

"Absolutely. Nothing could've soothed my fear of public speaking like a crowd full of applause and laughter."

"I'm kind of proud of you." I smiled.

"I'm kind of proud of me, too. Though, to be fair, everyone's been drinking and they probably would've cheered for the moon."

I laughed. "No, that was all you, Aus. Trust me. I thought you might say a sentence or two. Where'd you get the inspiration from anyway?"

At this, the smile slipped off Austin's face and his eyes flickered to mine. He picked at the label on his beer bottle. "Just came to me."

There was a heaviness in the air between us, something strong and tangible. I had an almost uncontrollable urge to wrap my arms around him and pull him close, maybe run my fingers through his hair.

But, I shook myself off. Austin was probably talking about one of his exes. Like the Hannah person he dated in LA.

I took a deep breath. "You sure you're not mad?"

"Well, I mean…" Austin shrugged. "You do owe me."

"Do I?" I asked, hands on my hips as we fell into our familiar banter. "Owe you what?"

Austin smiled as he glanced around the room. Carly and Ben were inviting more people onto the dance floor to join them after their perfectly practiced waltz. Austin took my hand and dragged me towards the center of the crowd. "A dance."

23

ELLA

*a*nd dance we did. Shamelessly and foolishly until our feet hurt and we were out of breath.

By the end of the night, I'd kicked off my flip flops, let my hair down, and was chicken-dancing around the floor. And Austin? He was chicken-dancing along with me. His blond hair fell over his forehead and his eyes sparkled as he grinned at me.

It still shocked me sometimes just how attractive he was. And, on top of that, he was the most down-to-earth, grounded, sweetest person. It was like God had blessed him at birth to be a perfect specimen of a human. I felt so lucky to call him my friend.

Even if my mind did occasionally wander in wayward directions. Like right now.

It was after midnight and Austin and I were parked in front of the Inn. We'd shut the party down—Carly and Ben had left hours ago, followed closely by my parents, and then the rest of the wedding party slowly trickled until it was just me, Austin, and a handful of others.

I had to be up early tomorrow for the wedding, and I

really should've gone straight to bed. But, I couldn't bring myself to do it. My skin still tingled with the memory of Austin's arm wrapped over my shoulder, the way his body pressed against mine when we laughed on the loveseat.

All I could think about was what it would be like if this had been a real date. Would he kiss me at the end of it?

Bad Ella. You shouldn't be having these thoughts about your best friend.

But, my breath quickened and I snuck a glance at Austin. He was leaning forward in his seat, his chest resting on the steering wheel. His nose was wrinkled as he squinted at the night sky.

I frowned. "What are you doing, Aus?"

"Looking for stars."

"Ooh!" I leaned forward, too, imitating his nose wrinkling and eye narrowing. If someone passed by, I was sure that we looked like a couple of overeager guinea pigs.

The sky was laden with gorgeous, twinkling stars. Hordes and hordes of them. I held up a finger to trace a constellation across the sky.

"You can't see stars like this in New York," I murmured, and the slightest tinge of sadness colored my voice. When I was in the city, seeing the stars was one of the things I missed most.

After a beat, Austin spoke. "Do you know when you're going back?"

I sat back in my seat with a sigh. His face was turned towards the window so I couldn't see his expression. "I haven't booked my flight, if that's what you're asking."

Austin chuckled. "I wasn't asking."

"I could blame the wedding, say that I've been too busy, but that isn't the truth."

The truth is that I'm not ready to leave Aston Falls. Leave you.

I pressed my lips shut. Where did *that* come from?

It might've been the headiness of the night, or the endorphins from all the dancing. But, it was the truth—I didn't want to leave Austin. Not again. I wasn't ready. And who knew when I'd be back for this amount of time? I wanted to soak up every moment with him.

Austin's eyes searched mine and I waited for him to ask what the truth was. Why I hadn't booked my flights yet.

Instead, he smiled. "Want to go for a drive, Els?"

My heart leapt at his sweet expression. "Always."

Austin started up his SUV and put it into gear. We pulled away from the curb and drove towards town. We didn't need to speak, and I stared out the window, my eyes on the stars. We drove down Center Street, through the forest and onto a road I hadn't been on since high school.

We drove up the gravel road, higher and higher as it wound through the mountains. Then, Austin pulled off and parked. We were at one of the viewpoints we used to visit when we were young. It was the place we came to when I got my driver's license, when I failed my math final, and when Austin's mom passed away. Grace used to join us, but, over the years, like the Cinema, the viewpoint had become another spot that was mine and Austin's.

Austin got out of the car and opened his arms towards the view. Below us, the bright lights of Aston Falls were perfectly mirrored with the myriad of stars overhead. The mountain ranges that surrounded our hometown formed an inky, impenetrable darkness.

Despite it being the dead of night, the air was warm and comfortable. As the dust from the road blew away, a fresh, humid smell took its place. The world was silent—blissfully, completely silent.

Like Austin and I were the only ones awake while the rest of the world slept.

He reached into the back seat and pulled out a couple of blankets. He spread one on the hood of his car, and I couldn't help but notice the way the veins in his forearms rolled. He gestured for me to sit.

"Well, this brings me back," I murmured.

"I can't let you head back to New York without doing *all* of our traditions at least once."

With a smile, I slipped out of my flip flops and wriggled myself onto the blanket. Austin shook out the other blanket and placed it on top of me, swaddling me. I giggled as he tucked me in.

Then, he hopped up next to me on the hood. Our upper arms pressed together and it took everything I had not to lay my head on his shoulder. That would be weird, right? High school Ella and Austin used to do stuff like that, but things felt... different now. Something between us had changed.

Or, maybe it was just me.

"Remember that time you brought your video recorder up here?" I asked.

"How could I forget?" Austin chuckled. "I wanted to film the stars, but I captured a whole lot of nothing. It wasn't until I did some googling that I learned you need—"

"Special photography equipment," I finished with a giggle.

"I truly thought my parents' ancient camcorder would do the trick."

"I do admire the fact that the bad filmography didn't stop you from trying."

"Oh, I gave up on filming the stars as soon as you whipped out your flute."

I placed my hands on my hips and pretended to be angry. "I fully maintain that I could've been a very successful flute player. Me and the flute? We were tight."

Austin burst into laughter and I snorted. We both knew that the chances of me being a pro flute player were less than none. I'd barely mastered "Hot Cross Buns" after years of trying.

I wiped a tear of laughter from my eye. "The only reason I brought the flute here was to do something nice for your birthday."

"So, instead of getting me my favorite sports jersey or a video game, like all my friends got on their birthdays, you decided to play me a song."

"Hey." I poked him in the side and my finger met with a very firm ab muscle. "It took me hours to write that song."

Austin took my poking finger and interlaced his fingers with mine, effectively disarming me. "And, it was beautiful. Truly. I appreciated it, Els. And now, it's forever memorialized on camera."

I shook my head. "I can't believe you kept my birthday song in your collection of home videos."

"That's the purpose of home videos—to capture your secrets and most embarrassing moments on camera so that you can relive them and cringe again in the future."

Our laughter faded into a comfortable silence as we watched the blinking lights overhead. I snuck a glance at Austin's profile. I could spend days looking at the guy, memorizing his every feature. His hand was warm around mine and I couldn't get past the sparks shooting up my arm. Did he feel it, too?

"It's funny, what your mom said tonight." Austin's voice broke the silence.

I frowned, thinking back to the moment before the dancing, before Austin's sweet words about Carly and Ben. When Mom had basically accosted the two of us and implied that we'd be getting married. If she had her way, I had no doubt that we'd be married and have kids on the way by next year.

"Sorry about that. Again." My cheeks heated. "She just gets carried away sometimes." I forced a laugh. "But, really, could you imagine us dating in high school?"

Austin smirked. "We would've gone to prom together."

"And you would've read all my articles for journalism class, and I would've gone to all your football games. Cheered you on." I laughed.

"We would've comforted each other when something bad happened."

"Shared all of our deepest secrets, too..."

My voice faded as my heart slammed. Because we *did* do those things. All of them. Sure, we never kissed, we never held hands, but Austin was one of the most important— scratch that, THE most important—person in my life at the time.

There was a heavy silence between us, so weighted that I felt I couldn't breathe properly. It was like we were on the precipice of something, approaching an edge or a cliff. But, instead of wanting to run away screaming, I found myself wanting to lean in, press into the void.

"There was one secret I never shared," Austin said, his voice low.

I didn't dare risk a glance in his direction. "What's that?"

Austin was silent for a long time. "It was a crush I had."

"A secret crush," I tried to joke to lighten the mood. "Do tell, Austin Bell."

He chuckled. "It was... well, it was you, Ella."

My smile immediately dropped off my face and I blinked. "I'm sorry, what?"

"In high school, I sort of had a crush on you," Austin repeated.

That's when my jaw hit the ground and my ears began to ring. A wash of emotions ran through my body. Austin Bell —Austin freaking Bell—had a crush on *me?*

There was no way.

"It was just a silly, light-hearted crush," he continued with a smile in his voice. "It meant nothing. But, I did. I liked you."

He shot me a nervous smile. I knew he was waiting for me to say something, but I couldn't speak even if I wanted to. It was all way, way too unbelievable. I pinched my arm to see if I was dreaming.

I didn't wake up, so I pinched harder.

Austin—our high school's star wide receiver, the guy every girl used to crush on, the town's most sought-after doctor—used to like me. Was he joking? Was he punking me right now?

"You're kidding, right?" I finally managed to croak.

At this, the smile fell right off Austin's face. His gaze met mine and his eyes sparkled with the reflection of the stars.

His expression made my heart stop.

"I'm not joking, Els. It was always you."

24

AUSTIN

*T*he silence from Ella's side of the blanket had never sounded so loud. I finally dared shoot a glance at her and she was frozen, her mouth open and her eyes wide. If I wasn't in the midst of the most terrifying moment of my life, I'd realize just how adorable she looked when she was gobsmacked.

Why did I tell her that? It was too much; I shouldn't have said anything. I blamed the wedding rehearsal—the loving moment on the dance floor between Carly and Ben combined with the adrenaline of my surprise speech.

That was the only explanation for my blatant overshare.

"Anyway, it's all in the past now." I chuckled dryly, my chest tight. "Things have changed since then. Those feelings are long gone now."

Or are they? A small, quiet voice whispered from the depths of my mind. A voice that threatened to change everything between us forever.

I couldn't go there.

I faced Ella. "Talk to me. What are you thinking?"

Finally, she cleared her throat and blinked, seeming to come back to life. "I just can't believe it."

"Why not?"

"Because..." Ella stared at her hands, clasped around the blanket. "Because I had a crush on you, too."

I physically shot back, almost falling off the car. "You did?"

"Uhm, obviously." Ella rolled her eyes and forced a laugh. "Did you see yourself in high school?"

I wasn't sure how to answer that.

"Come on, Aus. You were on the football team, gunning for med school, tall, handsome, smart. You even used to literally catch me when I fell, like you were some ridiculous, teenaged knight in shining armor."

I shook my head. "I thought... well, I didn't think you thought anything of me. You liked that other guy, Kevin—"

"Rodriguez." Ella winced. "Ms. Rodriguez's son. I liked him. But, not like I liked you."

I rubbed the back of my neck, genuinely surprised. Ella liked me all those years ago? I never had the slightest inkling. She'd always played it so cool, always treated me as nothing more than a friend.

"And, what about you? You were constantly dating people. Girlfriend of the week and all that." Ella's voice was low, and for the first time, I thought I detected a note of pain.

My heart sped. I knew I should stop. I knew we were approaching a line, the boundary of our friendship. But I couldn't.

"I think I was looking for something—*someone*—to make me feel the way you made me feel," I said quietly. "Someone who wasn't my best friend, and also best friends with my twin sister." I shot her another glance. "But, no matter who I dated, they were never you."

My words echoed through the night and Ella inhaled sharply. I bit the inside of my cheek as we fell into a slightly tense silence.

"Wow," Ella breathed. "So, we both liked each other at the same time. Imagine if things had worked out differently." She chuckled. "We might've gotten married, had kids—"

"Bought a big house on the outskirts of town," I finished. But, my heart skipped as I realized that that was exactly what I used to want. Before I pledged to never do forever.

I snuck a look at Ella and her face was turned towards the stars. She was quiet, her brow slightly furrowed. She gave nothing away as she tucked a strand of hair behind her seashell of an ear. My eyes grazed over the small pear-shaped birthmark on her shoulder, the extra prominent freckle on her nose.

I knew Ella. I knew almost everything about her... Or I thought I did. Hearing that she'd had a crush on me? Well, it was the last thing I expected.

We were in new territory now. And that was definitely making me feel things. Things I thought I'd locked away long, long ago.

My mind cast back over memories the two of us had shared—small things that made me realize just how precious and wonderful Ella was. Like when we went to prom together, or when she came to surprise me in LA, or when she returned to Aston Falls last year and helped Nicholas and Grace with the Farmer's Market.

When she'd played that song she'd written for my birthday on the flute.

Over the years, I got used to fighting those feelings. I tucked them away safely, in one of my securely locked boxes. She'd always been my friend first and foremost, and crossing that line was never an option. I wouldn't jeopardize what we had.

But, did I ever really stop fighting? Did I ever really, successfully, lock away those feelings?

Because now, the box was open and a weight was lifting off my chest. I could breathe easier as the liberation of truth hit me square in the face.

I fell for Ella Williams long, long ago, and, as much as I'd tried to fight it, that had never changed.

For the first time ever, I could admit that I was, indeed, crazy for this girl.

But, did she feel the same way? Or had I gone too far?

I knew I couldn't push her, and it would drive me mad to wait for her to speak. So, I closed my eyes and leaned back on the windshield, careful not to touch her.

25

ELLA

*M*y skin was covered in goosebumps, but I couldn't pull the blanket up. I was frozen, uncomprehending. I was stuck on one thing—Austin Bell used to have a crush on me.

Which meant that we could've held hands in the hallways, kissed before classes, shared food like those annoying couples in the cafeteria. We could've been together, just like I used to write about, dream about.

The tension between us was overwhelming as we sat on the hood of the car. His shoulder was mere inches from mine, and I wanted to bridge the gap. Or, maybe I didn't. Maybe I wanted to push him off the car and run away. Maybe I wanted to wrap my arms around him and have him cuddle me into the morning.

I'd never felt anything like it. But, I'd never felt anything like how I felt for Austin.

It all seemed way, way too good to be true that Austin Bell liked me back when I liked him, too. Because my feelings for Austin were in the past... weren't they?

Or, was it possible that I was feeling something more for my best friend?

I glanced at Austin and his eyes were closed, his hands clasped behind his head like he was sunbathing. I noticed the way his eyelids flickered, his long eyelashes resting on his cheeks. My gaze dropped to his lips and I had the almost irresistible urge to kiss him. To feel his full lips on mine. Just once, just for a moment.

As if this thought somehow stirred him, Austin lazily opened his eyes. He caught me staring at his mouth and he smirked. Then, his gaze dropped to my lips and he stopped smiling. The world slowed right down and my breath caught.

We sat, silent and still. Close, but not close enough.

Was Austin about to kiss me?

And did I want to kiss him?

Yes!

My heartbeat spiked and I almost leaned in.

But, at the very last second, my mind put up a flashing, blaring red alert sign.

Slow down. What's going on here? Am I really thinking about kissing Austin Bell?!

I blinked and shook my head. I had to think about our friendship. I had to consider what might happen between Austin and me... if we... if this...

If we kissed, it would automatically complicate everything for us. I couldn't take this lightly. Couldn't accost Austin with my lips, as much as I wanted to. Because even though I got the unmistakable sense that maybe he wanted to kiss me too, I was filled with doubt. Yes, maybe he used to have a crush on me in high school. But, Austin was also a serial dater. He wasn't a forever guy—he only ever did casual.

And I couldn't do casual. Especially not with him. Where did that leave us?

I wasn't sure I was ready to find out.

So, as the ever-so-graceful person I am, I punched Austin in the arm.

"Ah, it's all in the past now, just like you said." I laughed, slightly hysterically. "Grace would've killed you if you made a move anyway."

If Austin was put off by my reaction, he didn't show it. His trademark smirk spread across his face and he ran his fingers through his hair.

"I could've taken her," he said smoothly. Then, he checked the fitbit on his wrist. "It's getting late, though. I'll take you home."

He hopped off the hood of the car and started gathering the blankets. As soon as I handed him mine, my body broke into shivers. My stomach swirled and I realized that something in his statement sat badly with me.

As we pulled away from the viewpoint, I realized what had bothered me.

Austin referred to the Inn as "home," when in reality, I felt more at home with him than I did anywhere else.

26

AUSTIN

The next day, I woke up thinking of Ella. I thought of Ella as I made breakfast, and as I read the news, and as I did a workout in the small gym off the living room. I thought of Ella as I took a shower, got dressed, and went out the door.

I thought of her laugh, her smile, her sweet voice. It was like my senses were permeated with her. Even though she was miles away at the Inn, it felt like she was right there with me.

For the first time maybe ever, we barely texted—only to confirm the time I'd be picking her up for her sister's wedding.

And, when I pulled up in front of the Inn at that time, it was all I could do to stay put. Because I wanted so badly to go straight to her door and pick her up like this was a proper date. I wanted to open the passenger door of the car, hand her a single flower, find her glass slipper and slip it on her foot.

Fine, I stole that last part from *Cinderella*. But, needless to say, I wanted to be the prince she deserved, the one who made her dreams come true.

Because one thing was abundantly, embarrassingly clear. Christian, Nicholas, the gossips were right. All of them.

I was crazy about Ella Williams.

And, while I'd always loved everything about her, I didn't expect to fall for her. Again.

Last night's confession on the hood of my car took me by surprise, and it took everything I had not to lean in and kiss her. I almost did. And I think she almost leaned in, too.

At the last moment, though, she turned away, and she was right to do so. There was a lot on the line for us and she was leaving soon, which added yet another complication. I had no idea where this was going, or where it could go. But, I wanted to find out.

I drummed my fingers on the steering wheel and eventually decided to stand outside the car while I waited. I felt jittery and nervous, but anticipation drummed through my veins.

I leaned against the car, facing the Inn, and adjusted the jacket of my suit—the same maroon one all the ushers were wearing for Carly and Ben's wedding. Despite all of the drama at the bridal shop, I'd eventually gotten the suit fitted. Today, it felt a bit tight, but that could've been the nerves.

Right as I was about to text her again, the door of the Inn swung open and Ella swept out onto the sidewalk.

My heart stopped.

I'd seen Ella in a wide array of outfits over the past weeks, but this was something else entirely.

After Ella made her appearance as the purple loofah in the bridal shop, Carly had changed her mind on the dress. She tasked Ella to find a dress in the same purple color, and

Ella searched the shop dutifully. Eventually, she found this one—a stunning satin gown with an off the shoulder neckline that caressed her body and fell to her feet. The fabric shone and reflected with her every movement, making it look like she was moving through water. Gracefully, beautifully.

Until, she tripped on a section of sidewalk.

She fell forward, her arms windmilling around. "Arrrrrgh!"

I caught her before she hit the ground. Her arms were wrapped around my neck when she opened her eyes.

"Quite the entrance, Els."

She chuckled, a bit breathless. I lifted her to a stand and she patted her dress. "It's what I do."

I opened her car door for her and she slid into the passenger seat. Then, I went to my side.

"You look beautiful, by the way," I said. I couldn't help myself.

Ella snorted. "You don't look so bad yourself." She shifted in her seat. "You ready for another fake date?"

Her words landed funny and a deep discomfort shot through me. I forced a smile. "Born ready."

I started the car and snuck a glance Ella's way. I noticed that her hands were clasped tight in her lap as she stared out the window. There was a strange awkwardness in the air, the weight of words left unsaid. Like there was a very large elephant seated in the back of my SUV.

Fake date, she'd said. The words rolled through my mind, leaving a bitter taste in the back of my mouth.

Just like that, I had an idea. An idea that would've horrified me even a couple of weeks ago, an idea that would break every single one of my rules. But, something about it felt... right. I remembered what Ella said about getting out of my comfort zone, and if I didn't say this now, I wasn't sure I ever would.

I shut off the car, faced Ella, and took a breath. "Els, what if I don't want this to be a fake date?"

Her eyebrows shot up. "What?"

"What if I don't want this to be fake. What if I want this to be real?"

Ella was silent for a long moment. "Like you want to—"

"Date you, yes." I smiled, surprisingly calm. "What if, for today, we were more than just friends?"

My eyes searched Ella's face, waiting for her reaction. I didn't think I was wrong last night when I got the sense that she wanted to kiss me. And, now that things had changed so much between us, I didn't want to deny my feelings a moment longer. Did she feel the same?

But, as the agonizing seconds ticked by, I wondered if I'd made a huge mistake.

"If it fails and goes terribly, no harm, no foul," I added. "We'll go back to being friends like it never happened."

Finally, she looked at me. "You promise?"

"I promise," I said, seeing the worry in her eyes and unsure how to read it. "Ella, no matter what, I'll always be your best friend."

After a moment, she gave a slight nod. Smiled. "Okay."

That one little word was music to my ears. I beamed like an idiot as I started the car again and we pulled away from the curb. I grasped the steering wheel with one hand while my other arm rested on the center console. Part of me wanted to take Ella's hand, like it was the most natural, easy thing in the world.

I wasn't sure she was ready for that, though.

As we drove through Aston Falls, the sweet smell of her perfume filled the car and the sounds of country music played through the stereo. Then, I felt a warm, light touch on my hand. I looked down and Ella had placed her hand over mine. The pressure increased as she wrapped her fingers around mine.

Without a word, I removed my hand so I could take hers properly, pressing my palm to her soft one. My heart soared and I couldn't help but smile as I heard her take a sharp inhale. She didn't pull away.

We were crossing over into uncharted territory, and I didn't know where we were going next. But, when it came to Ella, it was a journey I wanted to make if she wanted to.

27

ELLA

*M*ore than just friends.

Austin Bell wanted to be more than just friends.

Someone pinch me.

I could hardly believe what had happened, and my stomach was full of nerves and excitement as Austin and I pulled up to the wedding venue, our hands intertwined. But, before either of us could say or do anything, I was swept away to the bridal suite, where Carly and the bridesmaids were getting ready.

Clouds of hairspray and excited chatter couldn't stop me from thinking about what might happen later at the reception. When Austin and I would be on a real date. But, as the ceremony got underway, I did everything I could to push all thoughts of Austin to the back of my mind and focus on the moment. Focus on my baby sister's wedding day.

Carly and Ben got married on the golden sand beach near the barn, with chairs for the wedding guests set up in the garden just beyond. The aisle featured a long, white carpet and bouquets of roses and lilacs at the end of every row. It was just after noon when the procession started, and despite it being a hot day, the breeze off the river was refreshing.

When my sister finally walked the aisle, my eyes stung with tears. She was beautiful, but the look on Ben's face—the one that showed how deeply in love he was? That was priceless.

As soon as the ceremony wrapped up, Carly stood front and center and, in true Carly fashion, commanded everyone to proceed into the barn.

"I have a surprise for y'all!" she shouted, and then winked theatrically. "Especially for the ladies."

My brow furrowed in curiosity. What surprise? I hadn't heard anything about this, and Carly was usually as bad as Mom when it came to keeping secrets.

It must be related to the band, I decided. Carly had assured me that she'd found someone for the wedding but flat-out refused to tell me who it was. Given that she listened to country music while I was more of a classic rock kind of girl, I doubted that I would have any idea who she'd booked anyway.

As the crowd almost physically carried me towards the barn, I caught Austin's eye and gestured that I'd be waiting for him inside. He smiled, a hand in his pocket like he was some kind of model, and my cheeks burned hot.

Apparently, this was something I was going to have to get used to. After last night, it was like I couldn't get my body temperature in check. I'd think about Austin's words when he told me he used to like me, and my entire head would heat up. Or, I'd think about how much I wanted to kiss him, the way his eyes dropped to my lips, and delicious chills would wash over my skin.

I barely slept last night, tossing and turning for hours.

All I could think about was him. Did I do the right thing in telling him I used to like him? Should I have gone ahead and kissed him?

But, here we were, on a date. And now, all I could wonder was—where would we go from here?

There was a kerfuffle on the stage next to the dance floor, and I craned my neck to see Carly grab the mic. A spotlight shone on her and she raised a hand to her eyes to peer over the crowd. I cast a quick glance around to find Austin, but I couldn't see him.

"Hey there! Everyone having a good time?"

Carly's question was met with raucous applause and cheering. She thanked everyone for coming and quickly went through a few basic announcements.

Then, her voice dropped to a conspiratorial tone. "Without further ado, I am very excited to introduce the band for this evening... or rather, the musician." She was practically bursting with excitement and I smiled to see her so happy. "Ladies and gentlemen, I am proud to present— CHRISTIAN WEST!"

Pandemonium ensued and incredible shrieks almost deafened me as Christian West—yes, *that* Christian West— walked out on stage.

Christian was not at all what I expected for a country star. He wore a slouchy forest green t-shirt, black jeans, and loafers. His brown hair was swept to the side, and around his neck, he wore a silver chain. He looked cool and confident, but somehow didn't seem the least bit arrogant. He seemed like your garden-variety friendly neighbor—if your neighbor had classic Hollywood looks and a sweet, lopsided grin.

My mouth fell open as he lifted a hand in a wave and smiled at the crowd. How did Carly get Christian West to play for her wedding? And why on earth wouldn't she tell me beforehand?

Unless... she knew of someone who happened to be good friends with Christian West. Someone who had a particularly handy knack for showing up right when people needed him most.

"Hi."

Speak of the devil.

I whirled around to face Austin. I lifted a hand awkwardly. "Hi."

He smiled down at me and my heart skipped a beat. Was I really on a date with this beautiful man? His blue eyes were playful but cautious, and his smile made me smile reflexively.

"Did you do this?" I asked, more than a little breathless.

"I might've called in a little favor."

"This..." I gestured towards the stage, where Christian was singing the opening verse to one of his most popular songs. "Is more than a *little* favor. How'd you manage this?"

Austin shook his head. "A magician never reveals his tricks."

He held out an arm for me and I beamed as I took it. We walked to the bar while almost every woman in the venue dived towards the stage. Before long, there was a manic crowd of screaming, cheering, overexcited fans at Christian West's feet.

Austin and I each grabbed a ginger ale and stood off to the side, listening to the music. I cast a few secret glances his way, my heart fluttering. I felt entirely too aware of what I was doing and saying. Butterflies were flying in my stomach —the same happy, scared nerves you get before a date with someone you feel excited about. A thousand times over.

At one point, I noticed Christian nod at Austin through

the crowd. Austin returned the nod with a smile before sipping at his soda. I still couldn't believe he'd done this for Carly.

Talk about going above and beyond.

I was about to take a sip of my drink when someone bumped into my back. I fell forward, almost spilling my drink all over Austin.

"Oh dear, I'm so sorry—Ella!"

A manicured hand wrenched me around so I was facing Aunt Laura. She held three glasses of water, all of which were rapidly losing their contents as she flailed about.

"Wasn't it just the most beautiful ceremony?" she gushed, eyes bright. "I knew it. I told Carly to go with roses in her bouquet, and would you believe it? I'd say it was the best part of the entire wedding. Roses truly are..."

As Aunt Laura went on about flowers, I shot Austin a sneaky glance. He winked at me and I grinned back.

Aunt Laura knocked her hip against mine. "Aren't you two planning on dancing? It's a party out there."

"Soon." I laughed. "You're enjoying it?"

Aunt Laura threw her head back as though to flip her bobbed hair over her shoulder. "Obviously. Now stop being sticks in the mud!"

With a final whoop, Aunt Laura turned on her heel and headed back towards the stage with her three—now, mostly empty—glasses of water. Austin looked at me and I shrugged. With a sweet smirk, he put down his soda and held out a hand.

"Shall we dance?" he asked.

I placed my hand in his. "We shall."

He led me through the crowd to a vacant spot on the dance floor. It was hard to believe that we'd been dancing at this very spot just last night. So much had changed since then.

Deftly, Austin turned me around and took my hands. Though there were hordes of people bustling around, the room might as well have been empty. All I was aware of was the feeling of his hands on mine, his grip around my fingers.

Then, right when I was painting a picture of how adorably romantic this moment was, Austin broke out into the most awkward, bizarre jig.

"What are you doing?"

"Isn't it obvious? I'm dancing."

"You look like an overzealous leprechaun."

Austin made a goofy face and I burst into laughter. He smiled as he pulled me close and segued into a slightly more normal waltz.

"So, how am I doing?" he asked as he twirled me.

"Not bad," I teased. "Could be worse."

"Well, this is pretty much exactly what you asked for on a first date." His eyes sparkled. "Dancing in a barn under twinkling lights. We aren't barefoot, though."

My heart squeezed and I shyly inched closer to him. "We were last night."

At this, Austin smiled wide. He twirled me, then dipped me low towards the ground.

"Awwww."

From my spot near the floor, I noticed Carly and Ben had appeared next to us. Austin returned me to my feet so I could hug my little sister. Carly seemed frazzled but deliriously happy, and the smile Ben wore might just split his face.

"You know, you two are very cute together," Carly said, and then placed her hands on her hips. "But, I'm just not buying it."

My happy mood vanished in an instant and my hands dropped from Austin's shoulders. I shrunk back, self-conscious. I knew it—it simply wasn't realistic to think that a guy like Austin could go for a girl like me. I picked at my fingernails, wanting nothing more than to run away. But, Austin kept his hands firmly on my hips, tethering me in place.

Carly tutted. "I haven't seen you guys kiss yet!"

My eyebrows shot up. "What?"

"Every time I've seen you guys together, you're, like, all over each other. But, you haven't kissed."

I looked at Austin right as he looked at me, and we blinked at each other. That was *not* what I expected.

Then, without permission, my eyes fell to his lips.

Of course I wanted to kiss him, I'd been aching to kiss him last night. But, I remembered the restrictions I'd put into our fake relationship agreement—we couldn't kiss on the lips. Though, technically, the agreement was currently void seeing as we were on a real date and not a fake date.

Austin was calm and collected as ever as he turned to Carly. "Sure you have, Car. Els and I kiss all the time."

Carly raised a perfectly plucked brow. "Do you? Because I haven't seen it. Not once."

"It's your wedding day." He laughed. "Don't you have other things to focus on?"

"I'm just saying." Carly put her hands up. "You guys are sweet and all, but there hasn't been one teeny, tiny kiss."

"Kiss her, kiss her," Ben chanted. Oh, so helpfully.

"Guys, seriously." Austin shook his head. "You don't need to see me give Ella the best kiss of her life."

Despite the annoyance I felt towards my overly intrusive sister and brother-in-law, I couldn't ignore the tingles that went all the way down to my toes at Austin's words. *The best kiss of my life, you say?*

Undeterred by Austin's rejections, Carly and Ben stared at us, sly smiles on their faces. Clearly, neither of them were going to drop the subject.

I bit my lip. Over the past twenty-four hours, Austin and I had crossed so many lines. Admitting we used to have feelings for each other, almost kissing, and now, we were on an actual date. Everything we were doing felt like a giant freefall.

I glanced at him and his eyes searched mine. I knew he was turning Carly and Ben down for my sake, to respect what we'd agreed upon when we started the whole fake relationship thing. But, I wanted to kiss him. And, if we were more than just friends today, didn't that justify a kiss?

So, I smiled. Austin shrugged helplessly, and our decision was made.

He faced me and slowly wrapped his arms around my waist. My heart raced as I linked my hands behind his neck and pressed close to him.

His eyes met mine and it suddenly didn't matter where we were or who was around us. Austin's gaze was strong, sure and confident, and I got lost in the deep ocean blue of his irises. The smell of his cologne intoxicated me, and in his arms, I felt completely at ease.

Something about this was right, was home. I felt it all the way in my bones.

He reached up and traced his fingers down my cheek, lighting a fire on my skin. He tucked a strand of hair behind my ear, then moved his hand so it cupped the back of my head.

A final smile crossed his lips as his eyes flickered once to my mouth.

Time stopped as he slowly, slowly, leaned towards me.

I tilted my head up and closed my eyes.

And when his lips finally pressed against mine, it truly was as good—better—than I ever could've imagined. The world was achingly quiet as Austin pressed one kiss, and another, and another, on my lips. His arms wrapped tighter around me and I pulled him closer, eager to deepen the kiss...

Until he took a step away, breaking the connection. His hands were still firmly on my waist, and, for a moment, he looked just as out of sorts as I felt.

But then, he faced Carly with a smile. "Happy now, Car?"

"Delirious." Carly giggled. She grabbed Ben's hand and they disappeared into the crowd.

Meanwhile, my head was spinning. I knew without a shadow of a doubt that Austin was right—I'd just had the best kiss of my entire life.

And I'd never been more terrified.

28

AUSTIN

*W*hoa.

My chest rose and fell quickly with the pace of my breaths as I turned back to Ella. The room faded as I got lost in her stunning chocolate eyes.

Then, she turned on her heel and ran away.

Like, literally picked up the bottom of her dress and ran into the crowd.

I stared after her in bewilderment, and was immediately overcome by burning hot regret. I shouldn't have kissed her. I shouldn't have taken her in my arms like that. I must've misread her smile. Did I make a horrible mistake? Overstep a boundary I never should've breached?

I deliberated for a moment or two. Then, I went after her. Even if she didn't want to see me, I had to make sure she was okay.

I pushed through the crowd and my eyes met Christian's on the stage. He shrugged, then tilted his head in the direction of the barn door. I nodded once before diving out the door after Ella.

By now, the sun was setting and the world was bathed in

a warm, healthy glow. I looked around the garden and towards the beach, but all I could see were couples on a stroll or groups of kids playing games.

Then, a flash of purple caught my eye. I turned towards the gazebo and spotted Ella looking away from me, at the river. I jogged towards her and came to a stop in the entrance of the gazebo.

"Els?"

She whirled around, eyes wide. Her arms were wrapped around herself and she was shivering slightly in the breeze coming off the river.

Reflexively, I took off my suit jacket and held it out to her. "Cold?"

She took the jacket hesitantly. "Thanks."

I smiled, feeling a little like I was approaching a baby deer. "Anytime."

I came to stand next to her and we both faced the river. The sun was shining through the leaves of the trees as it approached the horizon. The air smelled floral and fresh, and the chill of the river was welcome after the heat in the barn.

"So, are you going to tell me what's wrong or do I have to guess?" I eventually asked.

Ella frowned and bit at her pinky nail. It was painted purple to match her dress.

"Guessing it is," I murmured. "You're upset because of Carly and Ben?"

Ella shook her head.

"All right. You didn't like us dancing together?"

Another shake.

"Okay." My stomach twisted as I ventured my next guess. "You feel badly about the kiss?"

Ella didn't even hesitate. She shook her head adamantly and sweet relief filled my veins.

"So, what's the problem?"

She took a deep breath. Exhaled. Then, she opened her mouth. "It's just... none of this is real."

I furrowed my brow, my eyes scanning her profile. "What's not real?"

"This, us!" Ella burst out, gesturing between the two of us. "It's all fake."

My eyebrows shot up and I blinked. When I spoke, my voice was grave with sincerity. "No. We might've done the whole fake relationship thing, but that kiss was real."

Ella pressed her lips together and faced the river again.

"Els, I thought, for today, we were more than just friends. That was the best kiss I've ever had. I know you felt it, too."

Her cheeks flamed. "Of course I did. But, what happens tomorrow? And the day after that?"

My eyes scanned her profile, trying to understand. "I meant what I said earlier, and today just solidified that for me. I want to date you tomorrow, and the day after that, and—"

"Why?" Ella turned to me and her eyes flashed passionately. She brushed the corners and it was all I could do to not wrap my arms around her and comfort her.

I took a step back and leaned against the railing of the gazebo. Her expression was firm and her jaw was set. Her walls were up, and there was only one thing I could do.

So, my heart in my throat, I faced the river.

"Did I ever tell you why I came back to Aston Falls after LA?"

Ella sniffed. "You know you didn't. You were taking your reasons to the grave or whatever."

I smirked at her flippant tone. "Well, I want to tell you now. If you want to hear it."

She was silent for a long, long moment and I wondered whether I'd lost her. But then, she turned towards me, eyes curious. Ella was a Williams—she never could resist a secret.

I bent forward so I could lean my forearms on the railing of the gazebo. My stomach was twisted into a knot, but it was time to be honest. To tell the truth I hadn't told anyone. "Yesterday, I mentioned that I had a crush on you in high school, right? What I didn't tell you was that my crush went on a little longer than that. Part of the reason I went to LA was to... get over you. I hoped I'd move on there."

Ella shifted, but I couldn't bring myself to look at her face.

"It worked for a while. Or, I thought it did," I continued before I could lose my nerve. "But then, when you came to surprise me in LA before my graduation, I made a decision." I squeezed my eyes shut and took another breath. "Ella, when I came back to Aston Falls two years ago, I wanted to be with you."

The silence following my confession seemed endless. My words rang in my ears, almost too loud.

Then, a small hand landed on my shoulder. Ella pulled me gently to face her. "You came back for me?"

I bit the inside of my cheek and nodded once. Twice.

There it was, the truth was finally out—I didn't leave LA for work, or for my career. It was for love.

The "never forever" guy had chased love all the way back to his hometown. Only to find that the person he came back for was leaving to pursue her own dreams.

"Ella," I murmured. "Whether I've admitted it to myself or

not, I've been crazy about you for years. Your heart of gold, your humor, your intelligence... I feel like I get you and you get me. And every day, I've counted myself lucky to have you in my life."

Her hand remained on my shoulder and I took a cautious step forward. She didn't take a step back. Instead, her lips parted. Full lips that I desperately wanted to kiss again. But I wouldn't. Respecting Ella and treating her as she deserved was my number one priority. I would wait forever if that was what it took.

"Why didn't you tell me?" Ella asked quietly, eyes searching mine.

I smiled sadly. "You were headed to New York to pursue writing. I couldn't stand in the way of that. If you'd decided to stay and give up your dream, I never would've been able to live with myself."

Ella moved her hand to my cheek and I pressed mine against hers.

"I'm crazy about you, too," she whispered, almost so quietly I couldn't hear her.

My breath caught as the intensity of the moment built around us.

Her gaze dropped to my lips. "You can kiss me now."

Warmth radiated under my skin and I chuckled lightly. "Oh, can I?"

Her eyes lingered. "Yes."

She didn't need to tell me twice.

I placed my hands on her waist to bring her close as she locked her arms behind my neck. Our bodies fit together perfectly, like two pieces of a jigsaw puzzle, and my heart rate spiked.

All thoughts went out the window as I pressed Ella against the railing of the gazebo. She tugged me closer and our lips crashed, feverishly, heady, hungry. She tasted like honey and sunshine and I just wanted more.

I tilted her head back to deepen our kiss and her hands tangled in my hair.

Ella and I were no longer just friends. This kiss sealed our fates.

We were starting something completely new, and I didn't know where we would go. But, as long as I was with Ella, it didn't matter. None of it mattered.

29

AUSTIN

*H*eaven. That's what I would call the week after Carly's wedding.

Ever since our first (and second) kiss, Ella and I were inseparable. We spent all of our free time together, and each individual moment felt electrically charged, filled with so much beauty and promise.

We'd spend hours just chatting, cuddling, kissing. She'd come by my practice right after my last patient, and we would make dinner at my apartment before she returned to the Inn. Or, I'd meet her on my lunch breaks and we'd have picnics by the river. Even the simplest of things, like walking along Center Street together at twilight, or reading on the couch, our limbs intertwined, were the best parts of my days.

It was official—kissing Ella Williams was the best thing I'd ever done, and I never wanted it to stop.

"Just make sure to ice her ankle for 15 to 20 minutes every three hours for the next few days," I told Mrs. Clarke as I carefully finished bandaging the ankle of her daughter,

Beth. I cut off the extra wrap with a flourish. "And take lots and lots of rest."

Eight-year-old Beth Clarke daintily retracted her leg as her mom squeezed her hand. Beth's little brother hid behind their mom, sucking his thumb. Beth had fallen while playing a game with her youth soccer team, and dirt was streaked across her uniform. Her cheeks were tear-stained, her hair was messy and her elbows were scraped, but thankfully, she seemed to be in pretty good shape.

"Beth, you've been very, very brave," I said seriously, looking into her still-glassy eyes. Her lower lip was in a pout. "I'm impressed with you, and I think you deserve a gift..."

I stood and turned towards the cabinet, taking something out and secretly showing it to Mrs. Clarke. She nodded with a grateful smile.

I turned back to Beth. "This is for your courage today."

Beth's eyes lit up and she grabbed the red lollipop right out of my hand. She tore off the wrapper and popped the sweet into her mouth, smiling around the white stick. Her little brother stepped forward, curious. Seeing that his sister got candy and he didn't, his tiny face crumpled into a grimace. But, right before he could burst into tears, I produced another lollipop, just for him.

The stormy clouds on his face disappeared as he grabbed it and hid behind his mom again. He smiled at me and Mrs. Clarke laughed.

"Thank you so much, Dr. Bell," Mrs. Clarke said as she patted her daughter's hand. "We so appreciate it. When Bethy fell in the middle of the soccer field, I didn't know what to do."

"You did the right thing." I ruffled Beth's hair and she giggled. "Her ankle will be just fine."

We both helped Beth to a stand, and Beth grinned at me shyly.

"I didn't know what to expect coming here." Mrs. Clarke sighed. "Beth *hates* going to doctors, as does Brody. They usually have tantrums right as we step into the exam room. But, not today."

She smiled at her children fondly and I followed her gaze. I wondered briefly what it would be like when I had my own kids someday. Kids with unruly dark hair and adorable little glasses. I hoped they would look more like their mom—

Woah, reel it in.

I forced myself to push any of *those* kinds of thoughts to the back of my mind as I grabbed my clipboard.

"You were quick with the bandages," Mrs. Clarke said as she took her children's hands. "You must get a lot of sprained ankles here."

My heart skipped and I looked up from my notes to shoot her a smile. "A few. But I've actually had plenty of practice because of my... well, my girlfriend. She's been spraining her ankles for years."

"Your girlfriend is one lucky lady." Mrs. Clarke laughed.

I offered to help bring the kids to the car but she declined the offer. With a final "thank you," a shy wave from Beth, and a dimpled smile from Brody, the three of them left the room.

I returned to my notes, wondering idly whether the family was from Aston Falls or just visiting. Right then, my phone vibrated with a message. I checked the screen, saw it was from Christian, and skimmed the text quickly.

Hey man, he'd written. *Thanks again for the gig. It was just what I needed. And, turns out that I'm staying in Aston Falls awhile. Josh saw some footage from the wedding and wants to*

stage a music video here. Could be up to a week, but I'm happy to
stay. Besides, I found out where my bossy mystery chick works. I
have a feeling I'll be bothering her a few more times before I head
home. Hope things are going well with Ella.

I smiled at the text and started to reply.

"Girlfriend, huh?"

I looked up and Ella was standing in the doorway, her cheeks flushed and her eyes dancing.

My heart thundered as I raced forward and wrapped her in my arms, swinging her around. She laughed, and I silenced the beautiful sound with a kiss.

"Might be a little fast, don't you think?" Ella whispered, pressing her forehead against mine. "But, then again, we haven't done anything conventionally."

I chuckled and held her closer. "Not a thing."

I'd learned one thing time and time again this week— that our relationship was so easy and natural, it felt at times like we'd been together for years. We were so comfortable with each other, we might as well have been an old, happily married couple.

Which was why, after years and years of being single and casually dating, calling Ella my girlfriend had come so easily.

Of course, I didn't want to rush her or anything. So, I stepped back and tucked her brown hair behind her ear. She was wearing a t-shirt and shorts today, and she looked fantastic. Ella immediately closed the gap between us as she placed a tender, sweet kiss on my lips.

"Funny you mention the girlfriend thing—"

I laughed. "We don't have to make it official yet, if you don't want to."

Ella bit her lip to hold back a smile, and her cheeks

shone pink. "Official or not, I do have a bit of a favor to ask you."

"What kind of favor?"

She hopped up on the exam table and sighed, her face serious. "My parents want to spend more time with you. Specifically, they want to eat dinner with you. And me. But you'd be there in the context of being my... boyfriend."

"I'd love to. Have dinner with your family, that is." I winked.

Ella flushed and it took everything I had to keep from sweeping her off her feet in another kiss. But, I restrained myself. Even if Becca and Dr. Rob had gone home for the day, this was still my workplace.

I shrugged out of my doctor's coat as Ella told me about her day. She spoke about Carly and Ben's honeymoon in Hawaii, her mom's obsession with planning a party for their return, and about going to see Grace and Nicholas. She also told me about a surly, brooding guy who'd gone into Sweets n' Sundaes and annoyed the pants off of JJ.

"And another exciting thing happened," she said, almost shyly, as I locked the door of the clinic.

"What's that?"

"I was looking at job postings—as per usual—and I came across a staff writer position at an online magazine called *The Weekly Best*. They're based in New York, and get this—their mission statement is that they value meaningful, high-quality work. They believe in the power behind words."

"Els, that sounds perfect for you."

"It's almost exactly what I'm looking for, honestly. My dream job. But, what are the chances I'd ever get something like that?"

"You have to try," I said immediately. If anyone could do this, it was her.

"I don't know, Aus. They must have a million applications."

"But, they just need one." I smiled. "Yours."

Ella bit her bottom lip and tucked her hair behind her ear. Her cheeks were slightly pink. "Okay, maybe I'll try and see what happens. I'm not in any big rush to return to New York anyway." Then, she shook her head. "Anyway, enough about me. We're only a week away from the medical conference. Excited for your speech?"

I chuckled dryly. "'Excited' might be stretching it. I do feel better about it, but still nervous."

"You have no reason to be. You'll do great. Every time you've practiced with me, you've nailed it."

"Only because you've been there, Els. You've been my lifesaver. Presenting to a group without you is going to be a very different story..."

I trailed off as an idea came to me. Though I was more than happy to call Ella my girlfriend, neither of us had really spoken about what we were planning on doing when Ella returned to New York.

If Ella got this job, it would throw a few things into question. Our future was the one topic we hadn't properly addressed. But, perhaps, this might buy us more time.

"Do you want to come with me?" I asked.

Ella blinked. "To the NAFP conference?"

"That's right." I nodded, getting excited about the prospect of a weekend away together. "We can take the train from Aston Falls to Bozeman, then fly to Seattle for it."

Ella's brow furrowed as she turned the idea over in her mind. "I've never been to Seattle, but I'm always happy to have an adventure with you." Her smile turned devilish.

"And, speaking of the conference, I have another idea to prepare you for your speech. Can you meet me next Saturday evening?"

"Sure." My smile faltered. "Does it involve more public speaking?"

Ella's smirk remained. "Maybe."

I put on a serious expression and shook my head as if to say no.

But, Ella saw right through my charade. She launched herself on me and her lips met mine before we proceeded to my apartment to make dinner.

30

ELLA

"Come on, Aus!" I was practically buzzing with excitement as I dragged Austin down Center Street. It was evening and the street was deserted, but Austin was being purposely slow. Dragging his feet and holding back specifically to bug me. "Don't make me find a wheelbarrow."

Austin chuckled, but didn't pick up his pace. "A wheelbarrow?"

"Yes." I grunted. "So I can force you into it and wheel you down the street."

To my consternation, my threat did little. If anything, Austin just laughed harder. And slowed even more. He was literally going at a snail's pace.

"Els, we both know how the wheelbarrow race went at Dad's barbecue a couple years ago—"

"It's not my fault your legs are so darn heavy."

Austin continued. "Do you really think you can push me to this mystery place?"

I turned and placed both hands around his massive one, tugging him harder. "Absolutely."

"Look." Austin stopped and I ground to a halt in front of him. When he spoke, his tone was all too reasonable. "I'll pick up my pace if you tell me where we're going. Deal?"

I gave up and placed my hands on my waist. I stared at him quizzically. "And if I don't?"

Austin's ocean eyes bore into mine, warm and intense. "Then, that only means one thing..."

He took one step towards me. Then another.

His presence electrified me and I held my breath, my skin sparking at his proximity.

He reached out and his hands met my waist.

Then, he began to tickle me.

I exploded into cackles and I screeched as Austin wrapped his arms around me, securing me in place so he could tickle me more. I laughed and laughed, but when Austin's lips met mine, I wasn't laughing anymore.

After a solid couple minutes of making out in the middle of Center Street, I placed a hand on Austin's chest and took a step back, steadying myself.

"Fine, I'll tell you," I said, breathless. "We're headed to the Express Restaurant. Happy?"

Austin smiled mischievously. "Exceedingly so."

Something in his voice made me break out into a full-body blush and I shyly took his hand as we continued down Center Street and towards the Aston Falls Express. I snuck secret glances at Austin while we walked and my chest filled with warmth.

The past week and a half had been indescribable. Truly, there were no words for how perfectly things were going with us. I was worried to even try to find the words in case I accidentally jinxed it and this amazing dream came to an end. We'd crossed the line into something more, and it had paid off. A trillion times over.

I'd extended my stay at the Aston Glow Inn again, but I spent most of my time with Austin. No matter what we did, I wanted to squeeze my eyes shut and savor it. From the most mundane things, like reading together and watching TV on his couch, to fun dates, like going for ice cream in the evenings.

Anytime we were apart, I actively missed him. It was almost embarrassing. Like, whenever he left, he took a part of me with him. Tucked away safely in his back pocket.

Yesterday, I also had a phone interview with *The Weekly Best*. It all happened so fast—Austin encouraged me to apply, and the magazine called for a phone interview a couple of days later. I'd been over the moon... and completely terrified. But, I sat in Austin's apartment, his hand around mine, and the interview had gone well. Exceptionally well.

At the end of the call, the hiring manager informed me that, while it was tough to hire over a phone interview, she thought I would be an amazing fit. She said that I would hear back in a week or two. To celebrate, Austin and I had a picnic at the Aston River Park.

I still smiled at the memory. Everything was going so well. And, in less than a week, Austin and I would be taking a big step—a weekend trip to Seattle. When he'd first asked me, I didn't know what to think. My feelings for him were growing by the day, and a trip together felt suitably serious. I chose to focus instead on the fact that we were going for his work. For the conference.

And, on that, I was hopeful that my idea for tonight would pan out. Either that, or it would flop terribly, and Austin would hate me, and I'd be required to hide away in a hole somewhere.

So, I was crossing my fingers.

Nonetheless, my stomach filled with nerves as we walked into the Express Restaurant and passed through to the last car of the train. There, we met with a rather large, bouncer-looking figure.

"Hello," I said, and offered a feeble smile. "We're here for the open mic night?"

I was aware of Austin shifting on his feet next to me. I didn't dare look at his face as the bouncer checked his list. "Reservation?"

"No?" I squeaked.

The bouncer glanced at me and then at Austin. He sized him up, taking in his height and athleticism, and then, apparently approving, smiled. "It ain't too busy tonight. Go right on in."

"Amazing," I breathed, before taking Austin's hand and wrenching him through the door.

The open mic night always took place on Saturdays, when the last train car of the Express was transformed into a cozy and intimate lounge. The passenger seats were made into booths, and the lights were dimmed to classic red and blue hues. At one end, a small stage was lit by a single spotlight and featured a stool and a mic.

As Austin and I tumbled into the darkened train car, I was thrown back to the open mic nights and comedy nights my friends in New York had dragged me to. Those events were always loud, bustling and altogether a bit much. Though, to be fair, my friends did go for the social atmosphere rather than to see the performances.

The Aston Falls version was quieter, more low-key. Perfect for getting someone out of their comfort zone...

"What're we doing here, Els?" Austin said, voice low. "I'm not really big on open mic nights."

"I know you're not. And that's why we're here."

Before Austin could ask any more questions, I took his hand and dragged him towards the front. We sat at the table nearest the stage and I looked around. Small groups and couples were already seated and murmuring in low voices while waiting for the show to start. The smells of incense and perfume permeated the space, giving the train car an even more intimate quality.

Finally, the host stepped onto the stage to introduce the first acts of the evening. They were regulars—the guy who played guitar and sang a little pitchy, the aspiring stand-up comedian, the person doing a spoken word poem, the woman who played the flute in such a way that put my high school attempts to shame.

I whispered to Austin to pay attention to how the performers behaved, how they carried themselves. I pointed out a few things—like the fact that they faced the crowd and made eye contact with audience members, how they took pauses and regulated their breathing.

"That's a lot to remember," Austin murmured. "I might not even be able to get through my keynote speech, I'll just be thinking of what I have to do to present properly."

I giggled. "You're going to be amazing, Aus. These are just suggestions to make you feel more sure of yourself."

There was a break in the performances and I turned to Austin. "Having fun?"

Austin stretched his arms. I knew exactly how he felt about open mic nights—he'd never attended one because even the thought of watching someone struggle onstage gave him second hand discomfort. But, I was gratified to see him smile. "I'm not going to lie, Els. It's not the worst way I've spent an evening."

"Admit it. You're enjoying yourself."

Austin looked around and then leaned in. He got so

close that I could see the flecks of gray in his eyes. "Alright, I'm having a good time. Getting out of my comfort zone with you is fun."

I blushed as he kissed the sensitive spot below my ear.

"I will say that this wasn't what I expected," he said. "I thought you'd take this opportunity to throw me into the deep end again. Force me to perform or something."

I bit my lip and averted my gaze. Tried to feign an innocent expression.

Unfortunately, he knew exactly what that meant. That was the problem with dating your best friend—they already knew everything about you.

"Unless that was your plan..." His eyes scanned my face. "Els, what did you do?"

I took a deep breath and reached into my purse. I took out a single sheet of paper, folded over eight times. *Here goes.*

"Okay, you got me. I put your name down for a performance later tonight. I thought, maybe, you could do a reading of that same scene from high school. The one that didn't go well." I fiddled with the paper, not daring to look at Austin. "But, of course, if you don't want to, I completely understand and that's totally fine."

Silence from his direction. When I finally hazarded a glance towards him, Austin was... smiling.

"Of course you did." He chuckled and took the paper, slowly unfolding it. He skimmed the page, then folded it back up again. His expression was unreadable as he faced the stage once more and the lights dimmed for the next set of performers.

"Sooo?" I whispered. His silence was too much.

He looked at me and his eyes gleamed. My heart started again.

"I'll do it," he replied. "But, on one condition."

"What's that?"

"That the next time we come, you have to do a flute solo."

By the time Austin was called up to perform, you wouldn't think the guy was the least bit nervous. He strode to the front of the room, exuding confidence and calm. The crowd fell into a polite silence as he walked onstage, and all eyes turned to him.

Austin approached the mic and ran his fingers through his blond hair. He smiled as he gazed into the crowd, and my stomach flip-flopped.

"How y'all doing tonight?" he drawled into the microphone and whoops erupted around the room.

He unfolded the paper and bit the inside of his cheek as he looked at the words. The little crack in his facade exposed his shyness and vulnerability, and it almost did me in. I was in awe of him, of his bravery.

Austin took a breath, faced the crowd, and cleared his throat. "Tonight, I'm going to read Shakespeare's Sonnet 18."

He cleared his throat again and I could sense him getting nervous. I wished I could do something to help him, find some way to show him he could do this. I shifted in my chair, and the noise made him glance up. His eyes locked with mine and he smiled. Just a little smile. But my heart did about fifty somersaults.

Then, he began to speak. "Shall I compare thee to a summer's day? Thou art more lovely and more temperate..."

Of course, the sonnet spoke of love. I hadn't even thought about it, or considered what that might do to my insides.

Because, as Austin spoke, his deep chocolatey voice melting over each and every word, the sentences came alive. He took measured pauses so every sentiment hit home. Though he occasionally looked at the crowd, his gaze always returned to me and, at times, it felt like he was speaking to me. The whole thing made my heart race.

Though I'd printed the thing and Austin hadn't prepared at all, he might as well have spent days rehearsing. And, judging by the absolute silence around the train car— not even the creak of a chair, or the scrape of a glass on a tabletop—I wasn't the only one who was captivated.

As the sonnet came to an end and Austin folded the paper, the room was deathly quiet. He shifted and then, like the crash of thunder, the space exploded into raucous applause.

Austin's cheeks turned the slightest bit pink as he waved at the audience and stepped down from the stage. He fist-bumped the host, then jogged back to our table.

He kissed me on the cheek and I blushed a furious shade of red. I was lightheaded and dazed. I'd never been so attracted to someone in my life.

"You were amazing," I breathed. "You should read Shakespeare more often."

Austin laughed. "Thanks, Els. I'm going to grab a drink. Thirsty?"

"Am I," I blurted, and Austin took off towards the bar at the back of the train car.

I turned towards the stage, smiling stupidly. I was completely, overwhelmingly proud of Austin, and totally blown away by him. He managed to take every challenge, every hardship, in his stride. No, he did more than that—he took challenges and squared up to them. Destroyed them. All with a killer smile.

As the host announced the next performer, I felt a light tap on my shoulder.

"Pssst."

I turned to see Ms. Rodriguez, leaning so far she was basically falling out of her chair. She smiled and gave me the thumbs up.

"Lucky girl," she whispered.

"Thanks." I smiled.

I turned to look for Austin by the bar and noticed that he was speaking to someone—Sophie Moore.

I remembered what she'd said the night she found out Austin and I were "together," the skepticism in her reaction to us as a couple. Though I never would've admitted it aloud, it felt pretty nice to show up my school bully.

Little did Sophie know that, because of that evening, Austin and I were a real couple now. I was beyond happy with him, and I couldn't remember the last time I'd felt so strongly for someone.

I was about to face the front again when Sophie laughed in response to something Austin had said. She threw her head back so her pearly hair cascaded down her back, and then touched his arm. Her hand lingered a moment too long on his bicep and my jaw clenched.

Austin didn't seem to notice this obvious flirtation. Instead, he nodded at her and made his way back through the crowd.

He smiled at me as he approached, ocean eyes dancing, and the tinge of jealousy disappeared.

"Sorry, got caught up with Sophie." He rolled his eyes and placed a ginger ale in front of me before scooting his chair closer. "She was looking for tips on performing, believe it not. I told her that she'd better look somewhere else, I barely survived myself."

Austin chuckled and the sound was warm and inviting. His words soothed me, and I berated myself. Why did I jump to such conclusions? Whether or not the girl was interested in Austin, it didn't matter. I trusted Austin with every fiber of my being.

I took his hand and linked my fingers through his as the next performer came onstage and settled on the stool. She was an older woman with flowing gray hair and a frilly leather vest over a floral dress.

As she began her performance, I sipped my ginger ale, completely content. I was sitting with an amazing man, his hand around mine, and things were finally looking up. Sure, I hadn't yet heard from *The Weekly Best*, and I didn't want to think about what the job would mean for Austin and me. But, I knew that we could get through anything. A little long distance wouldn't hurt us.

I focused on the woman's performance. She was reciting a poem she'd written about the pain of love lost. Her words were deep and emotional and I found myself leaning forward as she spoke, drawn in.

The poem was about regret and the pain of losing someone you loved. But, more than that, she spoke of friendship lost. The crux of it was that her partner, the one she'd addressed the poem to, was her best friend, the person who knew everything about her. When they broke up, she lost everything that mattered to her.

I shifted in my seat as her words landed funny. Her poem was beautiful, but it sent unwelcome pin pricks over my skin. Something about what she said felt... familiar. Uncomfortably familiar.

It felt like the woman was looking right at me, speaking directly to me. Like she knew something I didn't.

I looked away, towards Austin. But, he was on his phone, texting.

I assessed him—the way he smiled and bit his lip, the way his fingers flew across the screen. He wasn't paying any attention to the lady's poem, and maybe that was for the best.

I'd always heard stories about best friends becoming romantically linked, about how important it was to be friends with the person you were dating. But, how often did you hear the other types of stories? The stories of friends who tried for something more and it didn't work out? The stories of couples who went back to being just friends?

I was crazy about Austin, there was no way around it. But, was there a chance we wouldn't get our happy-ever-after? That we wouldn't be so lucky?

My eyes landed on Sophie, standing by the bar and leering unashamedly at Austin. I knew one person who was counting on us breaking up.

As though sensing my unpleasant thoughts, Austin placed his phone on the table. His eyes met mine and he smiled before taking my hand again. I let the warmth of his touch dispel the questions in my head, and I closed my eyes for a moment.

The next act took to the stage, and I resolved to forget it. Austin and I were great together, we were on solid ground, and that was all that mattered.

31

ELLA

*B*ut, just like the diet I'd started right after New Year's, my resolution didn't exactly go as planned.

For the next two days, I tried to move past my uncertainty, but like a wayward child reaching back into the cookie jar, my thoughts would sneakily return to the open mic night and the woman's poem. It was not a knock on her performance—if anything, judging by the way it stuck with me, her poem was exceedingly good.

But, it got me thinking. Were Austin and I doing the right thing? Would we get our happily-ever-after? If things didn't work out, would we be able to remain friends?

Apart from the annoyingly nagging doubts and anxieties, Austin and I still saw each other every day. We cooked dinners together, jogged through the park on his lunch breaks, and even took another drive to the viewpoint and watched the stars over Aston Falls.

Things were practically perfect.

Now, Austin and I were standing on the steps of my parents' little brownstone, and I had something else on my mind. Tonight was dinner with my parents, and I was filled with nervous jitters.

Reflexively, I checked my phone screen. No new notifications.

My phone interview was a week ago today. I hadn't heard from *The Weekly Best* and my hopes were slipping. If they wanted to hire me, wouldn't they have called by now?

I placed my phone back in my pocket and refrained from slipping my other hand out of Austin's. His grip was firm and sturdy, but my palm felt clammy. I kind of wanted to run away, but I didn't exactly know why.

"Els, you okay?" Austin asked.

I shot him a quick smile. "I'm fine."

It was a lie. I hoped he couldn't see through it.

His eyes scanned my face. "You sure? If you don't want to do this, just say the word. We can have dinner with your parents another time."

I pursed my lips. I'd been so excited for my parents to spend time with Austin now that we were truly together. I wouldn't let my niggling insecurities spoil this moment for us. So, I flashed him a smile I hoped was at least slightly brighter. "Totally ready. Let's do this."

Austin stared at me a beat longer. It occurred to me that, when I felt this way in the past—like before a job interview, or a big meeting, or a confrontation with a friend—I always turned to him first.

For the first time ever, I was holding back.

With a bright smile, I knocked on the door, and within seconds, Mom emerged. Her dark hair was held back with a white headband, and she wore pink lipstick that complimented her pink top. Her beige slacks and sandals gave her a very mom-at-the-summer-barbecue appearance.

"Ella, Austin!" she exclaimed. Like she hadn't been

standing behind the door awaiting our arrival. "So lovely to see you. Come in, come in!"

I dropped Austin's hand so I could step inside, and wiped my clammy palms on my shorts. I just had to get through this dinner. That was all I had to do.

What came after that? Well, who knew.

32

AUSTIN

*D*inner was going exceptionally well.

Though I'd essentially grown up with the Williams and they came to my clinic whenever they were ill, spending time with them in *this* setting was entirely differ-ent. Ella and I were together now, and I was getting the full boyfriend treatment.

It started with a stern gaze from her dad, followed by questions regarding my "intentions." I responded that Ella was her own person, and I intended to be with her as long as she wanted to be with me. Mr. Williams chuckled and that was the end of that.

Then, it was Mrs. Williams's turn.

I didn't even realize that she was grilling me at first. The lady was *that* good.

She started by asking when Ella and I knew that we liked each other, then she followed with questions about what I saw for myself and my future. Some of the questions got personal, diving into topics Ella and I had yet to discuss. Like, whether I wanted children and whether I wanted to settle down in Aston Falls.

For the record, it was a "yes" on both counts. Assuming that was what Ella wanted.

Luckily, Ella had my back and she swooped in whenever her mom's questions got a bit too intrusive.

Finally, the exam came to an end and we were all able to relax. Mrs. Williams spent most of dinner regaling us with hilarious anecdotes about her marriage and children. Her husband, meanwhile, had his arm around her shoulders, and he doted on her throughout the meal.

I had my arm wrapped around Ella, too. As conversation flowed easily, I had a very pleasant premonition of my future. Our future. Ella and I could host dinner parties like this, invite our closest friends and family.

I was new to this whole long-term relationship thing, but with Ella, I was ready to do it all.

"I always wondered whether you two would get together," Mrs. Williams said as we were finishing dinner. She steepled her fingers and gazed between Ella and me. "I'm just so delighted to see how happy you two are."

Ella rolled her eyes, pink rising to her cheeks. "Mo-om."

I kissed Ella's blush. "You're not the only one."

"I suppose you will have to work everything out if Ella gets that dream job of hers in New York."

Right. Ella's dream job.

My lips twitched and I glanced at Ella. Of course I wanted her to get the job at *The Weekly Best*, and I could never ask her to stay. But, I couldn't say I was looking forward to her leaving. I would do anything for her, and that included long distance, but I would miss seeing her every day, making her laugh, seeing her smile. Miss kissing her.

Ella was taking a long swig of her drink. She placed her glass on the table and wiped her lips. "Haven't heard anything yet."

Mrs. Williams placed her hand on Ella's. "I know you said your career is important, honey, but you and Austin are together now. There must be a job in Aston Falls that could work for you?"

"No," Ella responded immediately, shaking her head. "The staff writer position with *The Weekly Best* is exactly what I want."

"I see."

An awkward silence settled over the table. Even Mr. Williams looked uncomfortable. I couldn't say I felt excited at the prospect of Ella leaving again either, but as the boyfriend, it was my job to steer us away from heavier topics, right?

"Did Ella tell you about Seattle?" I asked brightly. Too brightly.

Ella cast a glance my way and her lips twitched. I could swear a shadow crossed her features, but the next moment, it was gone.

"No." Mrs. Williams smiled. "I didn't hear about that. You two are going to Seattle?"

I nodded. "Just for the weekend."

"That is fantastic news! Dad and I went to Seattle once, and it was great. We both loved it."

"I have lots planned for us. Museum tours, delicious food, hanging out by the ocean—"

At this, Ella's head snapped up. "It's just a work trip, though. We're going for Austin's medical conference."

My smile faltered. I mean, she wasn't wrong... but the conference wasn't the only reason I'd asked her to come with me. I wanted to explore Seattle together, just the two of us. Another adventure for us.

Ella's parents didn't seem to notice that anything was off. Mrs. Williams stood from the table to clear plates.

"Speaking of delicious food, I have a tasty dessert I've been waiting to share with guests. Want to help, dear?"

Mr. Williams did as she asked, and I stood with him, piling the plates. But, Mr. Williams waved me away. "Don't worry about the dishes. Enjoy yourself."

With a merry wink, he followed his wife through to the kitchen.

I sat back in my seat and put my arm loosely around Ella's shoulders. I may have imagined it, but I thought she stiffened. She'd seemed a bit off before dinner, but she'd been all smiles and laughter all evening. I wondered if something was bothering her, Ella was usually very forthcoming when something was on her mind.

"Dinner seems to be going well," I ventured.

Ella nodded enthusiastically. "Really well."

"So now, your parents know we're together."

"They do."

"JJ knows our relationship is real, and Christian knows." I counted down on my fingers, then I smiled. "So, what do you think about making this official? Telling Gracie and my dad that we're actually dating?"

Ella cleared her throat and stared intently at her water glass. "I'm not sure."

"Not sure about what?"

Her face crinkled, like she was scrambling for words. "It's just not a good time. Mom and Dad are only just getting comfortable with us. And, Grace and Nicholas are so busy with the house renovations. They won't want to hear about this."

My frown deepened. "Really? I think Gracie will be happy for us."

Ella fiddled with her fingers. Tapped her water glass. "I think we should wait. At least until after the conference."

An uncomfortable twinge radiated through my abdomen. Grace was one of Ella's best girlfriends, she went to her whenever anything boy or dating related came up. It was odd that Ella didn't want to talk to Grace about us, but if something was on Ella's mind, I trusted that she would talk to me about it. I probably just had to give her time to process her thoughts.

So, I waited. But, Ella carefully avoided my eyes, looking everywhere but at me.

The door to the kitchen swung open, breaking the awkward tension.

"Here it is!" Mrs. Williams announced as she swept into the room with two huge slices of tiramisu. "I hope you're ready for dessert."

I forced a smile as she placed the plates in front of Ella and me. My arm was no longer draped over Ella's shoulders and I could almost feel the chill from her direction.

Despite how delicious the cake looked, I suddenly wasn't hungry.

33

ELLA

I loved Shirley Temples. The drink was my adulthood guilty pleasure.

So, when I saw it on the drinks list of the Seaside Grand hotel conference center in Seattle, I ordered one. But, I couldn't bring myself to take a sip.

Instead, I cradled the drink as I walked back to my table, trying and failing to blend in with the crowd of doctors and medical experts. They bustled around me, their hair perfectly coiffed and their neutral-colored dresses and suits pressed to within an inch of their lives.

Meanwhile, I stuck out like a sore thumb in my coral dress, hair askew. I approached the table Austin and I were assigned to, but my heel caught on the carpet and I flew forward, spilling some of my Shirley Temple onto my dress.

Perfect.

With a grimace, I took a seat and swirled my straw around the drink. Austin had gone off with the conference organizer as soon as we'd entered the room, and in all honesty, it was probably for the best that we were apart.

Since the open mic night, I was having doubts about Austin and me, and when he mentioned to my parents that we were going to Seattle together, my doubts and anxieties solidified.

Austin was at the pinnacle of his career. And me? I was in a pretty stinky mood after the news I'd received earlier this morning.

We arrived in Seattle late last night and checked into our respective rooms at the Seaside Grand. Austin was staying down the hall from me and we said our good nights before heading to sleep.

Well, mostly slept. I had to admit that I was tossing and turning for a lot of the night.

The oh-so-delightful surprise had happened this morning, when I forced myself out of bed and checked my phone. An email had come through, and the message preview was enough to know that it was bad.

Dear Ms. Ella Williams, we appreciate your interest in our staff writer position. Unfortunately, you have not been...

And so on, and so forth.

All to say that the dream job I'd been hoping for with *The Weekly Best*—the one I thought I was a sure thing—wasn't going to be mine.

I was back to square one. Back to being unemployed and directionless.

On the bright side, this meant I could stay in Aston Falls longer, if I wanted. However, even this consolation seemed hollow as I considered telling Austin the bad news. There was no way I was going to tell him here, at his conference. I wanted to support him, celebrate his success and achievement. He'd more than earned it after years of hard work.

So, I had to keep this to myself for now. Tell him after we got back.

I continued to swirl my straw around my Shirley Temple, trying not to feel like a complete and utter failure.

"Is this seat taken?" A deep, slightly nasal voice pulled me from my spiral.

I looked up to see a guy with slicked back blond hair and a small mustache gesturing to the seat next to mine. Austin's seat.

"Technically," I said apologetically. "Are you sitting at this table?"

His eyes were weirdly intense as they met mine. "No, I'm across the room." He proffered his hand. "Dr. Willoughby. Head of Neurosurgery at Boston General. And, you are?"

I shook his hand. "Ella... Ella Williams."

"Nice to meet you, 'Ella Ella Williams.'" Willoughby gazed at me, unblinking. I felt uncomfortable under his rather eagle-eyed stare and I tucked my hair behind my ear.

Sensing that I wasn't about to offer up any more information about myself, Willoughby picked up the name card in front of him.

"Austin Bell," he read, and then his eyes went wide. "Like Dr. Austin Bell?"

I nodded. "That's him."

"People here seem to think he's a living legend." Willoughby pursed his lips. "Studied in LA? Spearheading the opening of a medical facility in a tiny town somewhere?"

"Yeah."

"Hmm, his speech should be... interesting. I heard he's afraid of public speaking. Wouldn't know anything about that myself."

Willoughby's tone sat badly with me and I frowned. "Austin's actually a really talented speaker. His keynote speech is going to be amazing."

The condescending smile dropped right off his face. "So, you've met him then?"

"Met him?" I laughed dryly. "We're... well, we're dating."

At this, Willoughby's entire demeanor changed. He dropped the name card onto the table like it burned him. He nodded once, stiffly, and smiled. "I see. Nice to meet you, Ella. I'll be around if you want to chat."

Yeah, right. "Sounds good."

As Willoughby vanished, my eyes lingered on the crowd. I was practically drowning in a sea of beautiful people, all nicely groomed and put together. Even Willoughby, aside from his unnerving stare, had a regal quality to him. Everyone was neatly dressed, and they smiled jovially. The kind of smile that said "I'm an adult and I'm in control."

These people had their lives together, had a purpose and direction.

So, what was I doing here?

I bit my lip as my fingers went slack around my glass. This was Austin's world. It was filled with successful people, and gorgeous, inspiring women. He could date anyone he wanted, so why on earth had he chosen me?

Surely, there had to be someone better for him out there. Someone who could walk without tripping and spilling her drink all over herself. Someone who could keep a job.

Maybe it really was insane to think that a guy like Austin could belong with a girl like me.

An awful booming noise echoed around the conference room as someone tapped the mic on stage. I shot back in my seat, nearly toppling onto the floor. Meanwhile, with a smile and no inclination of the distress he'd put the audience through, the host of the conference introduced himself and the agenda for the day.

First up? The keynote speech by Dr. Austin Bell.

I turned my attention towards the stage, waiting for my suitably beautiful best friend to take his place at the podium. Though I had doubts about whether we should be together, I had to be a friend to him now, first and foremost. He needed me and, no matter what, I believed in him.

So, my heart in my throat, I forced a smile and clapped as loud as I could.

34

AUSTIN

"And that is where cutting edge healthcare belongs —helping the communities that need it most. Thank you."

My voice echoed through the speakers of the conference room and the crowd burst into applause. I smiled as I collected my papers from the podium. A heady rush of happiness and pride filled my body as I stepped out of the spotlight.

Dr. Mendoza and the rest of the NAFP committee rushed forward. Mendoza took my hand and shook it enthusiastically. "Wonderful!"

His colleague patted me on the shoulder. "Truly marvelous. You could make a career out of lecturing, my boy."

I laughed, feeling like I could breathe easier. Like I could do anything. I shook the doctors' hands. "Thank you so much."

My speech had gone off without a hitch. I wasn't shaky, didn't stutter or scramble for words. I spoke to the crowd as though they were friends of mine, taking measured pauses and gazing around to make eye contact. It helped that the woman I was crazy about was seated in the audience, and anytime I felt unsure, I looked to her. Ella's smiles and nods were all the encouragement I needed. I couldn't have done it without her.

Mendoza took to the stage to introduce the next speaker for the evening—Dr. Albert Willoughby from Boston General.

A bitter taste filled my mouth as the man stepped forward. I knew Willoughby, I'd encountered him in passing a few times. He was one of those guys who used conferences as an excuse to cheat on his wife. On the very few occasions that we'd spoken to one another, his greasy attitude was enough to deter me from making a connection.

I had a feeling the guy was a bit intimidated by me now.

When I saw him approach Ella earlier, it was all I could do not to march over. Ella could handle herself, but the guy was scum and I didn't want him around her. Unfortunately, Mendoza and the NAFP committee were literally in my way, setting me up for my speech. By the time they'd finished briefing me, Willoughby had left the table.

Now, as I made my way through the bustling crowd— people were mingling instead of paying attention to Willoughby's speech—I tried to keep my eyes on Ella. She was smiling and waving, and I could understand why Willoughby had approached her, why almost every other man in here had their eyes on her. She looked stunning in her pink dress, lively and beautiful.

With her wide smile and warm gaze, I could almost believe that everything was right between us.

In truth, things between Ella and I had been rocky for a few days now. Ever since her parents' dinner, Ella seemed distracted and distant, like she was pulling away. And the worst part was, she hadn't talked to me about any of it.

I wondered whether I pushed her too hard—wanting to tell Grace and my dad about us, and inviting her to Seattle. On the train and plane yesterday, I hoped we could speak about it, but anytime I asked what was on her mind, she changed the subject.

Often to something weather-related, like how hot or cold the day was. You'd think she was interested in a career as a weather person.

Something was clearly on her mind, but what was bothering her? And why on earth wouldn't she talk to me about it? I wasn't used to Ella keeping these kinds of things from me, and there was a distance between us I absolutely did not like.

I just wanted to get back to our table, get back to her. Now that my speech was out of the way, maybe she would be more willing to tell me what was going on.

"Austin!"

I recognized the voice immediately, and I turned to face a tall, redheaded firecracker.

"Austin Bell, as I live and breathe." Hannah McAdams shook her head, her twangy Southern accent rolling over my name.

"Hannah." I smiled and we exchanged a quick hug. "It's so good to see you."

"You too, stud," she teased, flipping her hair over her shoulder. "Congrats on your speech, I thought you hated public speaking."

I chuckled. "Oh, I still do. But, I had help today."

I cast a glance towards Ella, but there was a wall of people in the way and I couldn't see her.

"It's been ages since I saw you. The last time was probably when we broke up. Right before I left for Florida."

I furrowed my brow, trying to remember. "That's right. When you got the surgeon job. How's it going, by the way?"

"Amazingly well." Hannah beamed. "I'm in the running for Head of Surgery, actually."

My jaw dropped. "Oh, Han. That's awesome."

"That's what Keith said, too." Hannah's eyes went dreamy and I noticed the wedding ring on her finger. I smiled, happy to see her so happy. Though Hannah had been my longest term relationship, she and I had ended on good terms. She leaned in and placed a hand on my arm, chuckling conspiratorially. "Who said that break ups have to be a bad thing, right?"

I laughed along with her. "I'm glad you're doing well, Han. I'd better get back to my date."

"Yes, I should find my husband." She rolled her eyes. "Lord knows that Keith is probably hunting down a TV to broadcast the game."

With a final wave, Hannah made her way towards the conference room doors.

I chuckled to myself, thinking how nice it was that Hannah had found her place in the world. I thought I'd found mine, too.

I continued towards our table, smiling and nodding as people patted my back and congratulated me on my speech. But, all I wanted was to see Ella. To thank her for helping with my speech, and for being my guiding light.

As I broke through the crowd around our table, though, Ella was gone.

35

ELLA

I plopped into a booth and the waiter appeared next to the table.

"Can I get you anything, miss?" he asked. His smile faded as soon as he saw my expression.

"Fries," I blurted. "All of your fries."

With a nod, the waiter disappeared and I shifted on the uncomfortable leather seat. It always baffled me when restaurants ordered leather booths and then insisted on keeping the temperature of the place practically scalding.

I glanced back towards the entrance of the hotel restaurant, but I didn't see anyone following me. Austin was probably still talking to Hannah, his perfect, effortlessly beautiful ex. The one who made me look like a dressed up garden gnome.

My phone vibrated on the table and I nearly jumped out of my skin. I checked the caller ID and, seeing that it was JJ, I picked up. "Hel—?"

"ELS!"

JJ's squeal nearly deafened me and I held the phone away from my ear.

"Where have you been?" she asked. "I've been dying to talk to you. I've gone to the Inn like twelve times and Ms. Rodriguez said you weren't there."

I counted back on my fingers. "JJ. I've been gone for less than twenty-four hours."

"Gone? Gone where?"

"Seattle?" I paused. "Remember?"

I told JJ about this trip a couple of days ago while I was hiding out at Sweets n' Sundaes, lightly avoiding Austin. To be fair, she'd been rather distracted at the time, watching Youtube videos on how to properly scoop ice cream. Apparently, she and some guy she'd met a few months back had gotten off very much on the wrong foot. Fast forward to a couple of weeks ago, and this same guy—she would only call him "scruffer"—came into Sweets n' Sundaes and insulted her scooping technique.

"Ohmygosh, of course." I heard JJ smack something through the phone. Likely, her forehead. "Is Austin being the most magical travel boyfriend or what?"

I ground my teeth. I wouldn't be upset, I wouldn't.

"Yep," I finally breathed, but my voice cracked.

JJ stopped laughing. "Els? What's going on?"

I sighed and leaned back in the booth, pressing my head into the leather seat. "You should've seen it, Austin's keynote speech was perfect! The audience loved it, and I'm so happy and proud of him."

"So?" JJ asked. "What's the problem?"

I shifted in the seat. "Well, his ex was there—"

"His ex? I thought Austin was like a "date 'em and leave 'em" kind of guy. That he didn't do relationships until he met you."

If our relationship could ever work.

I squeezed my eyes shut and shoved the thought far, far away.

"He dated this girl for a while back in LA. And JJ, she's beautiful. Like, a Danish supermodel with fiery red hair. You should've seen this silky silver dress she was wearing. And, she's incredibly smart. The last I heard, she's a surgeon. A *surgeon*!"

JJ was silent for a beat. "And?"

"Well!" I exclaimed passionately and my eyes stung. "She's got her life together. She's got it all figured out, just like Austin does. I bet she's the kind of person who wakes up early and meditates. The kind of person who sticks with their New Year's diets."

I thought back over their interaction. When I saw Hannah pull Austin aside, I intended to walk over and introduce myself. Then, a group of people walked by and, when they finally passed, I saw her lean in and place her hand on Austin's arm. They looked like an ad. Like a super tan, fit couple promoting some sporty drink. She was clean-cut and beautiful, while I had a Shirley Temple stain on my dress.

When I saw them laugh together, I couldn't stand there a moment longer.

I bolted. All the way to the hotel restaurant.

Because, one, Austin would've found me in my hotel room immediately. Two, I didn't know a single thing about Seattle and therefore couldn't leave the hotel. And three, after seeing *that* interaction, I needed a bucket of fries. STAT.

"Els, who cares that she has her life together?"

"I care." I shook my head. "Because I... don't. At all."

"What about that writing job in New York? Once you have that, I'm sure you'll feel better about all of this."

The pang of loss reverberated through my chest. It stung so much that I'd been passed over for the staff writer job, especially when the hiring manager had made it sound so promising. "Right. That."

I shook my head, breath held. I was about to tell JJ the painful truth when she continued speaking. "See? You're overreacting. This will sort itself out in no time."

I squeezed my eyes shut. I knew I'd have to tell her—tell everyone—sometime. But, for now, I wanted to keep pretending that everything wasn't falling apart around me. "Anyway, I'm being a terrible friend. What is it you wanted to talk about?"

JJ inhaled sharply. When she spoke, her voice was almost a whisper. "I found out who that annoying scruffer guy is. And you'll never believe it."

"You did?" I frowned. "I thought he lived out of town, and was mostly out of sight, out of mind."

"Except that he hasn't been. He visits Sweets n' Sundaes almost every day now."

"Wow." My eyebrows popped up as I peeked out of the booth to check the door. "So, who is it?"

Unfortunately, at that very moment, a familiar face entered the restaurant. Austin's blue eyes perused the booths and I leapt back into my seat.

"Okay, so I think he's—" JJ was saying.

"Gotta go," I cut her off, my voice a whisper. I sank deeper into the booth. "He's here."

"Who's there?" JJ sounded almost amused.

"You know who. I'll talk to you soon."

I ended the call and scooted over so I was basically pressed against the far wall of the booth. I sank down even lower and prayed that Austin hadn't seen me. Prayed that he might think this was just another empty booth and leave the premises. I couldn't handle seeing him right now.

I squeezed my eyes shut and held my breath. Waiting.

"Miss? Your fries?"

I opened one eye and the waiter was hovering next to my table with a confused, slightly worried grimace. In his hand, he held a massive basket of fries. But, I couldn't focus on those because, just behind him, Austin was staring at me.

And he did not look happy.

"Els. What the—" Austin cut himself off as he sat opposite me in the booth. He ran a frustrated hand through his hair and his eyes flashed. "Why'd you run off like that?"

I brought the fries close, cradling them to my chest. "I had a sudden, untamable craving for french fries?"

The question in my sentence didn't exactly help matters and Austin's face turned dark and stormy. Though Austin rarely ever got upset, he was undeniably hot when he was mad. It made me feel things that I really shouldn't have been feeling at this juncture.

"So. You decided to ditch me at the conference and come here."

I bit my lip. When he put it like that...

"I'm sorry," I said sincerely. "I'm so sorry, Aus. Your speech was incredible. Honestly, you were amazing. I'd never been so riveted by the topic of healthcare in rural—"

"Els, don't make jokes right now."

"I'm not. I know I gave you tips on writing it, and you rehearsed it with me and stuff. But, you were a natural up there."

"So, why'd you run away?"

My breath caught and, instead of answering, I shoved a handful of fries into my mouth. They were fresh out of the deep fryer and I grimaced in pain as they seared my tongue.

Austin raised an eyebrow. "Hot?"

"Ungg," I responded as I chewed through the discomfort, trying to enjoy the salty, fatty flavors. Judging by the way my tongue was burning, though, I likely wouldn't be able to taste anything for a couple of days.

As soon as I swallowed, Austin slid the fries to the side and pushed his water glass towards me. I downed the whole thing and then, gracefully, fanned my mouth.

"Are you ready to talk about it?"

"Talk about what?" I asked innocently.

He stared at me. "Why you ran away. Why you've been so off these days."

Austin's words hung in the air and heat rose to my cheeks. My stomach jolted uncomfortably and I wished I hadn't eaten the fries. I looked around, panicked, feeling a little like a hamster trapped in a cage. Then, my eyes settled on the window.

"Fine day outside, isn't it?"

Nice segue. Seamless.

"No," Austin said flatly. "We're talking about this. You can't avoid it anymore, Els. What's been going on with you?"

"Nothing." I wished my voice hadn't squeaked at the end. "I'm fine. Totally fine."

His eyes narrowed. "You're forgetting that I know almost everything about you. I know your tell when you're lying."

"What is it?" I asked, somewhat desperately. I was scrambling, and we both knew it.

"You pick at your nails. Just like you're doing right now."

I glanced at my hands and I was, indeed, picking at my nails. *Bad fingers.*

Austin's eyes scanned my face but I did everything I could to avoid looking at him. I stared at the walls, the ceiling, the floors, the waiter as he bustled about. I couldn't meet Austin's ocean eyes, I couldn't. Because, if I did, I would spill the beans.

And, I couldn't do that. I couldn't tell him that I was having doubts. That I knew, deep down, that I didn't deserve him. He belonged with someone like Hannah McAdams, or a fashion model, or a movie star. He shouldn't be with someone whose life was in chaos. Who was unemployed. Whose mom insisted on setting her up with weird men named Stevo.

I knew it, sure as anything. And, someday, he'd figure it out, too. It was inevitable.

"I just got off the phone with JJ, and she needs my help with something back in Aston Falls," I said in a rush. I clasped my hands together so my fingers couldn't do anything untoward. Like hint at the fact that I was absolutely lying.

Austin's face crinkled. "What?"

"You'll be okay without me for the next couple of days?" I asked, my voice tinny. I stood and hovered next to the table. "Really sorry. I just don't want to let her down."

Austin bit his lip and disappointment flashed in his eyes. "I guess."

"She's having trouble at Sweets n' Sundaes again. You know how it is." I laughed but the sound was false. Before Austin could say anything, I leaned down and kissed him on the cheek. "Anyway, the next flight to Bozeman is in a couple hours, so I better head out. I'll see you back in Aston Falls?"

He didn't open his mouth, just nodded at me wordlessly. I saw the caution in his expression, his walls going up, and my heart splintered.

I left the restaurant and took the elevator up to my floor. As soon as I stepped out, tears spilled down my cheeks. I barely made it back to my room before I was full-on crying.

This time, Austin didn't follow me. And I didn't blame him one bit.

36

AUSTIN

The rest of the weekend in Seattle was a write-off.

When Ella left to catch her flight to Bozeman, I returned to the conference and did my best to stay focused during the rest of the presentations. I laughed, chatted and mingled like nothing was wrong. But, as soon as I returned to my hotel room, all I could think about was Ella. I sent her a text to make sure she landed okay, and she responded that she had.

After that, I decided to leave her alone. What else could I say?

I didn't sleep that night. Ella said that she went back to Aston Falls to help JJ with something, but I knew it was a lie. There was something else going on. She was pulling away, and I needed to know why.

Growing up, Ella and I didn't have any secrets. We told each other everything—or, nearly everything. I knew how upset she felt when she asked out her first crush and he turned her down. I knew that she'd failed her driving test four times before getting her license. I knew how mad she was at Grace during The Big Fight of Sophomore Year.

Ella was my best friend, and I didn't take any of these things for granted. But, it was because I knew everything about her that I knew something about *us* bothered her. I wished that she would talk to me about it.

It was part of the reason why, when I returned to Aston Falls, I didn't go home. I went to the Aston Glow Inn, dropped my bags in the lobby, and ran to the front desk.

"What's Ella's room number?"

Ms. Rodriguez startled from her bent position over the guestbook. Her eyes widened a touch as she took in my bedraggled appearance. My clothes were rumpled, and my hair was a mess from raking my fingers through it. "Hello, dear."

"Hi, Ms. R." My face relaxed a touch. "Sorry for being so abrupt. Can I get Ella's room number, please?"

"Last name?"

As if she had to ask. But, I knew that she took her business seriously, and I respected that. "Ella Williams."

Ms. Rodriguez perused her list of guests, tapping a pencil to her lips as she went. Finally, she pressed her pencil to paper and seemingly underlined Ella's name. "Yes, she's staying here tonight, but I'm afraid I cannot give you her room information. It's hotel policy. Privacy issues and all that."

"Please, Ms. R? I need to talk to her about something."

"I wish I could. Truly, I do." She shrugged and turned away, putting an end to the conversation.

But, I persisted. "There must be something you can do. Maybe we can call her room?"

"She's not here right now, I'm afraid. Can't you call her, or text her, or email, or whatever you kids do these days?"

I grimaced as a bitter taste filled my mouth. "She's stopped returning my calls."

"I'm sorry to hear that, dear, but I cannot help you." Ms. Rodriguez pressed her lips together, and she truly did seem to feel bad. Then, she smiled helpfully. "You're welcome to stay in the lobby as long as you like, though. You might run into her on her way back to her room."

"Alright." I nodded. "Thanks, Ms. R."

I returned to the lobby and sat on a plushy couch near the window, my eyes focused on the Inn's front door. The scent of lilacs and lavender floated through the air—a normally lovely smell that now made me want to sneeze. The soft sounds of the acoustic guitar playing through the lobby speakers were barely audible beneath Ms. Rodriguez's humming.

She bustled around the front desk before sneaking to the back office, and I wondered briefly why she was working today. Though Ms. Rodriguez had renovated and opened the Inn herself, she didn't do much work these days. Grace often said that Ms. Rodriguez and Mrs. Applebaum had made new careers for themselves as the town gossips.

I was looking at the paintings in the lobby—one too many bouquets of roses, in my opinion—when I heard the front door open. I shot to a stand, heart beating manically.

But, it wasn't Ella who entered the lobby. Instead, I spotted a familiar flop of dark hair and a silver chain blinking in the light.

"Christian?" I asked, surprised.

He looked up from his phone, and smiled a lopsided grin. "Austin. What's up, man?"

Christian strode towards me and held up his fist for a bump. I obliged. "I thought you'd be back in LA by now."

"I thought so, too." Christian shrugged. "Josh received the footage for the music video and wants us to reshoot a few things. The guy's relentless. I told him to come out here if he has so much feedback, but he flat-out refuses. Something about how LA needs him."

Christian rolled his eyes and I couldn't help but snort.

"We did a few more takes this morning, and I think we got some good stuff." Christian's room key clanged as he spun it around his fingers. "Josh is reviewing it all now, and I'm distracting myself by going for ice cream just as soon as I get changed. I want this thing over with, you know?"

"I get it." Then, I raised an eyebrow. "You've been going for ice cream an awful lot these days."

"I like the flavors." Christian smiled wide. "Plus, that's where my mystery chick works."

I tilted my head. The mystery chick worked at Sweets n' Sundaes? I only knew one girl our age who worked there.

"She just goes off every time I walk in," Christian continued. "It sounds bad, but it's pretty entertaining. I haven't had someone get that mad at me since my album took off." He laughed, shaking his head, and then seemed to register my crumpled appearance. "What are *you* doing here, Aus? You look like you slept in your clothes. Penthouse got a leak or something?"

When I was renovating the penthouse, Christian was often subject to my complaints about the plumbing. Eventually, I got everything working, but it took a few burst pipes, a couple of broken faucets, and one unfortunate flooding incident. "Not this time."

Christian crossed his arms. "So, what? Trouble in paradise?"

I grimaced. "Something like that. Things with Ella have been... weird."

"Weird how?"

"Like, she's been avoiding me. I know something's bothering her, but she refuses to talk to me about it for some reason. She's been off ever since we went to her parents' house. No, before that. Since the open mic night—"

"I still can't believe you went to one of those." Christian shook his head. "This girl must be something if she got you to an open mic night."

I chuckled dryly. "But, aren't you glad I texted you a photo while I was there?"

"Yeah, yeah." Christian laughed, waving his hands. "Because of you, we decided to stage the music video there, and it's going to blow the minds of everyone the entire world over etc etc."

I rolled my eyes before proceeding to give Christian a rundown on the past few days with Ella. How distant she felt during her parents' dinner, and her bizarre behavior at the conference. I knew Ella had a bit of a penchant for running away when things got tough, but I never thought she'd leave without talking to me about what was bothering her.

"She ended up coming back to Aston Falls early to help her friend." I bit the inside of my cheek. "I don't get it. I came straight here to talk to her."

Christian pressed his lips together. "And, you're sure that's the right call?"

"What do you mean?"

"I mean... This is all new for Ella, isn't it? She's probably never really considered you guys being together. She's never seen you as a romantic partner before."

I frowned. "Well, this is new for me, too."

"Sure. But you've loved this girl for what, like, ever?" Christian shrugged. "Ella is clearly into you too, but it's possible she just doesn't know how to handle the change in your relationship. Maybe the thing to do is to give her space. Give her time to figure out what she wants."

Christian's words sank in and my heart beat echoed dully in my ears. He was right. Just not in the way he meant.

I hadn't considered the guys Ella had dated in the past—she'd often decided, fairly quickly, that they weren't a good fit. Ella was particular about the people she spent time with, rightfully so, and she'd broken up with guys for far less than having to do long distance. Which we would likely have to do when Ella got the job in New York.

Was it possible that she thought our relationship wasn't worth pursuing?

My stomach churned as I realized that maybe I'd misinterpreted everything. Misinterpreted Ella's distance and her pulling away. Maybe, the problem was simply that, after a couple of weeks together, she decided she didn't want to be with me.

"Anyway, chin up, man," Christian said brightly. "Think about it. Ella will come around, I know she will. Just give her time."

Christian issued a soft punch to my upper arm, but I barely felt it. A rush of realization was hitting me square in the chest, and my mind raced as I considered Ella's behavior with this new lens—her avoiding me, her distraction, her leaving me in Seattle. Was it all her way of showing that she didn't want to be with me? That she didn't want to do long distance?

Was Ella trying to tell me that she wanted to be friends and nothing more?

37

ELLA

I woke up late on Monday morning and blinked blearily at the sun outside the curtains. My head felt heavy and my eyes were groggy. It was like I'd barely slept, though I'd been feeling that way the past couple of nights. Ever since the conference... where I'd left Austin. Alone.

As soon as I set foot in the airport in Seattle, I wondered whether I'd done the right thing. I felt terrible for leaving him—who does that? And to their best friend?—but, the very thought of going back to the hotel made me physically freeze. Like, I was unable to move in the Departures line and the people behind me started to complain and tap on my shoulder to shoo me forward.

I was a coward. I should've stayed and owned up to how I felt. That, or swallowed my feelings entirely so I could finish the conference with him.

But, I saw how Austin's face lit up when he spoke to Hannah. I saw how comfortable and happy he seemed surrounded by his fellow doctors, the way everyone admired him or, in the case of Willoughby, was mildly intimidated by him. Dr. Bell was well-known in the medical community, and it blew my mind that the same guy I'd shared almost all my secrets with had this whole other side to him. I knew he was successful, but I never could've guessed just how successful.

Seeing him in that environment, surrounded by people who clearly respected him, was eye opening. I began to wonder what might've happened if Austin had stayed in LA, or gone to Switzerland or Australia or wherever else. Would he have been an even bigger deal? Could he have contributed even more to the medical community? When he came back to Aston Falls, was he held back?

The thought made me queasy. It didn't help to see the way those bright, poised women doctors looked at him—like he was a god sent to earth. And gods didn't belong with mere mortals like myself.

I knew he would want to talk whenever he got back from Seattle, so I went to the park to wait for him. Unfortunately, I'd unwittingly left my phone in my room, but I assumed he'd come by on a run. I was going to speak with him then, try to explain myself.

He never showed. It wasn't until I got back to my room and saw his missed calls and texts that I realized he'd waited for me at the Inn.

Maybe it was for the best that we had this time apart anyway. I needed to figure out what I would say to him. Because I knew one thing for sure—Austin Bell was the best thing that had ever happened to me, but he deserved to be with someone who would make him happy. And I didn't know if that person was me.

For now, all I could hope was that we could salvage our friendship.

My skin was prickly and cold as I slid into my fuzzy gray

sweats and matching hoodie. The sweat suit had once belonged to Austin. Back when things were simpler between us.

I couldn't spend the day moping about my room at the Aston Glow, or I'd drive myself crazy. I debated going to Morning Bell to see Grace, but Grace had a nose like a bloodhound when it came to sniffing out problems, and she would know immediately that something was wrong.

I was hit with another pang of guilt. Grace was one of my oldest friends, but she never did find out that Austin and I were dating. I felt awful for keeping this from her for weeks on end. I couldn't exactly barge into Morning Bell and say "guess what, I've been dating your twin brother for real, and now I'm heartbroken."

Which left Sweets n' Sundaes. It was the right thing to do given how abruptly I'd hung up on JJ the other day. She was in the middle of telling me something important, and I hadn't even thought to text or call her back.

I was racking up an awful lot of "bad friend" points these days.

I breathed deeply as I approached the door of Sweets n' Sundaes, hoping she'd forgive me. I pulled down the hood of my hoodie before wandering inside.

A couple of tables were occupied by the window, but I'd missed the lunch rush. JJ's back was to me as she wiped down a table, humming to herself. I approached her quietly.

"Need a hand?" I asked.

JJ yelped and whirled around, cloth dangling like a weapon.

"You!"

To my utter surprise, instead of whacking me with the cloth—which would've been warranted—JJ wrapped her arms around me. She squeezed tight.

"JJ," I gasped. "Can't. Breathe."

She dropped her arms and stepped back. "Els, where've you been? You went dark on me."

"I know, I'm sorry," I said, looking at the ground dejectedly.

I waited for the reprimand to end all reprimands—JJ was the kind of person who worried for her friends and cared for them almost like a mother would. I once went hiking in the Appalachians and, right before my trip, JJ emailed me a full trail guide, tips on what to do in case of any possible dangers, and an emergency preparedness checklist.

The fact that I hadn't answered her texts and calls for a couple of days surely had her worried. But, something in my expression must've tipped her off because, instead of getting angry, JJ placed a hand on my arm.

"Shall I get you the usual?" she asked.

I met her gaze and smiled flimsily. "Sure."

JJ bustled behind the ice cream display and I took a seat at the counter. She scooped a nice dollop—two dollops—of butter pecan ice cream into a cup, and topped the thing with an Oreo cookie. She set it down in front of me with a flourish, then she leaned over the counter, chin resting in her palms. "You look bad, Els."

"Thanks." I rolled my eyes. "Just what I needed to hear today."

"So, what's going on? Last I heard, a certain *someone* had found you."

I grabbed the Oreo and began breaking it into small chunks. "Well, that someone did end up finding me."

"And?"

"And nothing," I sighed. "Not anymore."

JJ frowned. "Hang on. We're talking about the same someone, right? Austin?"

"Yeah," I said. My stomach squeezed nauseatingly as I spoke. "I think we're about to break up."

JJ's eyebrows shot up. "What are you talking about? Why?"

"We're not going to work, JJ. We both wanted it, I know we did. But, we have to break up."

"Is this coming from you or him?"

I sighed shakily and screwed up my mouth. I was doing this *for* him—to set him free and let him live the life he deserved. "Both. Technically."

JJ's eyes scoured my face and I looked away, shoving the rest of the cookie into my mouth and swirling my ice cream around the cup.

"Are you sure this is what you want?" JJ asked.

My eyes stung, but I couldn't cry. Not here.

"I just... don't want to lose my best friend," I whispered.

"Have you talked to him? Maybe you guys can work through this."

I pressed my lips together and met JJ's gaze ruefully. "Is that what you and Ted do when you have issues?"

It was JJ's turn to look away. "Do as I say, not as I do."

My heart ached and I pushed my ice cream away.

Behind me, I heard the soft tinkling of a bell as someone entered the shop. Before my eyes, JJ's expression changed. It was like something out of a movie—her smile dropped off and her eyebrows pinched together. There was a fire in her eyes that I had never, ever seen before.

"Oh. It's you," she practically growled. "What are you doing here, scruffer?"

I was taken aback by JJ's tone, the contempt in it. This

was the guy who riled JJ up, the one who had insulted her scooping technique. The one JJ had recently identified.

I cast a glance over my shoulder to see the unfortunate victim of JJ's wrath.

I almost fell off my stool.

Because the person JJ was being so rude to was none other than Christian freaking West.

The musician stepped forward, his eyes riveted on JJ. He was wearing a faded navy tee and dark jeans, and for the first time, I noticed the dark studs in his ears. His hair was swept to the side, and he wore a lopsided smile that made him look both devilish and innocent as a lamb.

"It's okay, Jessica Jade," he shot back. "You can tell me you missed me."

No. He didn't.

My jaw dropped as I stared between the two. Christian didn't just go there with JJ's full name.

Her nostrils flared and her mouth pinched. She ground her teeth. "Nobody will be missing you when you've eaten so much cookie dough ice cream that you can barely fit through the door."

Christian had reached the counter at this point, and he leaned forward on his elbows next to me. JJ took a huge step away, glaring at him unashamedly. Meanwhile, I scooted back a couple paces. Clearly, the guy could handle himself around JJ's fiery side, and I didn't want to end up in the crossfire.

"Interesting that you've noticed my physique," he retorted smoothly. "Anything you like?"

Oh, the guy was a *flirt.*

JJ's cheeks went beet red and her brows drew together even more. "What can I get you so you'll leave?"

Christian stood straight and shrugged. "I'm headed out

of town soon and want to grab something for a friend. Have any of those little ice cream keychains?"

JJ sighed loudly, the sound full of frustration. "Maybe in the back."

She disappeared around the corner and Christian chuckled. Then, he noticed me staring at him, mouth wide open and arms slack by my sides. At once, his playful expression became kind and jovial and he held out his hand.

"Hey. Ella, right?"

My throat was dry. Christian West—award-winning musician, heartbreaking lyricist, man who's traveled the world on his concert tours—was extending his hand to me.

"That's right," I croaked as I robotically grasped his hand.

"Austin's told me a lot about you." Christian's eyes scanned my face, but it wasn't necessarily an uncomfortable feeling. He just seemed concerned. "He said you guys are in a bit of a rough patch."

I slammed my mouth shut, mortified. This Christian West guy sure got straight to the point; no beating around the bush here.

He leaned forward. "Listen, I know it isn't my place, and I know we don't know each other. But, I hope you and Austin can work things out. You two are great together."

"Agreed," JJ said as she whipped back around the corner, her hands full of dangling silver chains. She rolled her eyes as she added, "the one thing we agree on."

Christian chuckled and turned towards JJ as she handed him the keychains.

"These are all nice, Jessica. Have any favorites?"

"Even if I did, why would I tell you?"

"We could be keychain buds. That way, whenever I'm in LA, you'll think of me when you see yours."

"Like I'd ever think of you as anything but an annoying gnat who insists on visiting my workplace on the daily."

They continued to bicker while Christian picked through the selection, but I tuned them out. It wasn't often you had a world-famous country music star giving you relationship advice. Especially when, sadly, that advice didn't seem to apply.

I knew what I had to do now—I had to talk to Austin. It would break my heart, shatter it into a million pieces, but I had to do what was right for him. It was the only way I could hope to save our friendship.

38

AUSTIN

"*D*r. Bell, I'm done for the day." The words were followed by the abrupt smack of bubblegum.

I looked up and Becca was hovering in the doorway, wearing an oversized jean jacket and huge glasses. Despite her near-constant gum chewing and addiction to her cellphone, she'd proven herself to be a hard worker. She'd upgraded the clinic's phone system and often stayed late to help file paperwork.

Which was the case today. According to my Fitbit, her shift had ended thirty minutes ago.

"Of course, yes." I smiled. "Thanks, Becca. I appreciate your help today."

"No probs, Dr. Bell." Another smack of gum. "I'll see you tomorrow."

She shot me a peace sign before disappearing out the door and I chuckled to myself. The girl seemed so mature and put together, but I remembered myself at that age. I had no idea what I was doing about 95% of the time.

There were still moments when I didn't have a clue what I was doing. I was just much, much better at hiding it.

I had to admit, though, that it was fun to break down those walls sometimes and let loose. Like Ella always insisted I should.

A pang of discomfort tore through my chest at the thought of her. I ignored the feeling and popped my head out the door of my exam room just as Dr. Rob was locking up. "I'm headed out as well. Long day, wasn't it?"

"Longer than most."

"I'm glad to hear that construction's starting on the new center. And I can't thank you enough for squeezing in my twelve o'clock." He ran his fingers over his salt and pepper mustache. "Sherri was having a bit of a curtain crisis."

Dr. Rob and his wife, Sherri, were renovating their townhouse and, from what I'd heard, the process had been a nightmare. "No problem. I enjoyed the distraction today."

"Well, the patients love you. Mr. Devi asked how you were doing, and whether you were keeping up with the football pre-season. I told him you were so involved, you were practically running the thing by now."

I laughed along with Dr. Rob. He'd always had a great sense of humor, even during the busiest of days when we were dealing with loads of patients, and work for the medical center. I enjoyed chatting with him on the rare evenings we finished at the same time.

"Speaking of which, Sherri would love to have you over for dinner when the renovations are done."

"I'd love that." I nodded. "Sherri's cooking is out of this world."

"Don't I know it. The way to a man's heart really is through his stomach." Dr. Rob laughed and patted his rather sizeable belly. "Though, of course, I married her for several other reasons."

I leaned back on the doorframe. "Like what?"

"Well." A smile tugged at Dr. Rob's lips. "She makes me laugh constantly, and she makes any situation, no matter how dull, fun and exciting. She's the opposite of me, but I love it because I'm always trying new things when I'm with her. She's my best friend, and there's nothing so strong as a bond based on friendship. Know what I mean?"

I thought of Ella again, and my stomach twisted. "I do."

Dr. Rob patted my shoulder. "My boy, my advice is and will always be to marry your best friend. They're the only ones who'll put up with your complaining, and your bad days, and your morning breath." He rolled his eyes. "Trust me."

I forced a laugh but it felt like my chest was being squeezed.

With a wave, Dr. Rob said his goodbyes and I returned to my exam room to finish my paperwork. I closed up the clinic for the evening, moving slowly. By the time I entered my penthouse, dropped my bags, and turned on the light, it was way past dinnertime.

I undid my tie as I climbed the steel stairs, but as I looked around my home, I felt hollow. The place was quiet, and it might as well have been empty. Ever since Ella moved out, I'd realized just how lonely this place was. I missed her presence, her laugh, her smile. Even her grumpiness in the morning.

I missed her more than usual seeing as we'd barely spoken in almost a week. It was the longest we'd ever gone without talking. I didn't even know whether she'd heard back from that job in New York.

Every day, I wanted to reach out to her and see how she was doing, but I'd decided to take Christian's advice. If Ella wanted space and time, I'd give that to her.

Over the past few days, I'd been wondering exactly

where things had gone off the rails with us. Did she feel pressured or pushed into going to Seattle with me? I would never intend to do such a thing, but if Ella was pulling away to create distance, I felt foolish for trying to bridge that gap.

I turned on the radio to keep me company as I got changed. The station was playing Christian's newest single —"I'll Be Waiting for You." The beautiful guitar melody followed me to the bedroom, where I changed into black slacks and a white t-shirt, and then back out to the kitchen.

I was taking peppers, tomatoes, and lettuce out of the fridge when I heard something. A soft knock barely audible over the tail end of Christian's song.

Knock knock.

There it was again.

I wiped my hands on a dishcloth and went to the front door. Was it Christian? Nicholas? My bet was on Nicholas— I hadn't spoken to the guy in weeks. I'd been more or less avoiding him given the whole "dating Ella" situation. But, now that things between us were so up in the air, I really missed speaking to him. He was one of my best friends, after all.

I swung the door open, but as soon as I saw the person waiting on the doorstep, my smile disappeared.

"Ella?"

39

ELLA

*A*ustin's face dropped and my heart wrenched painfully. I was shivering, but I didn't know why—it wasn't a particularly chilly night, but the surface of my skin was freezing cold. I clenched my jaw to keep it from clicking.

"Hey Austin," I said quietly, managing a smile. "Can I come in?"

Say no. Please say no.

But Austin, being the kind and wonderful guy he is, stepped aside and gestured for me to come through. I nodded and walked stiffly past him. Everything about this moment felt awkward and jilted. Like we were two actors in a play and we'd both forgotten our lines.

Austin led me up to the living room, and I kept my focus on the stairs. One, because I didn't want to trip and fall. And two, because my stomach was swirling with dread at the thought of why I was here.

The worst part was that, judging by his demeanor and somber expression, Austin had an inkling as to why I was here, too.

He walked to the kitchen to turn off the radio and then crossed his arms. An empty silence filled the room and I found myself bustling towards the couch, just to fill the quiet.

"Can I get you a glass of water?" he asked, and his tone had the same professional lilt that he used when with his patients.

"I'm fine, thanks." I perched on the edge of the couch. My heart was beating like a jackhammer.

"I was just about to make dinner. Want any?"

"Oh, uh, no thanks," I stuttered. "I won't be here long."

Austin flopped onto the other side of the couch and crossed one ankle over his knee. He stared at me—just blatantly, openly stared at me—and I had to look away. He was waiting for me to say something, but where would I even start?

How could I tell my best friend—the man I felt so strongly for—that I didn't want to be with him? Especially when it was a huge lie. All I'd ever wanted was to be with him, grow old with him.

My throat was dry and cracked and I wished I'd taken him up on that water. I had an almost irresistible urge to flee back down the staircase.

Austin noticed me struggling and spoke first. "So, what's up? Are you going to tell me why you keep avoiding me and running away?"

A terrible heat raged through my veins and I dropped my head. "I'm so sorry, Aus. I feel awful for leaving you in Seattle. I should never have done it. I just felt... overwhelmed."

"Overwhelmed? With what?"

My breath was coming in short, ragged bursts and my blood was pounding in my ears, but I knew what I had to do.

It was the only thing I could do to ensure Austin's happiness. A guy like Austin didn't belong with a girl like me. As long as I kept that at the forefront of my mind, my next words would be much, much easier to say.

My fingers were clasped in my lap, knuckles white, when I finally opened my mouth. "We're not a good match."

Austin barely flinched. "What?"

"We're not good together. We don't belong together."

Every word broke my heart, every word felt deeply, horribly wrong. But, I had to do this.

Austin shook his head. "Are you hearing yourself right now? We both know that's a lie. Why are you doing this?"

The confidence in his tone, his certainty in our belonging together, broke my heart all the more. Why was he holding on so tight? I had to let him go.

"I'm not doing anything. It's just the truth. We're better off as friends and nothing more."

"I disagree."

"Aus, this isn't debatable." My voice was almost desperate. I so wanted to give in to what he was saying, but I had to see this through. "We shouldn't do this. There's someone better out there for you—for us."

Austin was shaking his head vehemently, but as soon as I said the word "us," he stopped. His gaze met mine and a dark, unreadable shadow flitted across his features. His mouth pressed into a thin line.

"For us," he repeated quietly. "There's someone better out there for... us."

I nodded slowly, watching his expression close up. The room fell into silence, an uncomfortable, dreadful silence, and the air was so heavy, I couldn't breathe. Austin's eyes bore into mine until I had to look away.

Tears gathered behind my eyelids and I felt sick, but I

didn't know what else to say. I was just trying to do the right thing for once.

Austin rose to a stand. "I completely understand where you're coming from, Ella."

His use of my name sent my head spinning and I scrambled to a stand as well. Austin extended his hand coolly. He was looking for a handshake, like we'd just made an agreement, or settled on a deal.

I shook his hand limply, trying to ignore how achingly wonderful his firm palm felt pressed against mine. In some dark corner of my mind, I wondered whether this was the last time Austin and I would hold hands like this. The thought made me unbearably sad.

"Friends?" I whispered, the word barely audible.

Austin grit his teeth. "Friends."

I took a shaky breath and left the penthouse. Austin didn't walk me out, didn't follow me to the top of the stairs. And I didn't look back. I knew that my resolve was moments away from crumbling to pieces.

I managed to make it a few steps down the street before I collapsed to the ground in a heap, tears spilling down my cheeks.

40

ELLA

So. This is what rock bottom feels like.

I stared at the ceiling of my room at the Inn, my eyes following each individual wood beam. The tears had dried on my cheeks in criss-cross patterns, and my stomach grumbled with hunger. When was the last time I ate?

My hands were clasped over my midsection and the fuzzy fabric of my gray sweat suit was soft under my fingers. I'd turned on the room's speakers and was playing "Heartbreak Hotel" on repeat—which felt absurdly accurate.

Okay, I had to admit that the whole scene was rather dramatic. JJ or Grace would take one look at me and kick my butt into gear.

If only they knew what had happened.

Tears welled up in my eyes again and I brushed them away. In the span of a week, I'd managed to lose out on my dream job, break up with the man of my dreams, and, in doing so, it appeared that I may have lost my best friend, too.

Every time I thought about leaving Austin's apartment

three days ago, I felt physically queasy. I couldn't move past the thought that irreparable damage had been done to our friendship. By trying to do right by him, did I actually lose him forever?

Austin and I had never said our "I love you's" and we hadn't even truly become girlfriend and boyfriend. And yet, Austin was by far the worst breakup I'd ever had. I'd never felt anything like it. I was heartbroken, truly heartbroken.

Knowing that I did the right thing offered little consolation.

Since we'd broken up, I'd barely left the Inn. I ordered in food, watched hours' worth of rom coms, and did my best to ignore my phone. It was one of the hardest things I'd ever done. All I wanted was to text Austin, and, every time I heard the *ding* of a text message, I literally leapt across the room. Unfortunately, it was usually just my mom, JJ or Grace. Never Austin.

I hadn't shared the details of our split with anyone. I just couldn't face that we were... what? Friends? Acquaintances? Nothing?

I squeezed my eyes shut against the pain just as my phone *ding*-ed. Once again, I flew towards my desk, taking down a couple of pillows, a lamp, and my desk chair in the process. I clicked open the message on my phone. But, it was just from my Janice, my roommate in New York.

Hey, girl! She wrote. *Just checking in. Holly is loving your room here and is super thankful that you let her extend her stay again. I think she'd move here if she could haha. Any idea when you're coming back?*

I pressed my lips together and put my phone down. I'd answer Janice later. Right now, I didn't have anything to say.

I'd been keeping an eye out for cheap flights back to New York for the past day or two. There wasn't any point in staying here now, and giving Austin space might be the best thing for our friendship.

Okay, I could call it like it is. Maybe a part of me was running away.

I'd also started up the dreadful job search again, but my heart wasn't really in it. None of the hiring magazines or newspapers offered anything like *The Weekly Best*. I just couldn't bring myself to apply for yet another dead-end job that would undoubtedly lead to a layoff before I could gain any real experience. I was tired of getting lost in the pile of resumes, tired of being just another needle in the haystack.

Because Austin had taught me something valuable—I knew what I wanted now. I didn't want to be just a data-gathering reporter, I wanted to own the stories I wrote. I wanted to feel proud of what I'd contributed. And the only opportunity I'd had slipped right out of my fingers.

I had to do something, however. Without a job, I wouldn't be able to pay rent, and I'd not only be unemployed, but homeless. Even though the prospect of going back to the city gave me no joy, it was the next logical step. I had to go.

There was nothing left for me in Aston Falls. Not anymore.

41

AUSTIN

*M*y feet pounded the pavement and I propelled myself forward, carried by the music blaring through my headphones. My muscles ached and burned but I pushed through the pain.

I'd been running a lot these days, and working a lot. Both at the clinic and for the medical center. Anything to keep me from texting Ella, anything to stop me from thinking about her.

I'd been through my fair share of breakups, but never anything like this. A part of me had always assumed that, if Ella and I could make it work, she was *it*. But, we'd been broken up for days now, and I still had no idea where to go from here.

Should I text her? Give her space and wait for her to text? What was the protocol? The uncertainty wasn't a feeling I was used to or particularly enjoyed. I didn't even know if Ella was still in Aston Falls or whether she was back in New York.

The thought made me push harder, run faster.

I rounded the corner towards the park and there was a

change in the song playing through my headphones. Over the pounding drum of my heartbeat and the whack of my feet on pavement, I thought I heard a voice. A muffled voice.

I slowed to a jog and the voice called again. "Austin!"

I ripped out my headphones and looked around. Across the park, Nicholas was jogging towards me, followed closely by a pack of young kids.

I waved as he approached and he gestured for the kids to return to the field, assuring them he'd be right back. The kids scattered across the park and started up another game of flag football.

"Aus, where've you been?" Nicholas held up a fist and I bumped it. "It's been weeks since we spoke."

"Sorry, man. Work's been super busy."

"Right, how was the conference in Seattle?"

I stopped walking as my chest squeezed painfully. The conference. Did Ella know, even then, that she wanted to break up? I took a breath and tried to recover. "Good."

Nicholas's smile disappeared. "Things going okay?"

"Just fine. Everything's fine and dandy."

There's an expression I never thought I'd say.

Nicholas crossed his arms and shot me a skeptical look. "You know who you're talking to, right? You and Ace both have the same little crinkle in your eyebrow when something's wrong."

"Nothing's wrong. I'm just stressed with work." I forced a bright smile.

Nicholas cocked an eyebrow. "You're never stressed with work. You're legendarily unflappable."

"Unflappable." I laughed. "That's a new term for you."

"Don't change the subject. What's going on?"

I shifted from foot to foot. Grabbed the bottom of my jersey and wiped my face. I weighed the pros and cons of telling Nicholas everything. Logically, I knew that I shouldn't tell him the full story with Ella in case it got back to Grace. But, Nicholas knew how I felt about relationships better than anyone. It seemed right that I would share this piece of my life with him.

But, that didn't mean I had to divulge the whole truth.

"Alright," I said slowly. "I was seeing someone. Someone I was really excited about. Someone I... loved."

Nicholas's mouth split into a wide smile. "Aus, that's great. That's honestly so—"

"But, things got messed up." I shook my head. "I think we're done forever."

He paused for a moment, frowning. "I thought you didn't 'do forever' anyway."

I looked at the river. The late summer sunshine bounced off the water, making it sparkle. "For her, I would."

"Forever isn't scary when you're going into it with the right person." Nicholas nodded. "And, in all honesty, what else matters? Love is funny like that. Simple, but complicated."

"You're telling me. We were complicated from the start."

"How so?"

"Because we were best friends first."

The words escaped me without thought, and my eyes went wide. I tore my gaze away from the river. I'd said way, way too much.

Predictably, Nicholas's brow furrowed in confusion. "You're talking about Ella."

I pinched the bridge of my nose, cursing myself. *I shouldn't have said that.*

But, as I looked at Nicholas, his gaze open and curious, I realized it was too late anyway. Nicholas wasn't dumb and I was pretty clearly torn up. Besides, I could've used his advice. The guy was happily married, after all.

I nodded once and Nicholas's frown deepened. "Weren't you guys just faking it?"

"It started that way," I said quietly. "Then, we broke up."

"Isn't that supposed to happen with fake relationships? I thought you guys talked about that."

"This was different, man." I ran my fingers through my hair. "This was... real. It became real. At least, it was for me. And our breakup was real, too."

I waited for the shoe to drop, for Nicholas to look shocked or surprised or have *some* reaction to this piece of news. I'd more or less just confirmed his high school suspicions. Confirmed that I'd been secretly dating and falling for the girl I'd always so steadfastly insisted was "just a friend." I expected him to, at the very least, look sympathetic.

Instead, he rolled his eyes. "Of course it was real. You and Ella are meant to be."

"You don't get it. Ella doesn't want to be with me."

"She told you that?"

I opened my mouth to say yes, to insist that I knew exactly what Ella was thinking. But, I had to stop myself. Because I didn't actually know, and Ella had never said those exact words.

"It was the gist of what she said." I shifted on my feet. "She thinks that there's someone better out there for us both. And, we all know what that means."

Nicholas shot me another look—one that looked suspiciously like his "you're being an idiot" look.

"You and Ella have to talk sometime," he said reasonably. "It's the only way to move forward. Whether you become friends again, something less, or something more."

I considered Nicholas's words. He wasn't wrong, of course. Ella and I would talk eventually because, as much as this breakup hurt, I wanted her in my life. Assuming she wanted that, too. She'd been my best friend for as long as I could remember and it broke my heart that I couldn't talk to her now, when I most wanted to.

But, things were different between us, there'd been a shift in our relationship. I'd never felt so far away from her.

I didn't know what Ella and I were to each other anymore.

42

ELLA

"*E*lla Bella, we haven't seen you in days! Your dad, Ben, Carly and I have been so busy. But, we miss you. Please come for dinner tonight, and bring Austin. I'm making your favorite—lasagna!"

Mom's voicemail message went on for another couple of minutes about the glories of lasagna, the latest gossip with my cousin Tara, and a full news update on Carly and Ben's house hunting.

My stomach twisted as I clicked out of her voicemail. It had been awhile since I'd seen or properly talked to my family. Mom still believed that Austin and I were together, and as much as I didn't want to break the news to her, I had to.

Especially seeing as I booked my flight to New York—I'd be leaving two days from now.

The thought of leaving Aston Falls, leaving Austin with our relationship in tatters, made my heart ache even more. It was for the best, though. Right?

I crafted a quick text back to my mom letting her know I'd be there, alone, and then dropped my phone on my bed.

I'd taken my suitcases out this morning to start packing for my return to the city. I hadn't packed much yet, except for my dresses and skirts.

I turned up the volume on "Heartbreak Hotel"—still playing on repeat—and hummed along as I threw things into my suitcase.

Knock knock knock.

The noise made me jump, and I almost dropped the books I was carrying. I placed them on the bed, wondering who was at the door. Housekeeping? Ms. Rodriguez?

I grimaced at my appearance—crumpled short shorts and a slightly stained hoodie. It wasn't my best look. I ran to my closet to take out a pair of jeans.

"Just a minute!" I shouted.

In response, there was a harsher, more insistent *knock knock!!*

They clearly weren't going to wait, so I patted down my hoodie, tucked a few stray hairs back into my messy bun, and approached the door.

With a smile, I swung it open.

"Finally!" Grace exclaimed as she swept past me and into my room. "I thought my knuckles might start bleeding from all the knocking."

I frowned. "How long were you out there?"

Grace sat on the lone square of bedspread that was free of clothing items and take-out containers. She poked an open pizza box with just the crusts left. "Long enough to hear you wail about the one who got away."

I froze. I hadn't even realized I'd started singing.

Grace pointed at my suitcases. "You're leaving? We barely hung out."

Her voice was sad and I gave her a hug. As I wrapped my arms around her, I realized just how much I'd missed seeing

Grace these last few weeks. She was one of my oldest and best friends, and I valued our friendship so much. Things had just gotten so complicated.

"I'll be back soon," I murmured into Grace's hair. "You won't even realize I'm gone."

"It's not me I'm worried about." Grace sighed dramatically. "It's Austin. What's he going to do without you?"

Heat rose to my cheeks and I had to look away. That was strangely pointed. Did she know something? I tried to keep my voice as level as possible. "What do you mean?"

Her face was carefully composed, giving nothing away. "I mean that you're his best friend. Right?"

Her green eyes bore into mine, her lips pressed together, and suddenly, it was clear as day.

Grace knew about Austin and me.

I averted my gaze towards the window and bit my pinky nail, heart racing. I felt sick with guilt. Grace should've heard about this from me, I felt awful for keeping this huge secret from her. All I could hope was that Austin had been the one to tell her.

"Gracie, I'm so sorry," I croaked, my throat dry. "I don't know what to say. Things just got away from me and I didn't know what to do and—"

"Shh," Grace said, and to my surprise, she wrapped her arms around me.

Her kindness overwhelmed me and, all at once, tears spilled down my cheeks. I'd been such a bad friend, I didn't deserve to have someone like Grace in my life. Or Austin. I tried to do the right thing, but instead, it felt like I'd made an even bigger, more painful mess.

"I'm so sorry," I whispered again, shaking my head.

"It's okay, Els."

"I should've talked to you about it."

Grace pulled away to take a tissue from the box on the desk. She wiped my eyes. "Ah, I heard from a good source anyway. Nicholas saw Austin yesterday, and Aus mentioned what happened between the two of you. He swore Nicholas to secrecy, but you know that boy can't keep a secret from me."

"Are you mad?" I asked quietly.

"Of course not. I mean, ideally you and Austin would've told me, but I can't be mad about this. Not if you two are happy and want to be together. I can't stand in the way of true love." She shot me a goofy smile, but then, just as quickly, her face turned stony. "Unless I should be mad? Did Aus hurt you? Tell me what he did and I'll go after him."

Despite the heaviness of the moment, I chuckled. "No, no. Austin was a perfect gentleman. The perfect boyfriend."

Grace relaxed, and she grabbed another tissue for me. "So, what's the problem?"

"It's just..." I stared at the tissue, searching for words. "Everything's fallen apart, Gracie. I didn't get that job with *The Weekly Best*, I'm not even sure I can afford my rent in New York, and now, I might've lost Austin." I picked off the corners of the tissue so they fell to the ground like snow. "I'm going back to the city in two days, but to what?"

"Ella." Grace's voice was low, her eyebrows raised. "You know what to do."

"Not a clue." I sniffed.

Grace sat in silence for a moment. Then, without warning, she shot to a stand. "You *do* have a clue. And it's about time you get your act together. No more of this whole 'feeling sorry for yourself' thing. I know you've been avoiding me and avoiding JJ, which likely means you're avoiding everything else. You have to get back on your feet."

I frowned. "How?"

"You tell me," she said passionately. "When everything seemed to be going wrong at Morning Bell, you encouraged me to put myself forward and try to run the place. I took a risk, and it was scary and hard, but it paid off. You need to take your own advice. You're braver than you give yourself credit for, Els. You need to face this."

I bit my lip. Bravery wasn't one of my stronger qualities, I tended to run away instead. I'd never been able to face challenges like Austin could.

I remembered his spontaneous speech at Carly's rehearsal dinner, and when he presented at the open mic night. I wished I could be like that—so self-assured and confident and brazen. I admired those qualities so much in him. Could I really do the same?

Maybe it was worth a try.

"I guess," I started. "I guess I could go to their offices and ask for an in-person interview. The hiring manager did say that it was harder to hire over the phone."

"Exactly. See? You know what to do. And, you know what you need to do with Austin, too."

"Gracie, it isn't that simple. Your brother and I are just too different."

"What are you talking about? You two are basically the same person."

"No, we're really not. He's handsome, and successful, and wonderful. And, I'm just me. Constantly unemployed, spilling everything everywhere... I'm a mess."

At this, Grace's eyes filled with a rage I'd never seen before. She took my hand. "Ella Williams. Don't *ever* speak about my best friend like that. You are not a mess."

I gestured towards the empty pizza box, the half-full suitcases. "What do you call this?"

Grace bit the inside of her cheek for a moment. Then,

she smiled. "*This* is the journey. No one has everything figured out. Not even my stinky twin brother. You're in good company."

"I'm not sure."

"Trust me, Els. I've seen the way the guy looks at you, the way he smiles when you enter the room. I was suspicious the moment you said your relationship was fake. When it comes to Austin, all he wants is you. 'Mess' and all."

She even had the decency to put air quotes around the word. What she said was unbelievably kind, and I wished more than anything that she was right.

"Don't believe me?" Grace asked, seemingly reading my mind. "Talk to him. I'm sure he'd say the same."

I bit my lip as I considered talking to Austin, being honest with him. I considered not running away to New York, but standing up and facing my fears head on. Just like he would.

It was by far the hardest, most terrifying option. Which meant that it was probably the thing I needed to do.

When I broke up with Austin, I thought I was doing the right thing. But, maybe, I was just running away again. It was time I laid my cards on the table, told him how crazy I was about him, told him about my fears and anxieties. I'd face up to the challenge, just like he would do, and I'd let the chips fall where they may.

Filled with a newfound—and very tentative—motivation, I glanced around my room. My eyes landed on my daily journal. "I think I have an idea."

43

AUSTIN

I rubbed my eyes and squinted at the papers in front of me. I was just coming off of a 16 hour shift—a patient had called me early this morning due to heart palpitations that, it turned out, were caused by caffeine. Thankfully, the afternoon had been relatively quiet.

I was no stranger to lengthy shifts, but they usually weren't coming off the back of a series of terrible sleeps. Ten days' worth, actually.

Every time I shut my eyes, all I could see was Ella. I missed her so terribly, it felt like I'd lost a limb, some part of myself that I could never retrieve. I thought about her constantly, wondering if she was thinking about me, too.

Life was definitely a lot more monotonous without her. I woke up early in the morning, went to work, walked by the medical center's construction site on my way home, then went for a run. I'd make dinner, and sit on the couch with a bucket of figs—a poor excuse for junk food, Ella was right about that—and watched TV.

Though, by "watching TV," I really meant that I was watching home videos.

I couldn't tell you what exactly had triggered me to go by Dad's house a few days ago and pick up a stack of them. But, as soon as I clicked "Play" and saw Mom's face on the screen, I understood. It was comforting to see her face again—see the way she ran across the grass with a younger Grace and me, the way she comforted us when one of us fell down. The way she and Dad were just so happy together.

Of course, Ella featured front and center in a lot of these videos, which probably didn't help with the whole sleep issue. As much as it pained me to think about how things had gone between us, I loved to see her contagious smile, hear her twinkling laugh. Even in her teenage years when she was awkward and gawky, she was so wonderfully *her*.

When I eventually went to sleep, my dreams were often fitful and restless. I'd dream of Ella, and I'd imagine for a moment that everything was fine. But then, there was the crushing realization—that she was unreachable.

There was a light knock and I looked up to see Becca standing in the doorway of my exam room. She'd recently dyed her hair pink, and she was wearing funky coke-bottle glasses. I would never understand the girl's style, but I had to admit she was daring.

"Dr. Bell, there's a final patient here to see you."

I took a heavy breath and refrained from yawning. Becca was practically blurring around the edges. "Who is it?"

She pursed her lips. "You'll never guess."

At this, my heart leapt. Could it be Ella?

"Send her in," I said, trying to remain calm.

Becca nodded once and disappeared around the corner. I raked my fingers through my hair, and straightened my dress shirt. I felt jittery, adrenaline coursing through me. Did Ella come to talk? Was she finally breaking the silence?

I heard footsteps clack down the hallway and I waited impatiently.

The person got closer and closer.

"Doctor, thank you for seeing me." Sophie swept into the room, floating amidst a cloud of perfume.

My hopes crashed to the ground in a splintering heap. I squeezed my eyes shut. Was this a nightmare? Please let this be a nightmare.

But, when I opened my eyes, Sophie was standing in front of me. A touch too close, actually.

I side-stepped away from her. Sophie hadn't visited my practice in weeks—the only time I'd seen her was at the open mic night. I did not miss her company. Or her various fake ailments.

"What are you doing here, Sophie?" My voice was tinged with exhaustion.

Sophie hopped onto the exam table and stared at me, eyes intent. "I heard that you and Ella broke up. So, I thought I'd come by and offer you a shoulder to cry on, if that's what you're looking for."

Her almost predatory smirk told me that she had other things than a shoulder in mind. She tossed her pearly hair aside, pouted her lips, and leaned towards me.

Suddenly, it all felt like too much—the pain of losing Ella, missing my mom, Sophie coming back into my practice like nothing had changed...

I couldn't do it anymore.

A headache was rapidly building behind my temples and I pinched the bridge of my nose. When I looked up, it took every ounce of self-restraint to keep composed. "Sophie. For the last time, I—"

"Dr. Bell?" Becca poked her head through the door.

I held my breath for a moment. Exhaled. "Yes, Becca?"

Becca didn't look the least bit bothered that she'd just about walked in on me giving Sophie a piece of my mind. Remarkably, she wasn't chewing gum, but her eyes were flat and bored, as always. "There's a package for you at the front desk. Just arrived."

I frowned. "A package from who?"

"Dunno. You should come see it."

I shot a glance at Sophie. At some point, she'd taken out a nail file and was filing away like this conversation didn't have anything to do with her. I rubbed the back of my neck, held back an exasperated sigh, and followed Becca into the hallway.

"Thought you needed that," Becca muttered.

I chuckled dryly. "Thanks. Exhaustion is clearly getting to me. I never lose my patience with my patients."

"If you're going to lose it with anyone, I'm not surprised it's Sophie. I heard she's been kicked out of doctor's offices across the county for making unwanted advances towards the staff."

"Why doesn't that surprise me." I exhaled a deep, calming breath. "I should get back to her."

"Don't you want to see the package?"

"You didn't make that up?"

Becca shook her head and we walked the rest of the way to the front desk. I assumed the package would be about the medical center, or about my practice. Instead, she handed me a bulky envelope with my name written in cursive across the front.

I recognized the handwriting as though it were my own.

Heart racing, I ripped open the envelope and a stack of papers fell out. I dropped to the floor and gathered them up.

The parchment-style pages were filled with handwriting in a variety of colors—the same cursive handwriting. They appeared to be pages of a journal.

Ella's journal.

I blinked, unsure if I should look. Ella never wanted me to read her daily journal. I wondered whether I should put the pages away, respect her privacy. Though, she did send them to me. My name was definitely on that envelope.

Forgetting all about Sophie lingering in my exam room, I took the bundle of paper to a waiting room chair and sat down. With hungry eyes, I scanned the pages, starting with one dated at the end of June. When Ella had first arrived back in Aston Falls.

I dove in, my eyes skimming each and every beautiful word that Ella had written. The pages documented how and when she'd fallen for me. Each moment that had made her smile or her heart skip a beat. Every word demonstrated how Ella felt—how much she cared, how much she valued our friendship and, finally, our relationship. It was like reading the most wonderful love story, because it was ours.

And then, I read the pages that led up to our trip to Seattle. Ella recalled all of the times she'd tripped and fallen, every time she was rejected from a job in New York, every time she felt she wasn't good enough. And, when she eventually lost out on the job with *The Weekly Best*...

My stomach curdled as I understood. I finally understood. Ella didn't break up with me because she wanted to date other people. She broke up with me because she wanted *me* to date other people.

Everything fell into place. The open mic night when Sophie and I were talking, the dinner with her parents, the NAFP conference... Ella had convinced herself that she wasn't good enough to date me, so she wanted to preserve our friendship for when I—inevitably, in her eyes—saw it, too.

I sifted back through the papers, wanting to read them again. And, that's when I discovered one final paper at the bottom of the stack. The page was smaller than the rest, clearly from a different journal, and slightly wrinkled from time.

I scanned its contents, frowning. Ella had documented a day in high school, just any regular day. But, at the bottom, she'd written one thing and underlined it three times.

"I think I might be hopelessly and completely in love with my best friend."

44

ELLA

I popped another piece of popcorn into my mouth and shifted in my seat at the Aston Falls Cinema. I felt good. Better than I expected. Better than I'd felt in a long, long time.

For the first time in months, I finally felt that I had some direction, I was taking back control of the chaos and mess in my life. Grace's kick in the pants was exactly what I needed because I had a plan now, and it might've been foolish, but I felt excited about it.

Tomorrow, when I got back to New York, my first task would be to go to the head office for *The Weekly Best* and ask for an in-person interview. I wouldn't take no for an answer because, after all, what did I have to lose? This was my dream job, and I was going for it.

I also felt happy knowing that I'd done the most terrifying thing I ever could've imagined—I dropped my journal pages off at Austin's office.

The knowledge that he would read my innermost thoughts made me squirm a little, but I didn't regret my decision for a moment. I hoped that he would understand where I was coming from and why I did what I did. Maybe, when he saw my perspective, he'd finally agree with me. And, maybe, we could at least remain friends.

I was trying to be brave, just like he always was. I drew inspiration from his strength and courage, and I faced my deepest fears.

Last night, I went to my parents' house for dinner and told them the whole story. I told them about the stress of losing my job, and about how disappointed I'd been when this new opportunity fell through. And, I told them the truth about Austin—that our relationship had started fake, but had quickly become real.

It was probably the most honest I'd ever been with them.

By the end of the meal, Mom had tears in her eyes and she hugged me as she reassured me, over and over, that all she wanted was for me to be happy. I hugged her back twice as hard and promised her that I would come back to Aston Falls whenever I could.

It felt good to tell my parents the truth, to speak honestly with Gracie. I'd also gone by Sweets n' Sundaes this morning to give JJ the rundown on what had been going on.

I couldn't get over just how kind and supportive my friends and family were. I was going to miss them and Aston Falls, more than I ever would've imagined. It occurred to me that I would love to live here again someday. But, who knew if that would ever happen.

After saying my goodbyes and dropping off my envelope at Austin's medical clinic, I checked out of the Inn. I came straight to the movie theater to wait for the last train of the day, and I sat in back to back shows. I turned off my phone because I didn't want to be checking it constantly for a message from Austin. After the way I treated him, I wouldn't be surprised if he wanted some time. But, I told Grace and JJ where I was in case anyone needed me.

I wasn't running away anymore. From here on out, I was going to be brave.

"Excuse me," someone whispered from just behind my right shoulder. "Anyone sitting there?"

I turned to see Mrs. Applebaum in the aisle next to me, gesturing towards a couple of seats down my row. Behind her, Mr. Applebaum carried two huge buckets of popcorn.

Mrs. Applebaum smiled. "Hello dear, nice to see you. Mind if we sit next to you?"

I scurried out of my seat, pushing my bags to the side as I went. "Of course!"

While Mr. and Mrs. Applebaum took their seats, I gazed around the bustling, crowded theater.

It was busy. Like, really busy. Most of the seats were full.

Which was bizarre, seeing as the theater was never busy to begin with, and especially not at dinnertime on a Tuesday. Perhaps there was a new movie out? I hadn't bothered checking.

I was about to take my seat when I saw a couple across the room. The girl was wearing a pink sweater with the hood up and the guy wore a baseball cap. I could almost swear they looked like Grace and Nicholas, but I must've been imagining things. They were busy enough with Morning Bell and King's Kids these days.

I shook my head and took a seat before diving back into my popcorn.

The whispers and murmurs were almost deafening as we waited for the movie to start. I heard a high-pitched voice I would've known anywhere, and I whirled around in my seat. But, JJ was nowhere to be found.

Still, as I glanced around, I recognized a lot of faces. I

saw Ms. Rodriguez and Mayor Davis, and even Austin's dad. I could've sworn I saw a couple who looked remarkably like my parents ducking behind their brochures.

"Ice cream, miss?" An usher appeared to my right and I almost jumped out of my seat. The man smiled, amused, and held a cup my way. "It's butter pecan. On the house."

I frowned, more confused than ever. "Sure?"

The usher handed me the ice cream and disappeared back up the aisle. I opened the cup slowly and took a small bite using the spoon provided.

Man, it was delicious. But, this was *definitely* out of the ordinary for the Aston Falls Cinema.

The lights went out and a hush settled over the crowd as the screen came to life. But, the opening scenes weren't anything like a regular movie. There were no logos flying around, no grand introductory music, no flashing movie title.

Instead, I saw a yard... a yard that looked eerily familiar.

My mouth dropped open.

It was the yard at my parents' house.

I stared at the screen, uncomprehending.

What was going on? Why was my parents' yard in the movie? Was their house discovered by a location scout, and they didn't tell me about it?

No. There was no way.

Mom was the absolute worst at keeping secrets. Especially a secret like *that*.

Then, I heard laughter and a young Marc and Phil burst onto the screen, chasing each other with water guns. Carly appeared next, sporting a pink bathing suit and arm floats.

She had a tiny water gun as well, and was trying to keep up despite her tiny, chubby toddler legs.

And, suddenly, there I was. A younger me, running across the yard and followed closely by an equally young Austin.

My mouth was dry and I couldn't even blink as I stared at the two of us, running around. We couldn't be more than eight. Austin laughed as he caught up to me and knocked me to the ground, his light blond bowl cut all too familiar. Screen-me started to cry from the shock of the impact, and he took my hand, helping me to a stand.

Then, the movie cut to another moment. This video featured five-year-old Austin and I at the playground, going down the slide and laughing uncontrollably. Another video showed Austin and I playing cards, our faces twisted in concentration. Another one had us fighting in the mud. There was even a video of us at eleven, building blanket forts and telling scary stories. And one of the two of us and Gracie—the Three Musketeers—baking cookies in frilly pink aprons.

I remembered that day clearly. We were fourteen and Austin had started muscling up from all of his football practices. I remembered thinking just how hot he looked in the pink apron—he managed to pull it off seamlessly, with full confidence.

Then, the movie cut once more. Here, Austin and I were teens and we'd built a treehouse. I was inside, reading, and Austin was bugging me to play football with him. I was clearly getting annoyed, but then screen-Austin got down on one knee and proffered a blade of grass folded to look like a flower—the same trick I'd used with the carrot flower.

Teenaged me rolled her eyes and agreed to join him. He

took my hand, smiled, and even though the moment was in the past, shivers erupted on my skin to see it.

Video after video flew across the screen, better than any other movie. It was like I was traveling back in time. This was a montage of our childhood. Our friendship.

But, why on earth was the theater playing home videos of Austin and me? What was going on?

I blinked a few times and glanced around the theater. The rest of the audience likely didn't come to the Aston Falls Cinema to see something like this. I waited for a reaction, waited for protests. All I saw were smiling faces and odd glances in my direction.

At that moment, I caught the eye of the hooded girl. She was staring right at me, and as I looked back at her, she removed her hood.

My breath hitched. It was Grace! And, the guy in the baseball cap was Nicholas.

What were they doing here? Why were we all watching these home videos?

A spotlight shone bright onto the small stage before the projection screen.

Someone walked up onto the stage.

The man faced the crowd.

"Austin?" I breathed.

Austin Bell stood tall, holding a lone sheet of paper. He stared at the page with barely a glance at the crowd, and my first thought was that he was swallowing his fears to stand in front of a huge crowd of people again. But, why?

He cleared his throat and raised his eyes. He seemed nervous, but calm.

"Thanks, everyone, for coming tonight," he started, bouncing on his heels.

I shifted in my seat and one of my suitcases toppled into

the aisle. I scrambled to pick it up, but the noise drew Austin's attention. His eyes locked on mine, and my body filled with warmth. Then, he smiled that trademark smirk of his, and the theater, the crowd, everything disappeared.

"I'm sure many of you know this, but I'm not a fan of public speaking." He ran his fingers through his hair, as chuckles rippled through the audience. "It wasn't until recently that I started to venture out of my comfort zone and try new things. That I started making exceptions."

I leaned forward.

"I've always lived strategically and practically. There was a place for everything, compartments for every part of my life, and I never made room for exceptions... until I realized I'd already fallen for someone exceptional. I was in love with my best friend."

I froze. Austin's eyes met mine again and I almost melted on the spot.

"Ella Williams," he murmured. "I've loved you as long as I've known you. I loved you before I even knew what love was. I've told you a thousand times all of the things that make you wonderful, but now, I want to tell you some of the moments that stood out for me."

He smiled and looked at his paper. But, it was clear that he didn't need it.

"I loved you when you chose to stay in and read instead of come to Philip Hannigan's homecoming party in high school. I loved you when you played that birthday song for me on the flute. I loved you every time you were grumpy in the mornings, and when you made me overcooked mac n' cheese. Every single day that we've spent together, every moment, just reaffirms that where I belong is with you. And where you belong is with me."

His words echoed around the theatre and I almost fell

out of my chair from leaning so far forward. Was this real? Was any of this happening? Or was I just having the best dream of my life?

Austin took a deep breath. "In recent years, I've held firmly onto one belief—that I was a 'never forever' kinda guy. And there, again, I've made an exception, because I see forever when I'm with you, Ella. I see our future, and our family, and I see growing old with you. I see all of life's beauties and challenges. I've loved you, and I'll keep loving you. Because the truth is, if you'll have me, I'm already yours forever."

Austin folded the paper and his eyes met mine again. The room was so silent, you could hear a pin drop.

Without a word, I stood. My legs were shaky and my heartbeat was in my ears, but I'd never felt so calm, so sure of anything. I walked down the aisle until I reached the stage, and started climbing the set of stairs.

Then, I tripped on the carpet and went flying.

The crowd gasped as I flailed, arms windmilling around.

But, once again, Austin caught me right before I hit the ground.

When I opened my eyes, he was staring at me, a smile tugging at his lips. My heart nearly exploded.

"Quite the entrance," he murmured.

"I love you, too," I said at the same time.

Austin smiled wide, eyes dancing. "I know."

Before I could say anything else, Austin's hands were in my hair and mine wrapped around his shoulders, pulling him closer. Our lips met and, with that kiss, I allowed myself to see what he saw—our future, our past, everything. Austin and I belonged together, we were always meant to be.

Beyond our happy bubble, the room burst into applause.

Loud, raucous applause. Through the noise, I could hear JJ screech, "Finally!"

Austin broke our kiss so he could plant a small one beneath my ear. I hugged him close, knowing I was home. He pressed his forehead against mine and it didn't matter whether we were surrounded by the whole town or alone. With Austin, I was exactly where I needed to be.

"Forever?" I whispered.

He smiled. "Forever and always."

45

ELLA

One Year Later...

"*L*et's go, Els!" Austin hollered from the living room. "This isn't *your* baby shower, you know."

I smiled at myself in the mirror. "Be there in two minutes."

I applied another coat of lip gloss, then tucked a strand of hair behind my ear. I envisioned the nude kitten heels that would go with my airy white dress. It was the one dress I enjoyed wearing, and I had to admit that maybe Carly had a point after all. *Some* dresses could be comfortable.

Not that I would ever tell her that.

As I adjusted the gold necklace Austin had gotten me for my birthday, he appeared in the mirror behind me. My face split into a beaming smile, my cheeks slightly pink. He was wearing dark slacks and a white shirt, and he looked gorgeous as ever. He wrapped his arms around me and kissed my neck. I leaned back against him and closed my eyes, completely happy.

"You look beautiful, as always," he murmured. "Mrs. Bell."

Ooh, that still sent delicious shivers up and down my spine.

"Mmmh," was all I could manage in response.

That's right. A little over three months ago, to the delight of my parents and Carly, I had officially become Mrs. Ella Bell. The name still made me laugh, but I loved it because it was mine. It was perfectly mine.

After the home video montage at the Aston Falls Cinema, everything had fallen into place for Austin and me. Austin opened the medical center and had hired a few more doctors to help with the patient load. Meanwhile, I'd faced my fears and, with Austin's encouragement, went to New York to visit the offices of *The Weekly Best*.

I'd been working there for almost a year now and, recently, was promoted to Lead Editor.

The best part? They allowed me to work remotely so I could live in Aston Falls, close to my friends, family, and the love of my life. Holly was more than happy to take over my lease in New York, and I'd gone to visit her and Janice a couple of times.

Everything was perfect, especially between Austin and me. When he proposed to me at Christmas, I'd never been so pleasantly surprised.

We were married in a beautiful, unique ceremony at the Aston Falls Cinema. The movie theater had gone all out, and it truly was my dream wedding. Decorations lined the theater's aisles and an altar had been set up by the stage. Music pumped through the speakers, and Christian West made an appearance—much to JJ's frustration.

After the wedding, I moved back into Austin's penthouse, but I didn't stay in the guest room this time. We were even talking about finding a sweet, little house for ourselves. For our future.

My life was still messy and chaotic. I was scatter-brained and busy, and I still tripped and fell on nearly everything. But, I couldn't help but feel grateful because my journey brought me here—to a life with Austin.

"They're going to be upset if we're late," he said now, and the vibration of his chest along my back was supremely comforting.

I turned in his arms and stood on my tip-toes. I pressed a kiss on his lips and he responded immediately, holding me close to his body and tangling his hands in my hair.

"Okay," he murmured. "Being a little late won't hurt anything."

It took every ounce of self-control to step back and out of his arms. I pressed a hand firmly to his chest. "Says you. Do you know your sister at all?"

Austin smiled and bit his lip, and my resolve almost crumbled. But, he pulled away, his hand around mine. "I'll be in the living room whenever you're ready."

Austin and I pulled up in front of Morning Bell Cafe and my body buzzed with excitement. No sooner had he parked the car than I leapt out and ran up the sidewalk. It was a blistering hot late August day, and I got a few funny looks as I ran, but I didn't care.

I burst through the door, eyes wide, and zeroed in on my best friend.

Grace was literally glowing. Her blonde hair was curled in an updo, and her green eyes sparkled as she spoke with her dad and Nicholas's mom. She was wearing a long aqua-marine dress that skated down her body.

Her hand rested on her baby bump, the ring on her finger gleaming in the sunlight.

"Gracie!" I shrieked and ran forward. "Happy baby shower!"

Grace laughed as I wrapped my arms around her. "Thank you, Els."

"You look beautiful."

"I feel anything but." Grace fanned her face. "I could really use—"

"Water?" Nicholas appeared next to Grace and handed her a tall glass packed with ice cubes. Grace accepted it and took a huge swig. Nicholas then leaned down and kissed her on the cheek.

I smiled at the two, unbelievably happy for them.

A warm hand wound around my waist and Austin pressed a kiss to the side of my head. I giggled, my cheeks turning bright red.

Grace wrinkled her nose. "Still not quite used to that."

"What?"

"You two. Making out." Grace shook her head and laughed. "I should be used to it, seeing as you guys got married and are obviously meant to be together. You're just... really cute."

Austin and I shared a glance, our hands intertwined. The four of us caught up for a few minutes, talking about everything and nothing as more guests arrived. Austin, JJ and I had tag-teamed planning the party, and we'd invited Nicholas and Grace's closest relatives and friends.

Soon enough, Nicholas and Austin peeled off to talk about house renovations or something, and it was just Grace and me.

"Imagine," I murmured. "You'll soon have a mini Nicholas or Grace running around."

"I can't wait!" she squealed. "I just hope our baby has Nicholas's hand-eye coordination."

"They'll be on King's Kids in no time."

Grace chuckled along with me, then her eyes grew intense. "Do you and Aus have any baby plans?"

I looked across the room at Austin. The way he smiled, the way he laughed... he was kind, and playful, and so good with kids. He was going to make a wonderful dad. "Well, actually, I—"

"Sorry we're late, Gracie!" JJ burst through the door, presents piled high in her arms. She strode forward and dropped them on the counter next to the others. Then, she patted the front of her teal dress and brushed her hair back. "Ted's just parking the car."

"Don't worry about it." Grace hugged our friend.

"I told him we had to leave early, but he texted saying that something came up at his parents' house," JJ continued, rolling her eyes. "Twenty minutes later, he finally picked me up, and here we are." She glanced around. "Pretty busy, isn't it?"

At that very moment, the door to the cafe opened. But, instead of Ted walking in, it was none other than Christian West.

JJ's eyes narrowed to slits. "Ugh. *He's* back in town? Why?"

I snorted and Grace and I exchanged a glance. JJ's feud with Christian West was practically legendary. Though she used to belt out his song lyrics with abandon, she now changed the radio station if a song of his came on in Sweets n' Sundaes.

That being said, I had caught her absentmindedly

humming along to his songs on more than one occasion. I sometimes wondered whether she listened to his music when no one was around.

"He and Nicholas have gotten pretty close," Grace explained as we watched Christian approach our husbands, fist bumping them both.

"Ridiculous," JJ hissed, arms crossed.

Then, like he could sense our eyes on him, Christian glanced across the room. His gaze locked in on JJ's and he smiled a slow, lopsided grin that would make any other girl weak at the knees.

JJ? She just glared back harder.

Christian came towards us, closely followed by Austin and Nicholas, and the crowd parted around them. Christian was dressed casually, his hair grown out and shaggy. He'd shaved his scruff so the angles of his jawline were more pronounced than ever. As was his chin dimple.

"Hey Jessica Jade," he said with that famous low, gravelly voice. "Long time no see."

JJ played it cool, placing a hand on her hip. "Has it been awhile? I hadn't noticed."

Christian smirked. "Your scooping technique gotten any better?"

"Your facial hair decided you weren't worth its time either?"

I rolled my eyes as Christian and JJ continued to bicker. The verbal ping-pong went on until Ted appeared next to JJ.

The conversation dried right up, as it often did around Ted. I liked the guy well enough, but he wasn't exactly great in social settings. It was like his expression of perfect boredom put a damper on the entire group. Where JJ was lively and colorful, Ted was gray and rather dull.

Of course, I would never tell JJ that. Opposites did attract, right?

"Oh." JJ grabbed Ted's arm. "Have you met my *fiancé*, Ted Bigby?"

Christian smiled and held out his hand. "Nice to meet you, man."

If Ted recognized Christian West, he didn't show it. In fact, his reaction was flat as could be. He didn't even take Christian's hand, just smiled flimsily as he checked his phone. "Sorry, babe. John's calling. Better take it."

Without waiting for JJ's response, Ted disappeared towards the back of the cafe.

There was a tense, slightly awkward silence around our group of six. JJ stared at Ted's back, her expression like thunder.

Christian broke the silence. "Grace, Nicholas, congratulations, by the way. This baby's going to be one lucky little guy."

"Guy?" JJ whirled towards Christian. "What makes you say that?"

He winked. "I have a feeling."

We laughed while JJ rolled her eyes. She went after Ted, and Nicholas and Grace peeled off to speak with their guests. Christian was pulled aside by a fan and, soon, it was just Austin and me.

He wrapped an arm around me and pulled me close. "What are you thinking, Els?"

I stared at Grace and Nicholas, so happy together. "Honestly?"

"Always."

"I'm thinking," I started shyly. "I'm thinking that I'm ready to start our family. I'm ready for the next step in our forever."

Austin faced me and locked his arms behind my back. I rested my hands comfortably on his shoulders. His ocean eyes were endless and I got lost in them. "I was thinking the same thing."

I bit my lip and my heart leapt. I placed a hand on my belly.

"I have some good news, then," I whispered.

Austin's eyes met mine again and understanding flashed across his features. He smiled a huge, beaming smile, then leaned down and kissed me. I was breathless with happiness. My skin still tingled with electricity at his touch, and I knew that, as Austin and I entered the next stage of our lives, we would always find our way. Together.

Because he was right about one thing. He belonged with me, and I belonged with him.

And it all started when we became more than just friends.

Thank you for reading!

If you enjoyed the story, I'd appreciate if you were able to leave a review! As a new author, reviews mean everything to me, and I'm so grateful for each and every one of them.